Francis Marion Crawford

Corleone

A Tale of Sicily. Vol. 1

Francis Marion Crawford

Corleone
A Tale of Sicily. Vol. 1

ISBN/EAN: 9783337026080

Printed in Europe, USA, Canada, Australia, Japan

Cover: Foto ©Andreas Hilbeck / pixelio.de

More available books at **www.hansebooks.com**

CORLEONE

A TALE OF SICILY

BY

F. MARION CRAWFORD

AUTHOR OF "SARACINESCA," "PIETRO GHISLERI," "CASA BRACCIO,"
ETC., ETC.

IN TWO VOLUMES

VOL. I

New York

THE MACMILLAN COMPANY

LONDON: MACMILLAN & CO., LTD.

1897

Norwood Press
J. S. Cushing & Co. — Berwick & Smith
Norwood Mass. U.S.A.

CORLEONE

CHAPTER I

"IF you never mean to marry, you might as well turn priest, too," said Ippolito Saracinesca to his elder brother, Orsino, with a laugh.

"Why?" asked Orsino, without a smile. "It would be as sensible to say that a man who had never seen some particular thing, about which he has heard much, might as well put out his eyes."

The young priest laughed again, took up the cigar he had laid upon the edge of the piano, puffed at it till it burned freely, and then struck two or three chords of a modulation. A sheet of ruled paper on which several staves of music were roughly jotted down in pencil stood on the rack of the instrument.

Orsino stretched out his long legs, leaned back in his low chair, and stared at the old gilded rosettes in the square divisions of the carved ceiling. He was a discontented man, and knew it, which made his discontent a matter for self-reproach, especially

as it was quite clear to him that the cause of it
lay in himself.

He had made two great mistakes at the beginning of life, when barely of age, and though
neither of them had ultimately produced any serious material consequences, they had affected his
naturally melancholic temper and had brought out
his inherited hardness of disposition. At the time
of the great building speculations in Rome, several
years earlier, he had foolishly involved himself
with his father's old enemy, Ugo del Ferice, and
had found himself at last altogether in the latter's
power, though not in reality his debtor. At the
same time, he had fallen very much in love with
a young widow, who, loving him very sincerely in
her turn, but believing, for many reasons, that if
she married him she would be doing him an irrep-
arable injury, had sacrificed herself by marrying
Del Ferice instead, selling herself to the banker
for Orsino's release, without the latter's knowledge.
When it was all over, Orsino had found himself
a disappointed man at an age when most young
fellows are little more than inexperienced boys,
and the serious disposition which he inherited
from his mother made it impossible for him to
throw off the impression received, and claim the
youth, so to speak, which was still his.

Since that time, he had been attracted by women,
but never charmed; and those that attracted him

were for the most part not marriageable, any more than the few things which sometimes interested and amused him were in any sense profitable. He spent a good deal of money in a careless way, for his father was generous; but his rather bitter experience when he had attempted to occupy himself with business had made him cool and clear-headed, so that he never did anything at all ruinous. The hot temper which he had inherited from his father and grandfather now rarely, if ever, showed itself, and it seemed as though nothing could break through the quiet indifference which had become a second outward nature to him. He had travelled much, of late years, and when he made an effort his conversation was not uninteresting, though the habit of looking at both sides of every question made it cold and unenthusiastic. Perhaps it was a hopeful sign that he generally had a definite opinion as to which of two views he preferred, though he would not take any trouble to convince others that he was right.

In his own family, he liked the company of Ippolito best. The latter was about two years younger than he, and very different from him in almost every way. Orsino was tall, strongly built, extremely dark; Ippolito was of medium height, delicately made, and almost fair by comparison. Orsino had lean brown hands, well knit at the base, and broad at the knuckles; Ippolito's were slender and white, and rather nervous, with blue veins at the joints, the tips of the fingers pointed, the thumb unusually delicate and long, the nails naturally polished. The elder brother's face, with its large and energetic lines, its gravely indifferent expression and dusky olive hue, contrasted at every point with the features of the young priest, soft in outline, modelled in wax rather than chiselled in bronze, pale and a little transparent, instead of swarthy, — feminine, perhaps, in the best sense of the word, as it can be applied to a man. Ippolito had the clear, soft brown eyes which very gifted people so often have, especially musicians and painters of more talent than power. But about the fine, even, and rather pale lips there was the unmistakable stamp of the ascetic temperament, together with an equally sure indication of a witty humour which could be keen, but would rather be gentle. Ippolito was said to resemble his mother's mother, and was notably different in appearance and manner from the rest of the numerous family to which he belonged.

He was a priest by vocation rather than by choice. Had he chosen deliberately a profession congenial to his gifts, he would certainly have devoted himself altogether to music, though he would probably never have become famous as a composer; for he lacked the rough creative power which hews out great conceptions, though he possessed in a high degree the taste and skill which can lightly and lovingly and wisely impart fine detail to the broad beauty of a well-planned whole. But by vocation he was a priest, and the strength of the conviction of his conscience left the gifts of his artistic intelligence no power to choose. He was a churchman with all his soul, and a musician with all his heart.

Between the two brothers there was that sort of close friendship which sometimes exists between persons who are too wholly different to understand each other, but whose non-understanding is a constant stimulant of interest on both sides. In the midst of the large and peaceable patriarchal establishment in which they lived, and in which each member made for himself or herself an existence which had in it a certain subdued individuality, Orsino and Ippolito were particularly associated, and the priest, when he was at home, was generally to be found in his elder brother's sitting-room, and kept a good many of his possessions there.

It was a big room, with an old carved and gilded ceiling, three tall windows opening to the floor, two doors, a marble fireplace, a thick old carpet, and a great deal of furniture of many old and new designs, arranged with no regard to anything except usefulness, since Orsino was not afflicted with artistic tastes, nor with any undue appreciation of useless objects. Ippolito's short grand piano occupied a prominent position near the middle window, and not far from it was Orsino's deep chair, beside which stood a low table covered with books and reviews. For, like most discontented and disappointed people who have no real object in life, Orsino Saracinesca read a good deal, and hankered after interest in fiction because he found none in reality. Ippolito, on the contrary, read little, and thought much.

After Orsino had answered his remark about marriage, the priest busied himself for some time with his music, while his brother stared at the ceiling in silence, listening to the modulations and the fragments of tentative melody and experimental harmony, without in the least understanding what the younger man was trying to express. He was fond of any musical sound, in an undefined way, as most Italians are, and he knew by experience that if he let Ippolito alone, something pleasant to hear would before long be evolved. But Ippolito stopped suddenly and turned half round on the piano stool, with a quick movement habitual to him. He leaned forward towards Orsino, tapping the ends of his fingers lightly against one another, as his wrists rested on his knees.

"It is absurd to suppose that in all Rome, or in all Europe, for that matter, there is nobody whom you would be willing to marry."

"Quite absurd, I suppose," answered Orsino, not looking at his brother.

"Then you have not really looked about you for a wife. That is clear."

"Perfectly clear. I do not argue the point. Why should I? There is plenty of time, and besides, there is no reason in the world why I should ever marry at all, any more than you. There are our two younger brothers. Let them take wives and continue the name."

"Most people think that marriage may be regarded as a means of happiness," observed Ippolito.

"Most people are imbeciles," answered Orsino, gloomily.

Ippolito laughed, watching his brother's face, but he said nothing in reply.

"As a general rule," Orsino continued presently, "talking is a question of height and not of intelligence. The shorter men and women are, the more they talk; the taller they are, the more silent they are, in nine cases out of ten. Of course there are exceptions, but you can generally tell at a glance whether any particular person is a great talker. Brains are certainly not measurable by inches. Therefore conversation has nothing to do with brains. Therefore most people are fools."

"Do you call that an argument?" asked the priest, still smiling.

" No. It is an observation."

" And what do you deduce from it ? "

" From it, and from a great many other things, I deduce and conclude that what we call society is a degrading farce. It encourages talking, when no one has anything to say. It encourages marriage, without love. It sets up fashion against taste, taste against sense, and sense against heart. It is a machinery for promoting emotion among the unfeeling. It is a—"

Orsino stopped, hesitating.

" Is it anything else ? " asked Ippolito, mildly.

" It is a hell on earth "

" That is exactly what most of the prophets and saints have said, since David," remarked the priest, moving again in order to find his half-smoked cigar, and then carefully relighting it. " Since that is your opinion, why not take orders ? You might become a prophet or a saint, you know. The first step towards sanctity is to despise the pomps and vanities of this wicked world. You seem to have taken the first step at a jump, with both feet. And it is the first step that costs the most, they say. Courage! You may go far."

" I am thinking of going further before long," said Orsino, gravely, as though his brother had spoken in earnest. " At all events, I mean to get away from all this," he added, as though correcting himself.

"Do you mean to travel again?" enquired Ippolito.

"I mean to find something to do. Provided it is respectable, I do not care what it is. If I had talent, like you, I would be a musician, but I would not be an amateur, or I would be an artist, or a literary man. But I have no talent for anything, except building tenement houses, and I shall not try that again. I would even be an actor, if I had the gift. Perhaps I should make a good farmer, but our father will not trust me now, for he is afraid that I should make ruinous experiments if he gave me the management of an estate. This is certainly not the time for experiments. Half the people we know are ruined and the country is almost bankrupt. I do not wish to try experiments. I would work, and they tell me to marry. You cannot understand. You are only an amateur yourself, after all, Ippolito."

"An amateur musician — yes."

"No. You are an amateur priest. You support your sensitive soul on a sort of religious ambrosia, with a good deal of musical nectar. Your ideal is to be Cardinal-Protector of the Arts. You are clever and astonishingly good, by nature, and you deserve no credit for either. That is probably why I like you. I hate people who deserve credit, because I deserve none myself. But you do not take your clerical profession seriously, and you are an amateur, a dilettante of the altar. If you do not have distractions about the vestments you wear when you are saying mass, it is because you have an intimate, unconscious artistic conviction that they are beautiful and becoming to you. But if the choir responded a flat 'Amen' to your 'per omnia sæcula sæculorum,' it would set your teeth on edge and upset your devout intention at the beginning of the Preface. Do you think that a professional musician would be disturbed in conducting a great orchestra, by the fact that his coat collar did not fit?"

Ippolito smiled good humouredly, but did not answer.

"Very well," continued Orsino at once, "you are only an amateur priest. It does not matter, since you are happy. You get through life very well. You do not even pretend that you do any real work. Your vocation, as you call it, was a liking for the state of priesthood, not for the work of a priest. Now I do not care about any state in particular, but I want work of some sort, at any cost. I was never happy but once, during that time when I worked with Contini and got into trouble. I preferred it to this existence, even when we got into Del Ferice's clutches. Anything rather than this."

"I thought you had grown indifferent," said Ippolito.

"Indifferent? Yes, I am indifferent — as a machine is indifferent when the fire is out and there is no steam. But if the thing could think, it would want work, as I do. It would not be satisfied to rust to pieces. You ought to know a little theology. Are we put into the world with a purpose, or not? Is there an intention in our existence, or is there not? Am I to live through another forty or fifty years of total inactivity, because I happen to be born rich, and in a position — well, a position which is really about as enviable as that of a fly in a pot of honey? We are stuck in our traditions, just as the fly is in the honey — "

" I like them," said Ippolito, quietly.

"I know you do. So does our father. They suit you both. Our father is really a very intelligent man, but too much happiness and too much money have paralyzed him. His existence seems to have been a condition of perpetual adoration of our mother."

" He has made her happy. That is worth something."

"She has made him happy. They have made each other happy. They have devoured a lifetime of happiness together in secret, as though it were their lawful prey. As they never wanted anything else, they never found out that the honey of traditions is sticky, and that they could not move if they would."

"They are fond of us —"

"Of course. We have none of us done anything very bad. We are a part of their happiness. We are also a part of their dulness; for they are dull, and their happiness makes us dull, too."

"What an idea!"

"It is true. What have we accomplished, any of us four brothers? What shall we ever accomplish? We are ornaments on the architecture of our father's and mother's happiness. It is rather a negative mission in life, you must admit. I am glad that they are happy, but I should like to be something more than a gargoyle on their temple."

"Then marry, and have a temple of your own!" laughed Ippolito. "And gargoyles of your own, too."

"But I do not want that sort of happiness. Marriage is not a profession. It is not a career."

"No. At least, you might turn out a dilettante husband, as you say that I am an amateur priest." Ippolito laughed again.

Orsino laughed dryly, but did not answer, not being in a humour for jesting. He leaned back in his chair again, and looked at the carved ceiling and thought of what it meant, for it was one of those ceilings which are only to be found in old Roman palaces, and belong intimately to the existence which those old dwellings suggest. Orsino thought of the grim dark walls outside, of the forbidding gateway, of the heavily barred windows on the lower story, of the dark street at the back of the palace, and the mediævalism of it all was as repugnant to him as the atmosphere of a prison.

He had never understood his father nor his grandfather, who both seemed born for such an existence, and who certainly thrived in it; for the old Prince was over ninety years of age, and his son, Sant' Ilario, though now between fifty and sixty, was to all intents and purposes still a young man. Orsino was perhaps as strong as either of them. But he did not believe that he could last as long. In the midst of an enforced idleness he felt the movement of the age about him, and he said to himself that he was in the race of which they were only spectators, and that he was born in times when it was impossible to stand still. It is true that, like many young men of to-day, he took movement for progress and change for improvement, and he had no very profound understanding of the condition of his own or of other countries. But the movement and the change are facts from which no one can escape who has had a modern education.

Giovanni Saracinesca, Orsino's father, known as Prince of Sant' Ilario, since the old Prince Saracinesca was still living, had not had a modern education, and his mother had died while he was a mere child. Brought up by men, among men, he had reached manhood early, in close daily association with his father and with a strong natural admiration for him, though with an equally strong sense of personal independence.

Orsino's youth had been different. He was not an only son, as Sant' Ilario had been, but the eldest of four brothers, and he had been brought up by his mother as well as by his father and grandfather. There had been less room for his character to develop freely, since the great old house had been gradually filled by a large family. At the same time there had also been less room for old-fashioned prejudices and traditions than formerly, and a good deal less respect for them, as there had been, too, a much more lively consciousness of the outer world's movements. The taking of Rome in 1870 was the death-blow of mediævalism; and the passing away of King Victor Emmanuel and of Pope Pius the Ninth was the end of Italian romanticism, if one may use the expression to designate all that concatenation of big and little events which make up the thrilling story of the struggle for Italian unity. After the struggle for unity, began the struggle for life, — more desperate, more dangerous, but immeasurably less romantic. There is all the difference which lies between banking and fighting.

And Orsino was aware of qualities and feelings and opinions in his father and mother which he

did not possess, but which excited in him a sort
of envy of what he regarded as their simplicity.
Each seemed to have wanted but one thing in
life since he could remember them, and that was
the other's love, in possessing which each was satisfied and happy. Times might change as they
would, popes might die, kings might be crowned,
parties might wrangle in political strife, and the
whole country might live through its perilous joys
of sudden prosperity and turn sour again in the
ferment that follows failure,—it was all the same
to Giovanni and Corona. As Orsino had told his
brother, they had devoured a lifetime of happiness
together in secret. He would have added that
they had left none for others, and in a sense it
might have been true. But he preferred not to
say it, even to Ippolito; for it would have sounded
bitter, whereas Orsino believed himself to be only
indifferent.

Proud men and women hide their griefs and
sufferings, when they have any. But there are
some who are so very proud that they will hide
their happiness also, as though it might lose some
of its strength if anyone else could see it, or as
if it could be spoiled by the light like a photo-
graph not yet fixed. People sometimes call that
instinct the selfishness of love, but it is more
like a sort of respect for love itself, which is
certainly not vulgar, as all selfishness is.

It was not probable that either Giovanni or Corona should change in this respect, nor, indeed, in any other, for they had never been changeable or capricious people, and time had made solid their lives. To each other they were as they had always been, but to others Giovanni was a man advanced in middle life, and the beautiful Corona Saracinesca was a rose of yesterday.

She could never be anything but beautiful, even if she should live to extreme old age; but those who had known her in her youth had begun to shake their heads sadly, lamenting the glory departed, and seeing only in recollection a vision of it, while they could not see the value of what remained nor appreciate something which had come with years. Strangers who came to Rome and saw the Princess of Sant' Ilario for the first time, gazed in silent surprise at the woman who for nearly a quarter of a century had been the most beautiful in Europe, and they wondered whether, even now, anyone could be compared with her.

The degeneration of age had not taken hold upon her. The perfect features were as calm and regular as fate, the dark skin had still its clear, warm, olive tint, which very rarely changed at all perceptibly; her splendid eyes were truthful and direct still, beneath the strong black eyebrows. There were silver threads in the magnificent hair, but they were like the lights on a raven's wing. She was straight and strong and graceful still, she who had been compared to velvet and steel — slighter perhaps than in her full perfection, for she had in her some of that good Saracen blood of the south, which seems to nourish only the stronger and the finer tissues, consuming in time all that is useless; wearing away the velvet, but leaving the steel intact almost to the very last.

There could be but one such woman in one race, and it seemed in some way natural that she should have been sisterless, and should have borne only sons. But as though nature would not be altogether defeated and stayed out of balance, the delicate feminine element had come to the surface in one of the Saracinesca men. It was too fine to be womanish, too high to be effeminate, as it showed itself in Ippolito, the priest-musician. But it was unmistakably something which was neither in the old Prince, nor in Giovanni, nor in any of the other three brothers, and it made between him and his mother a bond especially their own, which the rest acknowledged without understanding, and respected without feeling that Ippolito was preferred before them. For it was not a preference, but a stronger mutual attraction, in which there was no implied unfairness to the rest.

It is one of the hardest things in the world to explain, and yet almost everyone understands it,

for it has nothing to do with language, and everything to do with feeling. We human beings need
language most to explain what is most remote
from our humanity, and those who talk the most
of feeling are often those that feel the least. For
conveying a direct impression, what is the sharpened conciseness of Euclid, or the polished eloquence of Demosthenes, what is the sledge-hammer
word blow of Æschylus, or the lightning thrust of
Dante's two-edged tongue, compared with a kiss,
or a girl's blush, or the touch of a mother's hand
— or the silent certainty of twofold thought in
one, which needs neither blush, nor touch, nor
kiss to say that love is all, and all is love?

And that bond which is sometimes between
mother and son is of this kind. It is not strange,
either, that the father who looks on should mis-
understand it, since it is the most especially
human feeling which is often the least compre-
hensible to those who do not feel it, for the
very reason that language cannot convey the impression of it to others. Nothing is less ridiculous than love, except death. Yet a man in love
is very frequently ridiculous in the eyes of his
friends and of the world, the more so in proportion as he shows the more plainly what he feels.
Yet most of those who laugh at him have probably
been in love themselves. A cynic would say that
the humour of it lies in the grim certainty which

others feel that it cannot last. Fear is terribly real to him who feels it, but a man who is frightened without cause is always laughable and generally contemptible. It is true that whereas we are all human and feel humanly, humanity is very hard to understand — because understanding is not feeling, any more than the knowledge of evil is temptation, or than the knowledge of good is virtue. The best description of a sunset cannot convey much to a man born blind, though it may awaken longings in him, and sharpen the edge of his old suffering upon the roughness of a new regret. And yet a description means very much more to most people than an explanation.

Sant' Ilario had long ago accepted the fact that his wife was in some mysterious way drawn to her second son, more than to the others. It would be saying too much, perhaps, to assert that Corona was glad when Ippolito took orders and the vow of celibacy. She was not an imaginative woman, nor nervous, nor in any way not normal. Nor were the Saracinesca by any means an excessively devout family, nor connected with the history of the church, as many Roman families are. On the contrary, they had in former times generally opposed the popes when they had not been strong enough to make one of their own, and the absence of any womanly element in the great house, between the untimely death of the old Prince's wife, and Giovanni Saracinesca's marriage with the Duchessa d'Astrardente nearly thirty years later, had certainly not favoured a tendency to devotional practices. When young Ippolito made up his mind to be a priest, the aged head of the family growled out a few not very edifying remarks in his long white beard. Even ten years earlier, he might have gone into a rage about it, which might have endangered his life, for he had a terrible temper; but he was near the end, now, and it would have taken more than that to rouse him. As for Giovanni, he was not especially pleased either, for he had never been fond of priests, and he assuredly did not care to have any in the family. Yet, in spite of this prejudice, there seemed to him to be a certain fitness in the event, against which it would be useless to argue, and after a little discussion with his wife, he accepted it as more or less inevitable.

But Corona was satisfied, if not glad, and what she felt was very like gladness, for, without reasoning at all, she knew that she should be jealous of any woman who came between her and Ippolito. She had never been able to think of a possible wife for him — as she often thought of wives for her other sons — without a sharp thrust of pain which could not be anything but jealousy. It was not exactly like what she should have felt, or fancied that she should have felt, if Giovanni had been momentarily attracted by some other woman. But it was not at all like anything else in the world.

She did not know how far Ippolito was aware of this, but she knew beyond doubt that he was instinctively drawn to her, as she was to him. She had that intuitive certainty, which women know so well, that in a moment of danger he would think first of her, precisely as her husband would. Such instincts are, perhaps, but shadowy inklings of the grey primeval past, when women and children knew to whom they must look for protection against man and beast; but they are known to us all in connexion with those we love best, though they may never cross our thoughts when we are alone.

There was between her and Ippolito a sort of constant mutual echoing of thought and feeling; that sort of sympathy which, between people of sensitive and unhealthy organization, leads to those things, not easily explained, to which the name of telepathy has lately been attached as a tentative definition. But these two were not unhealthy, nor morbidly sensitive, nor otherwise different from normal human beings. Corona had never been ill in her life, and if Ippolito had been thought delicate in his boyhood, it was by contrast with the rest of a family remarkable for most uncommon health and strength.

All this has seemed necessary in order to explain the events which at this time took place in the Sara-

cinesca household.   Nothing unusual had occurred
in the family for many years, excepting Orsino's
rather foolish and most unlucky attempt to occupy
himself in business at the time of the great building speculation, and his first love affair, to which
reference was made in the beginning of this somewhat explanatory chapter.

CHAPTER II

WHEN the notorious Prince of Corleone died without much ceremony in a small second-class hotel in Nice, and was buried with no ceremony at all worth mentioning, at the expense of the hotel keeper, his titles and what was left of his lands and other belongings went to his brother's children, since his brother was dead also. The Corleone people were never long-lived, nor had their alliances as a rule conduced to long life in others, who had been their wives and husbands. Superstitious persons said that there was upon the whole family the curse of a priest whom they had caused to be shot as a spy in order to save themselves during the wars of Napoleon in Italy. It was even said that they saw, or thought they saw, this priest when they were about to die. But as priests are plentiful in the south of Italy, it might very well be that their vision was not a vision at all, but simply some quite harmless living ecclesiastic who chanced to be passing at the time. It is true that they were said to notice always a small red hole in his forehead and another in his left cheek, but this also might have been only an effect of imagination. Nevertheless they were unfortunate, as a race, and several of them had come to violent or otherwise untimely ends within the century.

The name, Corleone, was only a title, and the town from which it was taken had long ago passed into other hands. The family name was Pagliuca d'Oriani. As often happens in Italy, they went by whichever one of the three names happened to be most familiar to the speaker who mentioned them.

At the time of thé Prince's death there were living his brother's widow and four children, consisting of three sons and one daughter; and there was another branch of the family, calling themselves Pagliuca di Bauso, with whom this history is not at present concerned.

The widowed lady was known in Sicily as Donna Maria Carolina Pagliuca. Her eldest son was Tebaldo, to whom came from his uncle the title, Prince of Corleone; and his two brothers were named Francesco and Ferdinando. Their sister, a girl seventeen years of age, was Vittoria, and was the youngest.

In the ordinary course of events, being of the south, the three sons as well as their father and mother would have each borne a distinctive title. Corleone, however, had begun life by quarrelling with his younger brother; and when the latter had died, and the property had been divided according to the code introduced after the annexation of Naples and Sicily, he had absolutely refused to allow his brother any title whatsoever. He could not prevent the division of the lands, of which, however, he had by far the larger share; but he could keep the titles, with which the law of succession does not concern itself, and he did so out of spite. Moreover, he injured and defrauded his brother by every means in his power, which was at that time considerable; and the result was that the said brother and his family became very poor indeed, and retired to live in a somewhat barbarous region of Sicily, very much in the manner of farmers and very little in the style of gentlefolks. He died of the cholera when his eldest son, Tebaldo, was barely of age, and Vittoria was a little girl at a convent in Palermo.

The three young men lived almost in the surroundings of Sicilian peasants, but with the pride and more than the ordinary vanity of a race of nobles. There might not have been much difference had their uncle been generous to them, instead of at once transferring and continuing to them his hatred of their father. But as they were placed, and with their characters, the result was inevitable. They grew up to be at once idle and vindictive, grasping and improvident, half cunning and half fierce, physically brave and morally mean. The many faults and the few virtues were not evenly distributed among them, it is true, for each had some greater or less share of them all. Tebaldo was the most cunning, Francesco the most licentious, Ferdinando was the boldest and the most rash of them all, — perhaps the best, or, at all events, the least bad.

The house which remained to them, with a little land around it, was known as Camaldoli to the peasants and the people of the neighbourhood, though its original name had been Torre del Druso — the Tower of the Druse, or of the fiend, as one chooses to interpret it. It was a good-sized, rambling, half-fortified old monastery, looking down from a gentle elevation in the high valley on one side, and having a deep gorge at the back, through which a torrent tumbled along over dark stones during three-quarters of the year. There was a sort of rampart above this chasm, and at one end rose a square tower with ruined crenellations, built of almost black tufo. It was evidently this tower which had given the place its more ancient name, before the monks had built their white plastered building against it and the rampart, with the little church in the inner court. The village of Santa Vittoria was about three-quarters of a mile distant, hidden by the spur of the hill, and separated from Camaldoli by a barren stretch of burnt lava and scoriæ, which had descended long ago from some lower crater of the volcano.

Far above all, Etna's enormous cone rose against the dark blue eastern sky like a monstrous, streaked sugar loaf. On each side of the great burnt strip between Santa Vittoria and Camaldoli, the woods and fields stretched north and south towards Messina and Catania, and westwards beyond the valley rose a great range of mountains covered high with forests of chestnut trees. No houses were visible from Camaldoli, nor any shed nor hut which could have served for a human habitation, for it was a wild and lonely country.

The three brothers lived with their mother at Camaldoli, and were served in a rough fashion by three men and four women, almost all of whom were expected to do almost anything, from stable work to cooking and waiting at table. There was a sort of slovenly abundance of coarse food and drink, but there was little else, and many a well-to-do peasant lived better than the sister-in-law and the nephews of Prince Corleone. Donna Maria Carolina scarcely ever left the house in winter or summer. She had been married from a convent, a mere child, had enjoyed a brief taste of luxury and something of happiness at the beginning of life, and had spent the years of subsequent poverty between spasmodic attempts to make gentlemen of her wild sons, bitter outbursts of regret for her marriage, and an apathetic indifference such as only comes upon women of southern races when placed in such hopeless situations as hers. She was a thin, dark woman, with traces of beauty, dressed generally in shabby black, but strangely fond of cheap and tasteless ornaments, which contrasted horribly with her worn-out mourning. As her sons grew up they acquired the habit of contradicting everything she said. Sometimes she argued her point, whatever it might be, and generally in total ignorance of the subject. Her arguments frequently ended in a passionate appeal to the justice of Heaven, and the right feeling of the saints, though the matter under discussion might not be more important than the planting of a cabbage, or the dressing of a dish of greens. Or else, as sometimes happened, she sullenly bent her brows, while her once handsome mouth curled scornfully, and from her scarcely parted lips one word came in an injured and dramatic tone.

"Villani!" she would exclaim.

The word may be translated 'boors,' and the three boys did not like it, for it is an outrageous insult from a man to a man. But it is worth noting that such rudeness to their mother did not go beyond flat contradiction in argument, and when she called her sons boors, they bore it in silence, and generally went away without a retort. There are no Italians without some traces of manners and of that submission to parents which belonged to the old patriarchal system of the Romans. It must be remembered, too, so far as this and the rest of their behaviour may be concerned, that although their father died when they were young, he had lived long enough to give them something, though not much, in the way of education, chiefly by the help of the parish priest of Santa Vittoria, and to teach them the rudimentary outward manners of young gentlemen. And these they were quite able to assume when they pleased. He had succeeded in having them taught at least enough to pass the very easy examination which entitles young men to serve but a year and a few weeks in the army, instead of the regular term; and he had taken first Tebaldo, then Tebaldo and Francesco, and then all three in successive years to Messina and Palermo for a fortnight at a time, so that they were not wholly ignorant of the world beyond Camaldoli, Santa Vittoria, and the one or two larger towns which lay within a day's ride of their remote abode.

It must not be forgotten, either, in order to understand how the brothers were able afterwards to make a tolerably decent appearance in Rome, that Italians have great powers of social adaptation; and, secondly, that the line between the nobility and the people is very clearly drawn in most parts of the country, especially in the matter of manners and speech, so that what little the young men learned from their father and mother belonged distinctively to their own class and to no other. Even had they been outwardly less polished than they really knew how to appear, their name alone would have admitted them to society, though society might have treated them coolly after a nearer acquaintance.

Vittoria, their sister, remained at the convent in Palermo after their father's death. He, poor man, seeing that his house did not promise to be a very fit place for a young girl, and especially not for one delicately organized as his daughter seemed to be, had placed her with the nuns while still a young child; and under the circumstances this was by far the wisest thing he could do. The nuns were ladies, and the convent was relatively rich. Possibly these facts had too much weight with Pagliuca, or perhaps he honestly believed that he should be able to pay regularly for Vittoria's education and living. Indeed, so long as he lived he managed to send small sums of money from time to time, and even after his death Donna Maria Carolina twice remitted a little money to the nuns. But after that nothing more was sent for a long time. Fortunately for herself, Vittoria was extremely unlike her turbulent brothers and her disappointed mother, and by the time she was ten years old she was the idol of the religious household in which she had been placed. Even had she been very different, of low birth, and of bad tem-

per, the nuns would have kept her, and would have
treated her as kindly as they could, and would have
done their best by her, though they would very
justly have required her to do something towards
earning her living under their roof when she grew
older. But apart from the child's rare charm and
lovable disposition, being of an old and noble name,
they would have considered her unfit for menial
work, though cast adrift and helpless, and they
would have thought her quite as worthy of their
sympathy as though she had belonged to the family
of one among themselves. All this, however, was
quite forgotten in their almost exaggerated affection for the child. They showed their love for her
as only such women could; for though there were a
dozen other daughters of nobles under their care, of
ranging ages, the nuns let no one know that Vittoria
was brought up by their charity after her father's
death. They gave her all she needed of the best, and
they even gave her little presents which she might
think had been sent from home. They told her that
'her mother desired her to have' a Book of Hours,
or a writing-case, or a silk handkerchief, or any such
trifles. Her mother, poor lady, doubtless did desire it, though she never said so. It was a pious
and a gentle fraud, and it prevented the other girls
from looking down upon her as a charity scholar,
as one or two of them might have done. In dress
there was no difference, of course, for they all

dressed alike, and Vittoria supposed that her parents paid for her things.

She was a very lovely girl as she grew up, and exquisite in all ways, and gentle as she was exquisite. She was not dark as her brothers were, nor as her mother. It is commonly said that all the region about Palermo is Saracen, but that the ancient Greek blood survives from Messina to Catania; and the girl certainly seemed to be of a type that differed from that of her family, which had originally come from the other side of the island. Vittoria had soft brown hair and clear brown eyes of precisely the same color as the delicate, arched eyebrows above them, a matching which always helps the harmony of any face. There was a luminous clearness, too, in the skin, which both held and gave back the light like the sheen of fine satin in shadow. There was about all her face the dream-like softness of well-defined outline which one occasionally sees in the best cut gems of the Greeks, when the precious stone itself has a golden tinge. The features were not faultless by any standard of beauty which we call perfect, but one would not have changed the faults that were there to suit rule and canon. Such as they were, they will appear more clearly hereafter. It is enough to say now that Vittoria d'Oriani had grace and charm and gentleness, and, withal, a share of beauty by no means small. And she was well educated and well cared for, as has been seen, and was brought up very differently from her brothers.

The existence of the Pagliuca at Camaldoli was not only tolerably wild and rough, as has been seen; it was, in a measure, equivocal; and it may be doubted whether all the doings of the three brothers, as they grew up, could have borne the scrutiny of the law. Sicily is not like other countries in this respect, and, at the risk of wearying the reader, it is better that something should be said at the outset concerning outlawry and brigandage, in order that what follows may be more clearly understood.

Brigandage in Sicily has a sort of intermittent permanence which foreigners cannot easily explain. The mere question which is so often asked — whether it cannot be stamped out of existence — shows a total ignorance of its nature. You may knock off a lizard's tail in winter with a switch, as most people know, but you cannot prevent the tail from growing again in the spring and summer unless you kill the lizard outright.

Brigandage is not a profession, as most people suppose. A man does not choose it as a career. It is the occasional but inevitable result of the national character under certain conditions which are sure to renew themselves from time to time. No one can change national character. The success of brigandage, whenever it manifests itself, depends primarily upon the almost inaccessible nature of some parts of the island, and, secondly, upon the helplessness of the peasants to defend themselves in remote places. It is manifestly impossible to arm a whole population, especially with weapons fit to cope with the first-rate repeating rifles and army revolvers which brigands almost invariably carry. It is equally impossible to picket troops all over the country, at distances not exceeding half a mile from station to station, in every direction, like cabbages in a field. No army would suffice. Therefore when a band is known to have formed, a large force is sent temporarily to the neighbourhood to hunt it down; and this is all that any government could do. The 'band,' as it is always called, may be very small. One man has terrorized a large district before now, and the famous Leone, when at last surrounded, slew nearly a score of men before he himself was killed, though he was quite alone.

Almost every band begins with a single individual, and he, as a rule, has turned outlaw to escape the consequences of a murder done in hot blood, and is, in all probability, a man of respectable birth and some property. It is part of the national character to proceed instantly to bloodshed in case of a quarrel, and quarrels are, unfortunately, common enough. The peasants break one another's heads and bones with their hoes and spades, and occasionally stab each other with inefficient knives, but rarely kill, because the carabineers are constantly making search for weapons, even in the labourers' pockets, and confiscate them without question when found. But the man of some property rarely goes abroad without a shot-gun, or a revolver, or both, and generally knows how to use them. He may go through life without a serious quarrel, but should he find himself involved in one, he usually kills his man at once, or is killed. If there are witnesses present to prove beyond doubt that he has killed in self-defence, he may give himself up at the nearest station of carabineers, and he is sure of acquittal. Otherwise, if he can get away, his only course is to escape to the woods without delay. This seems to be the simple explanation of the fact that such a large proportion of brigands are by no means of the lowest class, but have often been farmers and men of property, who can not only afford good weapons, but are able to get licenses to carry them. Brigands are certainly not, as a rule, from the so-called criminal classes, as foreigners suppose, though when a band becomes very large, a few common criminals may be found in the whole number; but the brigands despise and distrust them.

These things also account for the still more notable fact that the important bands have always had friends among the well-to-do landed proprietors. Indeed, they have not only friends, but often near relations, who will make great sacrifices and run considerable risks to save them from the law. And when any considerable number of brigands are caught, they have generally been betrayed into an ambush by these friends or relations. Sometimes they are massacred by them for the sake of a large reward. But to the honour of the Sicilian character, it must be said that such cases are rare, though a very notable one occurred in the year 1894, when a rich man and his two sons deliberately drugged six brigands at a sort of feast of friendship, and shot them all in their sleep, a massacre which, however, has by no means ended the existence of that particular band.

As for the practices of the bandits, they have three main objects in view : namely, personal safety, provisions wherewith to support life, and then, if possible, money in large sums, which, when obtained, may afford them the means of leaving the country secretly and for ever. With regard to the first of these ends, they are mostly young men, or men still in the prime of strength, good walkers, good riders, good shots, and not rendered conspicuous marks at a distance by a uniform. As for their provisions, when their friends do not supply them, they take what they need wherever they find it, chiefly by intimidating the peasants. In the

third matter they have large views. An ordinary
person is usually quite safe from them, especially
if armed, for they will not risk their lives for anything so mean as highway robbery. It is their
object to get possession of the persons of the richest nobles and gentlemen, from whom they can ex-
tort a really large ransom. And if they once catch
such a personage they generally get the money, for
the practice of sending an ear or a piece of nose as
a reminder to relations is not extinct. Few Sicilian
gentlemen who have lands in the interior dare
visit their estates without a military escort when a
'band' is known to be in existence, as happens to
be the case at the present time of writing.

It chanced that such a band was gathered together, though not a large one, within a few years
of Paglinca's death, and was leading a precarious
and nomadic life for a time not far from Santa
Vittoria. It was said that the Pagliuca men were
on good terms with these brigands, though of
course their mother knew nothing about it. In
the neighbourhood, no one thought much the worse
of the brothers for this. When brigands were
about, every man had to do the best he could for
himself. The Corleone, as many of the peasants
called them, were well armed, it is true, but they
were few and could not have resisted any depreda-
tions of the brigands by force. On the other hand,
they had the reputation of being brave and very

reckless young men, and even against odds might send a bullet through anyone who tried to carry off a couple of their sheep, or one of their mules. They knew the country well, too, and might be valuable allies to the carabineers, which meant that they could be useful friends to the outlaws, if they chose. Everyone knew that they were poor and that it would not be worth while to take one of them in the hope of a ransom, and no one was surprised when it was hinted that they sold provisions to the brigands for cash when they could get it, and for credit when the brigands had no money, a credit which was perfectly good until the outlaws should be taken.

There was very little direct proof of this alliance, and the Pagliuca denied it in terms which did not invite further questioning. To make a brilliant show of their perfect innocence, they led a dozen carabineers about for two days through a labyrinth of forest paths and hill passes, and brought them three times in forty-eight hours to places where a fire was still smouldering, and remains of half-cooked meat were scattered about, as though the brigands had fled suddenly at an alarm. It was very well done, and they received the officer's thanks for their efforts, with sincere expressions of regret that they should have been unsuccessful. In one of the camps they even found the skin of a sheep which they identified as one of their own, with many loud-spoken curses, by the brand on the back. It was all very well done, and the result of it was that the carabineers often applied for news of the brigands at Camaldoli, a proceeding which of course kept the d'Oriani well informed as to the whereabouts of the carabineers themselves.

It was certainly as well in the end that Vittoria should have stayed at the convent in Palermo during those years, until the death of the old Corleone suddenly changed the existence of her mother and brothers.

He died, as has been said, without much ceremony in a small hotel at Nice. He died childless and intestate, as well as ruined, so far as he knew at the time of his death. The news reached Camaldoli in the shape of a demand for money in payment of one of his just debts, from a money-lender in Palermo who was aware of the existence of the three Pagliuca brothers, and knew that they were the Prince's heirs-at-law.

It took a whole year to unravel the ruin of the dead man's estate. What he had not sold was mortgaged, and the mortgages had changed hands repeatedly during the tremendous financial crisis which began in 1888. There were debts of all kinds, just and unjust, and creditors by the hundred. The steward of the principal estate absconded with such cash as he happened to have in hand, as soon as he heard of Corleone's death. An obscure individual shot himself because the steward owed him money, and this also was talked of in the newspapers, and a good deal of printed abuse was heaped upon the dead rake. But one day Ferdinando Pagliuca entered the office of one of the papers in Palermo, struck the editor in the face, forced him into a duel, and ran him through the lungs the next morning. The editor ultimately recovered, but the Pagliuca had asserted themselves, and there was no more scurrilous talk in the press about poor dead Corleone.

Things turned out to be not quite so bad as he had imagined. Here and there, a little property had escaped, perhaps because he hardly knew of its existence. There was a small house in Rome, in the new quarter, which he had bought for a young person in whom he had been temporarily interested, and which, by some miracle, was not mortgaged. The mortgages on some of the principal estates in Sicily had found their way to the capacious desk of the Marchese di San Giacinto, whose name was Giovanni Saracinesca, and who represented a branch of that family. San Giacinto was enormously rich, and was a singular combination of old blood and modern instincts; a man of honour, but of terrible will and a good enemy; a man of very large views and of many great projects, some of which were already successfully carried out, some in course of execution, some as yet only planned. In the great crisis, he had neither lost much nor profited immediately by the disasters of others. No one called him grasping, and yet everything worth having that came within his long reach came sooner or later into his possession. When land and houses lost value and everything in the way of business was dull and dead, San Giacinto was steadily buying. When all had been excitement and mad speculation, he had quietly saved his money and waited. And in the course of his investments he had picked up the best of the Corleone mortgages, without troubling himself much as to whether the interest were very regularly paid or not. Before long he knew very well that it would not be paid at all, and that the lands would fall to him when Corleone should have completely ruined himself.

The Pagliuca family moved to Rome before the settlement of the inheritance was finished, and Vittoria was at last taken from the convent and accompanied her mother. Ferdinando alone remained at Camaldoli. The family established themselves in an apartment in the new quarter, and began to live well, if not extravagantly, on what was still a very uncertain income. Tebaldo, who managed all the business himself, succeeded in selling the house in Rome advantageously. Through San Giacinto he made acquaintance with a few Romans, who treated him courteously and regarded him with curiosity as the nephew of the notorious Prince Corleone. As for the title, San Giacinto advised him not to assume it at once, as it would not be of any especial advantage to him.

San Giacinto was on excellent terms with all his Saracinesca relations, and very naturally spoke to them about the d'Oriani. In his heart he did not like and did not trust Tebaldo, and thought his brother Francesco little better; but, in spite of this, he could not help feeling a sort of pity for the two young men, whose story reminded him of his own romantic beginnings. San Giacinto was a giant in strength and stature, and it is undoubtedly true that in all giants a tendency to good-nature and kindliness will sooner or later assert itself. He was advancing in years now, and the initial hardness of his rough nature had been tempered by years of success and of almost phenomenal domestic felicity. He was strong still, in body and mind, and not easily deceived; but he had grown kind. He pitied the Pagliuca tribe, and took his wife to see Donna Maria Carolina. He persuaded the Princess of Sant' Ilario to receive her and make acquaintance, and the Marchesa di San Giacinto brought her to the palace one afternoon with Vittoria.

Corona thought the mother pretentious, and guessed that she was at once bad-tempered and foolish; but she saw at a glance that the young girl was of a very different type, and a few kindly questions, while Donna Maria Carolina talked with the Marchesa, explained to Corona the mystery. Vittoria had never been at home, even for a visit, during the ten years which had elapsed since she had been placed at the convent, and her mother was almost a stranger to her. She was not exactly timid, as Corona could see, but her young grace was delicately nurtured and shrank and froze in the presence of her mother's coarse-grained self-assertion.

"Shall we marry her in Rome, do you think, Princess?" asked Donna Maria Carolina, nodding her head indicatively towards her daughter, while her eyes looked at Corona, and she smiled with much significance.

Vittoria's soft brown eyes grew suddenly bright and hard, and the blood sprang up in her face as though she had been struck, and her small hands tightened quietly on her parasol; but she said nothing, and looked down.

"I hope that your daughter may marry very happily," said Corona, with a kind intonation, for she saw the girl's embarrassment and understood it.

The Marchesa di San Giacinto laughed quite frankly. Her laughter was good-humoured, not noisy, and distinctly aristocratic, it is true; but Vittoria resented it, because she knew that it was elicited by her mother's remark, which had been in bad taste. Corona saw this also.

"You always laugh at the mention of marriage, Flavia," said the Princess, "and yet you are the most happily married woman I know."

"Oh, that is true!" answered the Marchesa. "My giant is good to me, even now that my hair is grey."

It was true that there were many silver threads in the thick and waving hair that grew low over her forehead, but her face had lost none of its freshness, and her eyes had all their old vivacity. She was of the type of women who generally live to a great age.

Donna Maria Carolina rose to go. In saying goodbye, Corona took Vittoria's hand.

"I am sorry that it is so late in the season, my dear," she said. "You will have little to amuse you until next year. But you must come to dinner with your mother. Will you come, and bring her?" she asked, turning to Donna Maria Carolina.

The Marchesa di San Giacinto stared in well-bred surprise, for Corona was not in the habit of asking people to dinner at first sight. Of course her invitation was accepted.

CHAPTER III

San Giacinto and his wife came to the dinner,
and two or three others, and the d'Oriani made a
sort of formal entry into Roman society under
the best possible auspices. In spite of Corona's
good taste and womanly influence, festivities at
the Palazzo Saracinesca always had an impressive
and almost solemn character. Perhaps there were
too many men in the family, and they were all
too dark and grave, from the aged Prince to his
youngest grandson, who was barely of age, and
whose black eyebrows met over his Roman nose
and seemed to shade his eyes too much. Ippolito,
the exception in his family, as Vittoria d'Oriani
was in hers, did not appear at table, but came
into the drawing-room in the evening. The Prince
himself sat at the head of the table, and rarely
spoke. Corona could see that he was not pleased
with the Pagliuca tribe, and she did her best to
help on conversation and to make Flavia San
Giacinto talk, as she could when she chose.

From time to time, she looked at Orsino, whose
face that evening expressed nothing, but whose
eyes were almost constantly turned towards Vit-

toria. It had happened naturally enough that he sat next to her, and it was an unusual experience for him. Of course, in the round of society, he occasionally found himself placed next to a young girl at dinner, and he generally was thoroughly bored on such occasions. It was either intentional or accidental on the part of his hosts, whoever they might be. If it was intentional, he had been made to sit next to some particularly desirable damsel of great birth and fortune, in the hope that he might fall in love with her and make her the future Princess Saracinesca. And he resented in gloomy silence every such attempt to capture him. If, on the other hand, he chanced to be accidentally set down beside a young girl, it happened according to the laws of precedence; and it was ten to one that the young lady had nothing to recommend her, either in the way of face, fortune, or conversation. But neither case occurred often.

The present occasion was altogether exceptional. Vittoria d'Oriani had never been to a dinner-party before, and everything was new to her. It was quite her first appearance in society, and Orsino Saracinesca was the first man who could be called young, except her brothers, with whom she had ever exchanged a dozen words. It was scarcely two months since she had left the convent, and during that time her mind had been constantly crowded with new impressions, and as constantly irritated by her mother's manner and conversation. Her education was undoubtedly very limited, though in this respect it only differed in a small degree from that of many young girls whom Orsino had met; but it was liberal as compared with her mother's, as her ideas upon religion were broad in comparison with Donna Maria Carolina's complicated system of superstition.

Vittoria's brown eyes were very wide open, as she sat quietly in her place, listening to what was said, and tasting a number of things which she had never seen before. She looked often at Corona, and wished that she might be like her some day, which was quite impossible. And she glanced at Orsino from time to time, and answered his remarks briefly and simply. She could not help seeing that he was watching her, and now and then the blood rose softly in her cheeks. On her other side sat Gianbattista Pietrasanta, whose wife was a Frangipani, and who was especially amused and interested by Vittoria's mother, his other neighbour, but paid little attention to the young girl herself.

A great writer has very truly said that psychological analysis, in a book, can never be more than a series of statements on the part of the author, telling what he himself fancies that he might have felt, could he have been placed in the position of the particular person whom he is analyzing. It is extremely doubtful whether any male writer can, by the greatest effort of imagination, clothe himself in the ingenuous purity of thought and intention which is the whole being of such a young girl as Vittoria d'Oriani when she first enters the world, after having spent ten years in a religious community of refined women.

The creature we imagine, when we try to understand such maiden innocence, is colourless and dull. Her mind and heart are white as snow, but blankly white, as the snow on a boundless plain, without so much as a fence or a tree to relieve the utter monotony. There is no beauty in such whiteness in nature, except when it blushes at dawn and sunset. Alone on snow, and with nothing but snow in sight, men often go mad; for snow-madness is a known and recognized form of insanity.

Evidently our imagination fails to evoke a true image in such a case. We are aware that maiden innocence is a state, and not a form of character. The difficulty lies in representing to ourselves a definite character in just that state. For to the word innocence we attach no narrow meaning; it extends to every question which touches humanity, to every motive in all dealings, and to every purpose which, in that blank state, a girl attributes to all human beings, living and dead. It is a magic window through which all good things appear clearly, though not often truly, and all bad things are either completely invisible, or seen in a dull, neutral, and totally uninteresting shadow of uniform misunderstanding. We judge that it must be so, from our observation. This is not analysis, but inspection.

Behind the blank lies, in the first place, the temperament, then the character, then the mind, and then that great, uncertain element of heredity, monstrous or god-like, which animates and moves all three in the gestation of unborn fate, and which is fate itself in later life, so far as there is any such thing as fatality.

Behind the blank there may be turbulent and passionate blood, there may be a character of iron and a man-ruling mind. But the blank is a blank, for all that. Catherine of Russia was once an innocent and quiet little German girl, with empty, wondering eyes, and school-girl sentimentalities. Goethe might have taken her for Werther's Charlotte. Good, bad, or indifferent, the future woman is at the magic window, and all that she is to be is within her already.

Vittoria d'Oriani was certainly not to be a Catherine, but there was no lack of conflicting heredities beneath her innocence. Orsino had thought more than most young men of his age, and he was aware of the fact, as he looked at her and talked with her, and carried on one of those apparently empty conversations, of which the recollection sometimes remains throughout a lifetime, while he quietly studied her face, and tried to find out the secret of its rare charm.

He began by treating her almost as a foreigner. He remembered long afterwards how he smiled as he asked her the first familiar question, as though she had been an English girl, or Miss Lizzie Slayback, the heiress from Nevada.

"How do you like Rome?"

"It is a great city," answered Vittoria.

"But you do not like it? You do not think it is beautiful?"

"Of course, it is not Palermo," said the young girl, quite naturally. "It has not the sea; it has not the mountains—"

"No mountains?" interrupted Orsino, smiling. "But there are mountains all round Rome."

"Not like Palermo," replied Vittoria, soberly. "And then it has not the beautiful streets."

"Poor Rome!" Orsino laughed a little. "Not even fine streets! Have you seen nothing that pleases you here?"

"Oh yes,—there are fine houses, and I have seen the Tiber, and the Queen, and—" she stopped short.

"And what else?" enquired Orsino, very much amused.

Vittoria turned her brown eyes full upon him, and paused a moment before she answered.

"You are making me say things which seem foolish to you, though they seem sensible to me," she said quietly.

"They seem original, not foolish. It is quite true that Palermo is a beautiful city, but we Romans forget it. And if you have never seen another river, the Tiber is interesting, I suppose. That is what you mean. No, it is quite reasonable."

Vittoria blushed a little, and looked down, only half reassured. It was her first attempt at conversation, and she had said what she thought, naturally and simply. She was not sure whether the great dark young man, who had eyes exactly like his mother's, was laughing at her or not. But he did not know that she had never been to a party in her life.

"Is the society in Palermo amusing?" he enquired carelessly.

"I do not know," she answered, again blushing. for she was a little ashamed of being so very young. "I left the convent on the day we started to come to Rome. And my mother did not live in Palermo," she added.

"No — I had forgotten that."

Orsino relapsed into silence for a while. He would willingly have given up the attempt at conversation, so far as concerned any hope of making it interesting. But he liked the sound of Vittoria's voice, and he wished she would speak

again. On his right hand was Tebaldo, who, as
the head of a family, and not a Roman, sat next
to Corona. He seemed to be making her rather
bold compliments. Orsino caught a phrase.

" You are certainly the most beautiful woman in
Italy, Princess," the Sicilian was saying.

Orsino raised his head, and turned slowly towards
the speaker. As he did so, he saw his mother's
look. Her brows were a little contracted, which
was unusual, but she was just turning away to
speak to San Giacinto on her other side, with an
otherwise perfectly indifferent expression. Orsino
laughed.

" My mother has been the most beautiful woman
in Europe since before I was born," he said, addressing Tebaldo rather pointedly, for the latter's
remark had been perfectly audible to him.

Tebaldo had a thin face, with a square, narrow
forehead, and heavy jaws that came to an over-
pointed chin. His upper lip was very short, and
his moustache was unusually small, black and
glossy, and turned up at the ends in aggressive
points. His upper teeth were sharp, long, and
regular, and he showed them when he smiled.
The smile did not extend upwards above the
nostrils, and there was something almost sinister
in the still black eyes. In the front view the
lower part of the face was triangular, and the low
forehead made the upper portion seem square. He

was a man of bilious constitution, of an even, yellow-brown complexion, rather lank and bony in frame, but of a type which is often very enduring. Such men sometimes have violent and uncontrolled tempers, combined with great cunning, quickness of intelligence, and an extraordinary power of taking advantage of circumstances.

Tebaldo smiled at Orsino's remark, not at all acknowledging that it might be intended as a rebuke.

"It is hard to believe that she can be your mother," he said quietly, and with such frankness as completely disarmed resentment.

But Orsino in his thoughts contrasted Tebaldo's present tone with the sound of his voice when speaking to the Princess an instant earlier, and he forthwith disliked the man, and believed him to be false and double. Corona either had not heard, or pretended not to hear, and talked indifferently with San Giacinto, whose vast, lean frame seemed to fill two places at the table, while his energetic grey head towered high above everyone else. Orsino turned to Vittoria again.

"Should you be pleased if someone told you that you were the most beautiful young lady in Italy?" he enquired.

Vittoria looked at him wonderingly.

"No," she answered. "It would not be true. How should I be pleased?"

"But suppose, for the sake of argument, that it were true. I am imagining a case. Should you be pleased?"

"I do not know — I think —" She hesitated and paused.

"I am very curious to know what you think," said Orsino, pressing her for an answer.

"I think it would depend upon whether I liked the person who told me so." Again the blood rose softly in her face.

"That is exactly what I should think," answered Orsino, gravely. "Were you sorry to leave the convent?"

"Yes, I cried a great deal. It was my home for so many years, and I was so happy there."

The girl's eyes grew dreamy as she looked absently across the table at Guendalina Pietrasanta. She was evidently lost in her recollections of her life with the nuns. Orsino was almost amused at his own failure.

"Should you have liked to stay and be a nun yourself?" he enquired, with a smile.

"Yes, indeed! At least — when I came away I wished to stay."

"But you have changed your mind since? You find the world pleasanter than you expected? It is not a bad place, I daresay."

"They told me that it was very bad," said Vittoria, seriously. "Of course, they must know, but I do not quite understand what they mean. Can you tell me something about it, and why it is bad, and what all the wickedness is?"

Orsino looked at her quietly for a moment, realizing very clearly the whiteness of her life's unwritten page.

"Your nuns may be right," he said at last. "I am not in love with the world, but I do not believe that it is so very wicked. At least, there are many good people in it, and one can find them if one chooses. No doubt, we are all miserable sinners in a theological sense, but I am not a theologian. I have a brother who is a priest, and you will see him after dinner; but though he is a very good man, he does not give one the impression of believing that the world is absolutely bad. It is true that he is rather a dilettante priest."

Vittoria was evidently shocked, for her face grew extraordinarily grave and a shade paler. She looked at Orsino in a startled way and then at her plate.

"What is the matter?" he asked quickly. "Have I shocked you?"

"Yes," she answered, almost in a whisper and still looking down. "That is," she added with hesitation, "perhaps I did not quite understand you."

"No, you did not, if you are shocked. I merely meant that although my brother is a very good man, and a very religious man, and believes that he has a vocation, and does his best to be a good priest, he has other interests in life for which I am sure that he cares more, though he may not know it."

"What other interests?" asked Vittoria, rather timidly.

"Well, only one, perhaps, — music. He is a musician first, and a priest afterwards."

The young girl's face brightened instantly. She had expected something very terrible, perhaps, though quite undefined.

"He says mass in the morning," continued Orsino, "and it may take him an hour or so to read his breviary conscientiously in the afternoon. The rest of his time he spends over the piano."

"But it is not profane music?" asked Vittoria, growing anxious again.

"Oh no!" Orsino smiled. "He composes masses and symphonies and motetts."

"Well, there is no harm in that," said Vittoria, indifferently, being again reassured.

"Certainly not. I wish I had the talent and the interest in it to do it myself. I believe that the chief real wickedness is doing nothing at all."

"Sloth is one of the capital sins," observed Vittoria, who knew the names of all seven.

"It is also the most tiresome sin imaginable, especially when one is condemned to it for life, as I am."

The young girl looked at him anxiously, and there was a little pause.

" What do you mean? " she asked. " No one is obliged to be idle."

" Will you find me an occupation? " Orsino asked in his turn, and with some bitterness. " I shall be gratified."

" Is not doing good an occupation? I am sure that there must be plenty of opportunities for that."

She felt more sure of herself when upon such ground. Orsino did not smile.

" Yes. It might take up a man's whole life, but it is not a career—"

" It was the career of many of the saints!" interrupted Vittoria, cheerfully, for she was beginning to feel at her ease at last. "Saint Francis of Assisi — Saint Clare — Saint —"

" Pray for us!" exclaimed Orsino, as though he were responding in a litany.

Vittoria's face fell instantly, and he regretted the words as soon as he had spoken them. She was like a sensitive plant, he thought; and yet she had none of the appearance of an over-impressionable, nervous girl. It was doubtless her education.

"I have shocked you again," he said gravely. " I am sorry, but I am afraid that you will often be shocked, at first. Yes; I have no doubt that to the saints doing good was a career, and that a saint might make a career of it nowadays. But you see I am not one. What I should like would be to have a profession of some sort, and to work at it with all my might."

"What a strange idea!" Vittoria looked at him in surprise; for though her three brothers had been almost beggars for ten years, it had never struck them that they could possibly have a profession. "But you are a noble," she added thoughtfully. "You will be the Prince Saracinesca some day."

Orsino laughed.

"We do not think so much of those things as we did once," he answered. "I would be a doctor, if I could, or a lawyer, or a man of business. I do not think that I should like to be a shopkeeper, though it is only a matter of prejudice—"

"I should think not!" cried Vittoria, startled again.

"It would be much more interesting than the life I lead. Almost any life would be, for that matter. Of course, if I had my choice—" He stopped.

Vittoria waited, her eyes fixed earnestly on his face, but she said nothing. Somehow she was suddenly anxious to know what his choice would be. He felt that she was watching him, and turned towards her. Their eyes met in silence, and he smiled, but her face remained grave. He was thinking that this must certainly be one of the most absurd conversations in which he had ever been engaged, but that somehow it did not appear absurd to himself, and he wondered why.

"If I had my choice—" He paused again. "I would be a leader," he added suddenly.

He was still young, and there was ambition in him. His dark eyes flashed like his mother's, a warmer colour rose for one instant under his olive skin; the fine, firm mouth set itself.

"I think you could be," said Vittoria, almost under her breath and half unconsciously.

Then, all at once, she blushed scarlet, and turned her face away to hide her colour. If there is one thing in woman which more than any other attracts a misunderstood man, it is the conviction that she believes him capable of great deeds; and if there is one thing beyond others which leads a woman to love a man, it is her own certainty that he is really superior to those around him, and really needs woman's sympathy. Youth, beauty, charm, eloquence, are all second to these in their power to implant genuine love, or to maintain it, if they continue to exist as conditions.

It mattered little to Vittoria that she had as yet no means whatever of judging whether Orsino Saracinesca had any such extraordinary powers as might some day make him a leader among men. She had been hardly conscious of the strong impression she had received, and which had made her speak, and she was far too young and simple to argue with herself about it. And he, on his part, with a good deal of experience behind him and the memory of one older woman's absolute devotion and sacrifice, felt a keen and unexpected pleasure, quite different from anything he remembered to have felt before now. Nor did he reason about it at first, for he was not a great reasoner and his pleasures in life were really very few.

A moment or two after Vittoria had spoken, and when she had already turned away her face, Orsino shook his head almost imperceptibly, as though trying to throw something off which annoyed him. It was near the end of dinner before the two spoke to each other again, though Vittoria half turned towards him twice in the mean time, as though expecting him to speak, and then, disappointed, looked at her plate again.

"Are you going to stay in Rome, or shall you go back to Sicily?" he asked suddenly, not looking at her, but at the small white hand that touched the edge of the table beside him.

Vittoria started perceptibly at the sound of his voice, as though she had been in a reverie, and her hand disappeared at the same instant. Orsino found himself staring at the tablecloth, at the spot where it had lain.

"I think — I hope we shall stay in Rome," she

answered. "My brother has a great deal of business here."

"Yes. I know. He sees my cousin San Giacinto about it almost every day."

"Yes."

Her face grew thoughtful again, but not dreamily so as before, and she seemed to hesitate, as though she had more to say.

"What is it?" asked Orsino, encouraging her to go on.

"Perhaps I ought not to tell you. The Marchese wishes to buy Camaldoli of us."

"What is Camaldoli?"

"It is the old country house where my mother and my brothers lived so long, while I was in the convent, after my father died. There is a little land. It was all we had until now."

"Shall you be glad if it is sold, or sorry?" asked Orsino, thoughtfully, and watching her face.

"I shall be glad, I suppose," she answered. "It would have to be divided among us, they say. And it is half in ruins, and the land is worth nothing, and there are always brigands."

Orsino laughed.

"Yes. I should think you might be very glad to get rid of it. There is no difficulty about it, is there?"

"Only — I have another brother. He likes it and has remained there. His name is Ferdinando.

No one knows why he is so fond of the place. They need his consent, in order to sell it, and he will not agree."

"I understand. What sort of man is your brother Ferdinando?"

"I have not seen him for ten years. They are afraid of — I mean, he is afraid of nothing."

There was something odd, Orsino thought, about the way the young girl shut her lips when she checked herself in the middle of the sentence, but he had no idea what she had been about to say. Just then Corona nodded slightly to the aged Prince at the other end of the table, and dinner was over.

"I should think it would be necessary for San Giacinto to see this other brother of yours." observed Orsino, finishing the conversation as he rose and stood ready to take Vittoria out.

The little ungloved hand lay like a white butterfly on his black sleeve, and she had to raise her arm a little to take his, though she was not short. Just before them went San Giacinto, darkening the way like a figure of fate. Vittoria looked up at him, almost awe-struck at his mere size.

"How tall he is!" she exclaimed in a very low voice. "How very tall he is!" she said again.

"We are used to him," answered Orsino, with a short laugh. "But he has a big heart, though he looks so grim."

Half an hour later, when the men were smoking in a room by themselves, San Giacinto came and sat down by Orsino in the remote corner where the latter had established himself, with a cigarette. The giant, as ever of old, had a villainous looking black cigar between his teeth.

"Do you want something to do?" he asked bluntly.

"Yes."

"Do you care to live in Sicily for a time?"

"Anywhere — Japan, if you like."

"You are easily pleased. That means that you are not in love just at present, I suppose."

San Giacinto looked hard at his young cousin for some time, in silence. Orsino met his glance quietly, but with some curiosity.

"Do you ever go to see the Countess Del Ferice?" asked the big man at last.

Orsino straightened himself in his chair and frowned a little, and then looked away as he answered by a cross-question, knocking the ash off his cigarette upon a little rock crystal dish at his elbow.

"Why do you ask me that?" he enquired rather sternly.

"Because you were very much attracted by her once, and I wished to know whether you had kept up the acquaintance since her marriage."

"I have kept up the acquaintance — and no

more," answered Orsino, meeting his cousin's eyes again. "I go to see the Countess from time to time. I believe we are on very good terms."

"Will you go to Sicily with me if I need you, and stay there, and get an estate in order for me?"

"With pleasure. When?"

"I do not know yet. It may be in a week, or it may be in a month. It will be hot there, and you will have troublesome things to do."

"So much the better."

"There are brigands in the neighbourhood just now."

"That will be very amusing. I never saw one."

"You may tell Ippolito if you like, but please do not mention it to anyone else until we are ready to go. You know that your mother will be anxious about you, and your father is a conservative—and your grandfather is a firebrand, if he dislikes an idea. One would think that at his age his temper should have subsided."

"Not in the least!" Orsino smiled, for he loved the old man, and was proud of his great age.

"But you may tell Ippolito if you like, and if you warn him to be discreet. Ippolito would let himself be torn in pieces rather than betray a secret. He is by far the most discreet of you all."

"Yes. You are right, as usual. You have a good eye for a good man. What do you think of all these Pagliuca people, or Corleone, or d'Oriani

— or whatever they call themselves?" Orsino looked keenly at his cousin as he asked the question.

"Did you ever meet Corleone? I mean the one who married Norba's daughter, — the uncle of these boys."

"I met him once. From all accounts, he must have been a particularly disreputable personage."

"He was worse than that, I think. I never blamed his wife. Well — these boys are his nephews. I do not see that any comment is necessary." San Giacinto smiled thoughtfully.

"This young girl is also his niece," observed Orsino, rather sharply.

"Who knows what Tebaldo Pagliuca might have been if he had spent ten years amongst devout old women in a convent?" The big man's smile developed into an incredulous laugh, in which Orsino joined.

"There has certainly been a difference of education," he admitted. "I like her."

"You would confer a great benefit upon a distressed family, by falling in love with her," said San Giacinto. "That worthy mother of hers was watching you two behind Pietrasanta's head, during dinner."

"Another good reason for going to Sicily," answered Orsino. "The young lady is communicative. She told me, this evening, that you were trying to buy some place of theirs, — I forget the name, — and that one of her brothers objects."

"That is exactly the place I want you to manage. The name is Camaldoli."

"Then there is no secret about it," observed Orsino. "If she has told me, she may tell the next man she meets."

"Certainly. And mysteries are useless, as a rule. I do not wish to make any with you, at all events. Here are the facts. I am going to build a light railway connecting all those places; and I am anxious to get the land into my possession, without much talk. Do you understand? This place of the Corleone is directly in my line, and is one of the most important, because it is at a point through which I must pass, to make the railway at all, short of an expensive tunnel. Your management will simply consist in keeping things in order until the railway makes the land valuable. Then I shall sell it, of course."

"I see. Very well. Could you not give my old architect something to do? Andrea Contini is his name. The houses we built for Del Ferice have all turned out well, you know." Orsino laughed rather bitterly.

"Remind me of him at the proper time," said San Giacinto. "Tell him to learn something about building small railway stations. There will be between fifteen and twenty, altogether."

"I will. But — do you expect that a railway in Sicily will ever pay you?"

"No. I am not an idiot."

"Then why do you build one, if that is not an indiscreet question?"

"The rise in the value of all the land I buy will make it worth while, several times over. It is quite simple."

"It must take an enormous capital," said Orsino, thoughtfully.

"It needs a large sum of ready money. But the lands are generally mortgaged for long periods, and almost to two-thirds of their selling value. The holders of the mortgages do not care who owns the land. So I pay about one-third in cash."

"What becomes of the value of a whole country, when all the land is mortgaged for two-thirds of what it is worth?" asked Orsino, carelessly, and half laughing.

But San Giacinto did not laugh.

"I have thought about that," he answered gravely. "When the yield of the land is not enough to pay the interest on the mortgages, the taxes to the government, and some income to the owners, they starve outright, or emigrate. There is a good deal of starvation nowadays, and a good deal of emigration in search of bread."

"And yet they say that the value of land is

increasing almost all over the country," objected Orsino. "You count on it yourself."

"The value rises wherever railways and roads are built."

"And what pays for the railways?"

"The taxes."

"And the people pay the taxes."

"Exactly. And the taxes are enormous. The people in places remote from the projected railway are ruined by them, but the people who own land where the railways pass are indirectly very much enriched by the result. Sometimes a private individual like myself builds a light road. I think that is a source of wealth, in the end, to everyone. But the building of the government roads, like the one down the west coast of Calabria, seems to destroy the balance of wealth and increase emigration. It is a necessary evil."

"There are a good many necessary evils in our country," said Orsino. "There are too many."

"*Per aspera ad astra.* I never knew much Latin, but I believe that means something. There are also unnecessary evils, such as brigandage in Sicily, for instance. You can amuse yourself by fighting that one, if you please; though I have no doubt that the brigands will often travel by my railway —and they will certainly go in the first class."

The big man laughed and rose, leaving Orsino to meditate upon the prospect of occupation which was opened to him.

CHAPTER IV

Orsino remained in his corner a few minutes,
after San Giacinto had left him, and then rose to
go into the drawing-room. As he went he passed
the other men who were seated and standing, all
near together and not far from the empty fireplace,
listening to Tebaldo Pagliuca, who was talking
about Sicily with a very strong Sicilian accent.
Orsino paused a moment to hear what he was
saying. He was telling the story of a frightful
murder committed in the outskirts of Palermo not
many weeks earlier, and about which there had
been much talk. But Tebaldo was on his own
ground and knew much more about it than had
appeared in the newspapers. His voice was not
unpleasant. It was smooth, though his words
were broken here and there by gutturals which he
had certainly not learned on his own side of the
island. There was a sort of reserve in the tones
which contrasted with the vividness of the language. Orsino watched him and looked at him
more keenly than he had done as yet. He was
struck by the stillness of the deep eyes, which
were slightly bloodshot, like those of some Arabs,

and at the same time by the mobility and changing expression of the lower part of the face. Tebaldo made gestures, too, which had a singular directness. Yet the whole impression given was that he was a good actor rather than a man of continued, honest action, and that he could have performed any other part as well. Near him stood his brother Francesco. There was doubtless a family resemblance between the two, but the difference of constitution was apparent to the most unpractised eye. The younger man was stouter, more sanguine, less nervous. The red blood glowed with strong health under his brown skin, his lips were scarlet and full, his dark moustache was soft and silky like his short, smooth hair, and his eyes were soft, too, and moistly bright, very long, with heavy drooping lids that were whiter than the skin of the rest of the face. Francesco was no more like his sister than was Tebaldo.

Orsino found himself by his father as he paused in passing, and he suddenly realized how immeasurably nearer he was to this strong, iron-grey, middle-sized, silent man beside him, than to any other one of all the men in the room, including his own brothers. Sant' Ilario had perhaps never understood his eldest son; or perhaps there was between them the insurmountable barrier of his own solid happiness. For it is sorrow that draws men together. Happiness needs no sympathy;

happiness is not easily disturbed; happiness that is solidly founded is itself a most negative source of the most all-pervading virtue, without the least charity for unhappiness' sins; happiness suffices to itself; happiness is a lantern to its own feet; it is all things to one man and nothing to all the rest; it is an impenetrable wall between him who has it and mankind. And Sant' Ilario had been happy for nearly thirty years. In appearance, as was to be anticipated, he had turned out to be like his father, as the latter had been at the same age. In temper, he was different, as the conditions of his life had been of another sort. The ancient head of the house had lost his Spanish wife when very young, and had lived many years alone with his only son. Giovanni had met with no such misfortune. His wife was alive and still beautiful at an age when many women have forgotten the taste of flattery; and his four sons were all grown men, straight and tall, so that he looked up to their faces when they stood beside him. Strong, peaceable, honest, rather hard-faced young men, they were, excepting Ippolito, the second of them, who had talent and a lovable disposition in place of strength and hardness of character.

They were fond of their father, no doubt, and there was great solidarity in the family. But what they felt for Sant' Ilario was perhaps more like an allegiance than an affection, and they looked to him as the principal person of importance in the family, because their grandfather was such a very old man. They were accustomed to take it for granted that he was infallible when he expressed himself definitely in a family matter, whereas they had no very high opinion of his judgment in topics and questions of the day; for they had received a modern education, and were to some extent imbued with those modern prejudices compared with which the views of our fathers hardly deserved the name of a passing caprice.

Orsino thought that there was something at once cunning and ferocious about Tebaldo's way of telling the story. He had a fine smile of appreciation for the secrecy and patience of the two young men who had sought occasion against their sister's lover, and there was a squaring of the angular jaws and a quick forward movement of the head, as of a snake when striking, to accompany his description of the death-blow. Orsino listened to the end and then went quietly out and returned to the drawing-room.

Vittoria d'Oriani was seated near Corona, who was talking to her in a low tone. The other ladies were standing together before a famous old picture. The Marchesa di San Giacinto was smoking a cigarette. Orsino sat down by his mother, who looked at him quietly and smiled, and then went on speaking. The young girl glanced at Orsino.

She was leaning forward, one elbow on her knee, and her chin supported in her hand, her lips a little parted as she listened with deep interest to what the elder woman said. Corona was telling her of Rome many years earlier, of the life in those days, of Pius the Ninth, and of the coming of the Italians.

"How can you remember things that happened when you were so young!" exclaimed Vittoria, watching the calm and beautiful face.

"I was older than you even then," answered Corona, with a smile. "And I married very young," she added thoughtfully. "I was married at your age, I think. How old are you, my dear?"

"I am eighteen — just eighteen," replied Vittoria.

"I was married when I was scarcely seventeen. It was too young."

"But you have always been so happy. Why do you say that?"

"What makes you think that I have always been happy?" asked the Princess.

"Your face, I think. One or two of the nuns were very happy, too. But it was different. They had quite another look on their faces."

"I daresay," answered Corona, and she smiled again, and looked proudly at Orsino.

She rose and crossed the room, feeling that she was neglecting her older guests for the young girl, who was thus left with Orsino again. He did not see Donna Maria Carolina's quick glance as she discovered the fact, and made sure of it, looking again and again at the two while she joined a little in the conversation which was going on around her. She was very happy, just then, poor lady, and almost forgot to struggle against the accumulated provincialisms of twenty years, or to be anxious lest her new friends should discover that her pearls were false. For the passion for ornament, false or real, had not diminished with the improvement in her fortunes.

But Orsino was not at all interested in Vittoria's mother, and he had seen too much to care whether women wore real jewelry or not. He had almost forgotten the young girl after dinner when he had sat down in the corner of the smoking-room, but San Giacinto's remark had vividly recalled her face to his memory, with a strong desire to see her again at once. Nothing was easier than to satisfy such a wish, and he found himself by her side.

Once there, he did not trouble himself to speak to her for several moments. Vittoria showed considerable outward self-possession, though it was something of an ordeal to sit in silence, almost touching him and not daring to speak, while he was apparently making up his mind what to say. It had been much easier during dinner, she thought, because she had been put in her place without being consulted, and was expected to be there, without the least idea of attracting attention. Now, she felt a little dizzy for a moment, as though the room were swaying; and she was afraid that she was going to blush, which would have been ridiculous.

Now, he was looking at her, while she looked down at her little white fan that lay on the white stuff of her frock, quite straight, between her two small, white-gloved hands. The nuns had not told her what to do in any such situation. Still Orsino did not speak. Two minutes had crawled by, like two hours, and she felt a fluttering in her throat.

It was absurd, she thought. There was no reason for being so miserable. Very probably, he was not thinking of her at all. But it was of no use to tell herself such things, for her embarrassment grew apace, till she felt that she must spring from her seat and run from the room without looking at him. The fluttering became almost convulsive, and her hands pressed the little fan on each side, clenching themselves tightly. Still he did not speak.

In utter despair she began to recite inwardly the litany of the saints, biting her lips lest they should move and he should guess what she was doing. In her suppressed excitement the holy personages raced and tumbled over each other at a most unseemly rate, till the procession was violently checked by the gravely indifferent tones of

Orsino's voice. Her hands relaxed, and she turned a little pale.

"Have you been to Saint Peter's?" he enquired calmly.

He was certainly not embarrassed, but he could think of nothing better to say to a young girl. On the first occasion, at dinner, he had asked her how she liked Rome. At all events it had opened the conversation. He remembered well enough the half dozen earnest words they had exchanged; and there was something more than mere memory, for he knew that he half wished they might reach the same point again. Perhaps, if the wish had been stronger and if Vittoria had been a little older, it might have been easier.

"Yes," she said. "My mother took me as soon as we came. She was very anxious that we should pay our devotion to the patron saint."

Orsino smiled a little.

"Saint Peter is not the patron of Rome," he observed. "Our protector is San Filippo Neri."

Vittoria looked up in genuine surprise.

"Saint Peter is not the patron saint of Rome!" she exclaimed. "But — I always thought — "

"Naturally enough. All sorts of things in Rome seem to be what they are not. We seem to be alive, for instance. We are not. Six or seven years ago we were all in a frantic state of excitement over our greatness. We have turned out to be nothing but a set of embalmed specimens in glass cases. Do not look so much surprised, signorina — or shocked — which is it?"

He laughed a little.

"I cannot help it," answered Vittoria, simply, her brown eyes still fixed on him in wonder. "It is — it is all so different from what I expected — the things people say —" She hesitated and stopped short, turning her eyes from him.

The light was strong in the room, for the aged Prince hated the modern fashion of shading lamps almost to a dusk. Orsino watched Vittoria's profile, and the graceful turn of her young throat as she looked away, and the fine growth of silky hair from the temples and behind the curving little ear. The room was warm, and he sat silently watching her for a moment. She was no longer embarrassed, for she was not thinking of herself, and she did not know how he was thinking of her just then.

"I wonder what you expected us to be like," he said at last. "And what you expected us to say," he added as an afterthought.

It crossed his mind that if she had been a married woman three or four years older, he might have found her very amusing in conversation. He could certainly not have been talking in detached and almost idiotic phrases, as he was actually doing. But if she had been a young married

woman, her charm would have been different, and
of a kind not new to him. There was a novelty
about Vittoria, and it attracted him strongly. There
was real freshness and untried youth in her; she
had that sort of delicacy which some flowers have,
and which is not fragility, the bloom of a precious
thing fresh broken from the mould and not yet
breathed upon. He wondered whether all young
girls had this inexpressible something. and if so,
why he had never noticed it.

"I am not quite sure," answered Vittoria, blushing a little at the thought that she could have had
a preconceived idea of Orsino Saracinesca. ·

The reply left everything to be desired in the
way of brilliancy, but the voice was soft and ex-
pectant, as some women's voices are, that seem just
upon the point of vibrating to a harmonic while
yielding the fundamental tone in all its roundness.
There are rare voices that seem to possess a distinct living individuality, apart from the women
to whom they belong. a sort of extra-natural musical life, of which the woman herself cannot control nor calculate the power. It is not the 'golden
voice' which some great actresses have. One
recognizes that at the first hearing; one admits
its beauty; one hears it three or four times. and
one knows it by heart. It will pronounce certain
phrases in a certain way, inevitably; it will soften
and swell and ring with mathematical precision at

the same verse, at the identical word, night after night, year after year, while it lasts. Vittoria's voice was not like that. It had the spontaneity of independent life which a passion itself has when it takes possession of a man or a woman. Orsino felt it, and was conscious of a new sensitiveness in himself.

On the whole, to make a very wide statement of a general truth, Italian men are moved by sense and Italian women are stirred by passion. Between passion and sense there is all the difference that exists between the object and the idea. Sense appreciates, passion idealizes; sense desires all things, passion hungers for one; sense is material, though ever so æsthetized and refined, but passion clothes fact with unearthly attributes; sense is singly selfish, passion would make a single self of two. The sensual man says, 'To have seen much and to have little is to have rich eyes and poor hands'; the passionate man or woman will 'put it to the test, to win or lose it all,' like Montrose. Sense is vulgar when it is not monstrous in strength, or hysterical to madness. Passion is always noble, even in its sins and crimes. Sense can be satisfied, and its satisfaction is a low sort of happiness; but passion's finer strings can quiver with immortal pain, and ring with the transcendent harmony that wakes the hero even in a coward's heart.

Vittoria first touched Orsino by her outward

charm, by her voice, by her grace. But it was his
personality, or her spontaneous imagination of it,
which made an indelible impression upon her mind
before the first evening of their acquaintance was
over. The woman who falls in love with a man
for his looks alone is not of a very high type, but
the best and bravest men that ever lived have
fallen victims to mere beauty, often without much
intelligence, or faith, or honour.

Orsino was probably not aware that he was falling in love at first sight. Very few men are, and
yet very many people certainly begin to fall in
love at a first meeting, who would scout the idea
as an absurdity. For love's beginnings are most
exceedingly small in the greatest number of instances. Were they greater, a man might guard
himself more easily against his fate.

CHAPTER V

At that time a young Sicilian singer had lately made her first appearance in Rome and had been received with great favour. She was probably not destined ever to become one of the chief artists of the age, but she possessed exactly the qualifications necessary to fascinate a Roman audience. She was very young, she was undeniably beautiful, and she had what Romans called a 'sympathetic' voice. They think more of that latter quality in Italy than elsewhere. It is what in English we might call charm, and to have it is to have the certainty of success with an Italian public.

Aliandra Basili was the daughter of a respectable notary in the ancient town of Randazzo, which lies on the western slope of Mount Etna, on the high road from Piedimonte to Bronte and Catania, within two hours' ride of Camaldoli, the Corleone place. It is a solemn old walled town, built of almost black tufo, though many of the houses on the main street have now been stuccoed and painted; and it has a very beautiful Saracen-Norman cathedral.

Aliandra's life had been very like that of any

other provincial girl of the middle class. She had been educated in a small convent, while her excellent father, whose wife was dead, laboured to accumulate a little dowry for his only child. At fifteen years of age, she had returned to live with him, and he had entertained good hopes of marrying her off before she was seventeen. In fact, he thought that he had only to choose among a number of young men, of whom any one would be delighted to become her husband.

Then, one day, Tebaldo and Francesco Pagliuca came riding down from Camaldoli, and stopped at the notary's house to get a small lease drawn up; and while they were there, in the dusty office, doing their best to be sure of what old Basili's legal language meant, they heard Aliandra singing to herself upstairs. After that they came to Randazzo again, both separately and together, and at last they persuaded old Basili that his daughter had a fortune in her voice and should be allowed to become a singer. He consented after a long struggle, and sent her to Messina to live with a widowed sister of his, and to be taught by an old master of great reputation who had taken up his abode there. Very possibly Basili agreed to this step with a view to removing the girl to a distance from the two brothers, who made small secret of their admiration for her, or about their jealousy of each other; and he reflected that she could

be better watched and guarded by his sister, who
would have nothing else to do, than by himself.
For he was a busy man, and obliged to spend his
days either in his office, or in visits to distant
clients, so that the motherless girl was thrown
far too much upon her own resources.

Tebaldo, on the other hand, realized that so
long as she lived in Randazzo, he should have
but a small chance of seeing her alone. He
could not come and spend a week at a time in
the town, but he could find an excuse for being
longer than that in Messina, and he trusted to
his ingenuity to elude the vigilance of the aunt
with whom she was to live. In Messina, too, he
should not have his brother at his elbow, trying to
outdo him at every turn, and evidently attracting
the young girl to a certain extent.

To tell the truth, Aliandra's head was turned
by the attentions of the two young noblemen,
though her father never lost an opportunity of
telling her that they were a pair of penniless
good-for-nothings and otherwise dangerous characters, supposed to be on good terms with the
brigands of the interior, and typical 'maffeusi'
through and through. But such warnings were
much more calculated to excite the girl's interest
than to frighten her. She had an artist's nature
and instincts, and the two young gentlemen were
very romantic characters in her eyes, when they

rode down from their dilapidated stronghold, on their compact little horses, their beautiful Winchester rifles slung over their shoulders, their velvet coats catching the sunlight, their spurs gleaming, and their broad hats shading their dark eyes. Had there been but one of them, her mind would soon have been made up to make him marry her, and she might have succeeded without much difficulty. But she found it hard to decide between the two. They were too different for comparison, and yet too much alike for preference. Tebaldo was a born tyrant, and Francesco a born coward. She was dominated by the one and she ruled the other, but she was not in love with either, and she could not make up her mind whether it would on the whole be more agreeable to love her master or her slave.

Meanwhile she made rapid progress in her singing, appeared at the opera in Palermo, and almost immediately obtained an engagement in Rome. To her father, the sum offered her appeared enormous, and her aunt was delighted by the prospect of going to Rome with her during the winter. Aliandra had been successful from the first, and she seemed to be on the high road to fame. The young idlers of rich Palermo intrigued to be introduced to her and threw enormous nosegays to her at the end of every act. She found that there were scores of men far handsomer and richer than the Paglinca brothers, ready to fall in love with her, and she began to reflect seriously upon her position. Artist though she was, by one side of her nature, there was in her a touch of her father's sensible legal instinct, together with that extraordinary self-preserving force which usually distinguishes the young girl of southern Italy.

She soon understood that no one of her new admirers would ever think of asking her to be his wife, whereas she was convinced that she could marry either Tebaldo or Francesco, at her choice and pleasure. They were poor, indeed, but of as good nobility as any of the rich young noblemen of Palermo, and she was beginning to find out what fortunes were sometimes made by great singers. She dreamed of buying back the old Corleone estates and of being some day the Princess of Corleone herself. That meant that she must choose Tebaldo, since he was to get the title. And here she hesitated again. She did not realize that Francesco was actually a physical coward and rather a contemptible character altogether; to her he merely seemed gentle and winning, and she thought him much ill used by his despotic elder brother. As for the third brother, Ferdinando, of whom mention has been made, she had rarely seen him. He was probably the best of the family, which was not saying much, and he was also by far the least civilized. He was undoubtedly in close communication with the brigands, and when he was occasionally absent from home, he was not spending his time in Messina or Randazzo.

Time went on, and in the late autumn Aliandra and her aunt went to Rome for the season. As has been seen, it pleased fortune that the Pagliuca brothers should be there also, with their mother and sister, Ferdinando remaining in Sicily. When the question of selling Camaldoli to San Giacinto arose, Ferdinando at first flatly refused to give his consent. Thereupon Tebaldo wrote him a singularly temperate and logical letter, in which he very quietly proposed to inform the government of Ferdinando's complicity with the brigands, unless he at once agreed to the sale. Ferdinando might have laughed at the threat had it come from anyone else, but he knew that Tebaldo's thorough acquaintance with the country and with the outlaws' habits would give him a terrible advantage. Tebaldo, if he gave information, could of course never return to Sicily, for his life would not be safe, even in broad daylight, in the Macqueda of Palermo, and it was quite possible that the mafia might reach him even in Rome. But he was undoubtedly able to help the government in a raid in which many of Ferdinando's friends must perish or be taken prisoners. For their sakes

Ferdinando signed his consent to the sale, before old Basili in Randazzo, and sent the paper to Rome; but that night he swore that no Roman should ever get possession of Camaldoli while he was alive, and half a dozen of the boldest among the outlaws swore that they would stand by him in his resolution.

Aliandra knew nothing of all this, for Tebaldo was far too wise to tell anyone how he had forced his brother's consent. She would certainly have been disgusted with him, had she known the truth, for she was morally as far superior to him and to Francesco as an innocent girl brought up by honest folks can be better than a pair of exceedingly corrupt young adventurers. But they both had in a high degree the power of keeping up appearances and of imposing upon their surroundings. Tebaldo was indeed subject to rare fits of anger in which he completely lost control of himself, and when he was capable of going to any length of violence; but these were very unusual, and as a general rule he was reticent in the extreme. Francesco possessed the skill and gentle duplicity of a born coward and a born ladies' man. They both deceived Aliandra, in spite of her father's early warning and her old aunt's anxious advice.

Aliandra was successful beyond anyone's expectations during her first engagement in Rome, and she was wise enough to gain herself the reputation of being unapproachable to her many admirers. Only Tebaldo and Francesco, whom she now considered as old friends of her family, were ever admitted to her room at the theatre, or received at the quiet apartment where she lived with her aunt.

On the night of the dinner-party at the Palazzo Saracinesca, Aliandra was to sing in Lucia for the first time in Rome. Both the brothers had wished that they could have been in the theatre to hear her, instead of spending the evening in the society of those very stiff and mighty Romans, and both made up their minds separately that they would see her before she left the Argentina that night. Tebaldo, as usual, took the lead of events, and peremptorily ordered Francesco to go home with their mother and sister in the carriage.

When the Corleone party left the palace, therefore, Francesco got into the carriage, but Tebaldo said that he preferred to walk, and went out alone from under the great gate. He was not yet very familiar with the streets of Rome, but he believed that he knew the exact situation of the palace, and could easily find his way from it to the Argentina theatre, which was not very far distant.

The old part of the city puzzled him, however. He found himself threading unfamiliar ways, dark lanes, and winding streets which emerged suddenly upon small squares from which three or four other streets led in different directions. Instinctively he looked behind him from time to time, and felt in his pocket for the pistol which, like a true provincial, he thought it as necessary to carry in Rome as in his Sicilian home. Presently he looked at his watch, saw that it was eleven o'clock, and made up his mind to find a cab if he could. But that was not an easy matter either, in that part of the city, and it was twenty minutes past eleven when he at last drew up to the stage entrance at the back of the Argentina. A weary, grey, unshaven, and very dirty old man admitted him, looked at his face, took the flimsy currency note which Tebaldo held out, and let him pass without a word. The young man knew his way much better within the building than out in the streets. In a few moments he stopped before a dingy little door, the last on the left in a narrow corridor dimly lit by a single flame of gas, which was turned low for economy's sake. He knocked sharply and opened the door without waiting for an answer.

There were three persons in the small, low dressing-room, and all three faced Tebaldo rather anxiously. Aliandra Basili, the young Sicilian prima donna who had lately made her first appearance in Rome, was seated before a dim mirror which stood on a low table covered with appliances for theatrical dressing. Her maid was arranging a white veil on her head, and beside her, very near to her, and drawing back from her as Tebaldo entered, sat Francesco.

Tebaldo's lips moved uneasily, as he stood still for a moment, gazing at the little group, his hand on the door. Then he closed it quickly behind him, and came forward with a smile.

"Good evening," he said. "I lost my way in the streets and am a little late. I thought the curtain would be up for the last act."

"They have called me once," answered Aliandra. "I said that I was not ready, for I knew you would come."

She was really very handsome and very young, but the mask of paint and powder changed her face and expression almost beyond recognition. Even her bright, gold-brown eyes were made to look black and exaggerated by the deep shadows painted with antimony below them, and on the lids. The young hand she held out to Tebaldo was whitened with a chalky mixture to the tips of the fingers. She was dressed in the flowing white robe which Lucia wears in the mad scene, and the flaring gaslights on each side of the mirror made her face and wig look terribly artificial. Tebaldo thought so as he looked at her, and remembered the calm simplicity of Corona Saracinesca's mature beauty. But he had known Aliandra long, and his imagination saw her own face through her paint.

"It was good of you to wait for me," he said.

"I daresay my brother helped the time to pass pleasantly."

"I have only just come," said Francesco, quickly. "I took our mother home — it is far."

"I did not know that you were coming at all," replied Tebaldo, coldly. "How is it going?" he asked, sitting down by Aliandra. "Another ovation?"

"No. They are waiting for the mad scene, of course — and my voice is as heavy as lead to-night. I shall not please anyone — and it is the first time I have sung Lucia in Rome. My nerves are in a state —"

"You are not frightened? You — of all people?"

"I am half dead with fright. I am white under my rouge. I can feel it."

"Poor child!" exclaimed Francesco, softly, and his eyes lightened as he watched her.

"Bah!" Tebaldo shrugged his shoulders and smiled. "She always says that!"

"And sometimes it is true," answered Aliandra, with a sharp sigh.

A double rap at the door interrupted the conversation.

"Signorina Basili! Are you ready?" asked a gruff voice outside.

"Yes!" replied the young girl, rising with an effort.

Francesco seized her left hand and kissed it.

Tebaldo said nothing, but folded his arms and stood aside. He saw on his brother's dark moustache a few grains of the chalky dust which whitened Aliandra's fingers.

"Do not wait for me when it is over," she said. "My aunt is in the house, and will take me home. Good night."

"Goodbye," said Tebaldo, looking intently into her face as he opened the door.

She started in surprise, and perhaps her face would have betrayed her pain, but the terribly artificial rouge and powder hid the change.

"Come and see me to-morrow," she said to Tebaldo, in a low voice, when she was already in the doorway.

He did not answer, but kept his eyes steadily on her face.

"Signorina Basili! You will miss your cue!" cried the gruff voice in the corridor.

Aliandra hesitated an instant, glancing out and then looking again at Tebaldo.

"To-morrow," she said suddenly, stepping out into the passage. "To-morrow," she repeated, as she went swiftly towards the stage.

She looked back just before she disappeared, but there was little light, and Tebaldo could no longer see her eyes.

He stood still by the door. Then his brother passed him.

“ I am going to hear this act,” said Francesco, quietly, as though unaware that anything unusual had happened.

Before he was out of the door, he felt Tebaldo’s hand on his shoulder, gripping him hard and shaking him a little. He turned his head, and his face was suddenly pale. Tebaldo kept his hand on his brother’s shoulder and pushed him back against the wall of the passage, under the solitary gaslight.

“ What do you mean by coming here ? ” he asked. “ How do you dare ? ”

Francesco was badly frightened, for he knew Tebaldo’s ungovernable temper.

“ Why not ? ” he tried to ask. “ I have often been here — ”

“ Because I warned you not to come again. Because I am in earnest. Because I will do you some harm, if you thrust yourself into my way with her.”

“ I shall call for help now, unless you let me go,” answered Francesco, with white lips. Tebaldo laughed savagely.

“ What a coward you are ! ” he cried, giving his brother a final shake and then letting him go. “ And what a fool I am to care ! ” he added, laughing again.

“ Brute ! ” exclaimed Francesco, adjusting his collar and smoothing his coat.

" I warned you," retorted Tebaldo, watching him. "And now I have warned you again," he added. "This is the second time. Are there no women in the world besides Aliandra Basili?"

"I knew her first," objected the younger man, beginning to recover some courage.

"You knew her first? When she was a mere child in Randazzo,—when we went to her father about a lease, we both heard her singing,—but what has that to do with it? That was six years ago, and you have hardly seen her since."

"How do you know?" asked Francesco, scornfully.

He had gradually edged past Tebaldo towards the open end of the passage.

"How do you know that I did not often see her alone before she went to Messina, and since then, too?" He smiled as he renewed the question.

"I do not know," said Tebaldo, calmly. "You are a coward. You are also a most accomplished liar. It is impossible to believe a word you say, good or bad. I should not believe you if you were dying, and if you swore upon the holy sacraments that you were telling me the truth."

"Thank you," answered Francesco, apparently unmoved by the insult. "But you would probably believe Aliandra, would you not?"

"Why should I? She is only a woman."

Tebaldo turned angrily as he spoke, and his eyelids drooped at the corners, like a vulture's.

"You two are not made to be believed," he said, growing more cold. "I sometimes forget, but you soon remind me of the fact again. You said distinctly this evening that you would go home with our mother—"

"So I did," interrupted Francesco. "I did not promise to stay there—"

"I will not argue with you—"

"No. It would be useless, as you are in the wrong. I am going to hear the act. Good night."

Francesco walked quickly down the passage. He did not turn to look behind him, but it was not until he was at the back of the stage, groping his way amidst lumber and dust towards the other side, that he felt safe from any further violence.

Tebaldo had no intention of following. He stood quite still under the gaslight for a few seconds, and then opened the door of the dressing-room again. He knew that the maid was there alone.

"How long was my brother here before I came?" he asked sharply.

The woman was setting things in order, packing the tinsel-trimmed gown which the singer had worn in the previous scene. She looked up nervously, for she was afraid of Tebaldo.

"A moment, only a moment," she answered.

not pausing in her work, and speaking in a scared tone.

Tebaldo looked at her, and saw that she was frightened. He was not in the humour to believe anyone just then, and after a moment's silence, he turned on his heel and went out.

CHAPTER VI

"What strange people there are in the world," said Corona Saracinesca to her husband, on the morning after the dinner at which the Corleone family had been present.

Giovanni was reading a newspaper, leaning back in his own especial chair in his wife's morning room. It was raining, and she was looking out of the window. There are not many half-unconscious actions which betray so much of the general character and momentary temper, as an idle pause before closed window panes, and a careless glance down into the street or up at the sky. The fact has not been noticed, but deserves to be. Many a man or woman, at an anxious crisis, turns to the window, with the sensation of being alone for a moment, away from the complications created by the other person or persons in the room, free, for an instant, to let the features relax, the eye darken, or the lips smile, as the case may be — off the stage, indeed, as a comedian in the side scenes. Or again, when there is no anxiety, one goes from one's work, to take a look at the outside world, not caring to see it, but glad to be away from the task · and to give the mind a breathing space. And then, also, the expression of the features changes, and if one stops to think of it, one is aware that the face is momentarily rested. Another, who has forgotten trouble and pain for a while, in conversation or in pleasant reading, goes to the window. And the grief, or the pain, or the fear, comes back with a rush and clouds the eyes and bends the brow, till he who suffers turns with something like fear from the contemplation of the outer world and takes up his book, or his talk, or his work, or anything which can help him to forget. With almost all people, there is a sudden change of sensation in first looking out of the window. One drums impatiently on the panes, another bites his lip, a third grows very still and grave, and one, perhaps, smiles suddenly, and then glances back to the room, fearing lest his inward lightness of heart may have betrayed itself.

Corona had nothing to conceal from Giovanni nor from herself. She had realized the rarest and highest form of lasting human happiness, which is to live unparted from the single being loved, with no screen of secret to cast a shadow on either side. Such a life can have but few emotions, yet the possibility of the very deepest emotion is always present in it, as the ocean is not rigid when it is quiet, as the strong man asleep is not past waking, nor the singer mute when silent.

Corona had been moving quietly about the room, giving life to it by her touch, where mechanical hands had done their daily work of dull neatness. She loosened the flowers in a vase, moved the books on the table, pulled the long lace curtains a little out from under the heavy ones, turned a chair here and a knickknack there, set the little calendar on the writing-table, and moved the curtains again. Then at last she paused before the window. Her lids drooped thoughtfully and her mouth relaxed, as she made the remark which caused Giovanni to look up from his paper.

"What strange people there are in the world!" she exclaimed.

"It is fortunate that they are not all like us," answered Giovanni.

"Why?"

"The world would stop, I fancy. People would all be happy, as we are, and would shut themselves up, and there would be universal peace, the millennium, and a general cessation of business. Then would come the end of all things. Of whom are you thinking?"

"Of those people who came to dinner last night, and of our boys."

"Of Orsino, I suppose. Yes—I know—" He paused.

"Yes," said Corona, thoughtfully.

Both were silent for a moment. They thought

together, having long been unaccustomed to think apart. At last Giovanni laughed quietly.

"Our children cannot be exactly like us," he said. "They must live their own lives, as we live ours. One cannot make lives for other people, you know."

"Orsino is so apathetic," said Corona. "He opens his eyes for a moment and looks at things as though he were going to be interested. Then he closes them again, and does not care what happens. He has no enthusiasm like Ippolito. Nothing interests him, nothing amuses him. He is not happy, and he is not unhappy. You could not surprise him. I sometimes think that you could not hurt him, either. He is young, yet he acts like a man who has seen everything, done everything, heard everything, and tasted everything. He does not even fall in love."

Corona smiled as she spoke the last words, but her eyes were thoughtful. In her heart, no thoroughly feminine woman can understand that a young man may not be in love for a long time, and may yet be normally sensible.

"I was older than he when you and I met," observed Giovanni.

"Yes — but you were different. Orsino is not at all like you."

"Nor Ippolito either."

"There is more of you in him than you think,

Giovanni, though he is so gentle and quiet, and fond of music.”

“The artistic temperament, my dear,— very little like me.”

“There is a curious tenacity under all that.”

“No one has ever thwarted him,” objected Giovanni. “Or, rather, he has never thwarted anybody. That is a better way of putting it.”

“I believe he has more strength of character than the other three together. Of course, you will say that he is my favourite.”

“No, dear. You are very just. But you are more drawn to him.”

“Yes — strangely more — and for ‘something in him which no one sees. It is his likeness to you, I think.”

“Together with a certain femininity.”

Giovanni did not speak contemptuously, but he had always resented Ippolito’s gentle grace a little. He himself and his other three sons had the strongly masculine temperament of the Saracinesca family. He often thought that Ippolito should have been a girl.

“Do not say that, Giovanni,” answered his wife. “He is not rugged, but he is strong-hearted. The artistic temperament has a certain feminine quality on the surface, by which it feels; but the crude creative force by which it acts is purely masculine.”

“That sounds clever,” laughed Giovanni.

" Well, there is dear old Gausche, whom we have known all our lives. He is an instance. You used to think he had a certain femininity, too."

" So he had."

" But he fought like a man at Mentana; and he thinks like a man, and he certainly paints like a man."

" Yes; that is true. Only we never had any artists in the family. It seems odd that our son should have such tendencies. None of the family were ever particularly clever in any way."

" You are not stupid, at all events."

Corona smiled at her husband. For all the world, she would not have had him at all different from his present self.

" Besides," she added, " you need not think of him as an artist. You can look upon him as a priest."

" Yes, I know," answered Giovanni, without much enthusiasm. " We never were a priest-breeding family either. We have done better at farming than at praying or playing the piano. Ippolito does not know a plough from a harrow, nor a thoroughbred colt from a cart-horse. For my part I do not see the strength you find in him, though I daresay you are right, my dear. You generally are. At all events, he helps the harmony of the family, for he worships Orsino, and the two younger ones always pair together."

"I suppose he will never be put into any position which can show his real character," said Corona, "but I know I am right."

They were silent for a few minutes. Presently Giovanni took up his paper again, and Corona sat down at her table to write a note. The rain pattered against the window, cheerfully, as it does outside a room in which two happy people are together.

"That d'Oriani girl is charming," said Corona, after writing a line or two, but not looking round.

"Perhaps Orsino will fall in love with her," observed her husband, his eyes on the newspaper.

"I hope not!" exclaimed Corona, turning in her chair, and speaking with far more energy than she had yet shown. "It is bad blood, Giovanni — as bad as any blood in Italy, and though the girl is charming, those brothers — well, you saw them."

"Bad faces, both of them. And rather doubtful manners."

"Never mind their manners! But their faces! They are nephews of poor Bianca Corleone's husband, are they not?"

"Yes. They are his brother's children. And they are their grandfather's grandchildren."

"What did he do?"

"He was chiefly concerned in the betrayal of Gaeta — and took money for the deed, too. They have always been traitors. There was a Pagliuca who received all sorts of offices and honours from Joaquin Murat and then advised King Ferdinand to have him shot when he was caught at Pizzo in Calabria. There was a Pagliuca who betrayed his brother to save his own life in the last century. It is a promising stock."

"What an inheritance! I have often heard of them, but I have never met any of them excepting Bianca's husband, whom we all hated for her sake."

"He was not the worst of them, by any means. But I never blamed her much, poor child — and Pietro Ghisleri knew how to turn any woman's head in those days."

"Why did we ask those people to dinner, after all?" enquired Corona, thoughtfully.

"Because San Giacinto wished it, I suppose. We shall probably know why in two or three years. He never does anything without a reason."

"And he keeps his reasons to himself."

"It is a strange thing," said Giovanni. "That man is the most reticent human being I ever knew, and one of the deepest. Yet we are all sure that he is absolutely honest and honourable. We know that he is always scheming, and yet we feel that he is never plotting. There is a difference."

"Of course there is — the difference between strategy and treachery. But I am sorry that his plans should have involved bringing the Corleone family into our house. They are not nice people, excepting the girl."

" My father remarked that the elder of those brothers was like an old engraving he has of Cæsar Borgia."

"That is a promising resemblance! Fortunately, the times, at least, are changed."

" In Sicily, everything is possible."

The remark was characteristic of Giovanni, of a Roman, and of modern times. But there was, and is, some truth in it. Many things are possible to-day in Sicily which have not been possible any-where else in Europe for at least two centuries, and the few foreigners who know the island well can tell tales of Sicilians which the world at large would hardly accept even as fiction.

CHAPTER VII

DURING the ensuing weeks Orsino saw Vittoria d'Oriani repeatedly, at first by accident, and afterwards because he was attracted by her, and took pains to learn where she and her mother were going, in order to meet her.

It was spring. Easter had come very early, and as happens in such cases, there was a revival of gaiety after Lent. There were garden parties, a recent importation in Rome, there were great picnics to the hills, and there were races out at the Capannelle; moreover, there were dances at which the windows were kept open all night, until the daylight began to steal in and tell tales of unpleasant truth, so that even fair women drew lace things over their tired faces as they hurried into their carriages in the cold dawn, glad to remember that they had still looked passably well in the candle-light.

At one of these balls, late in the season, Orsino knew that he should meet Vittoria. It was in a vast old palace, from the back of which two graceful bridges crossed the street below to a garden beyond, where there were fountains, and palms, and statues, and walks hedged with box in the old Italian manner. There were no very magnificent preparations for the dance, which was rather a small and intimate affair, but there was the magnificent luxury of well-proportioned space, which belonged to an older age, there was the gentle light of several hundred wax candles instead of the cold glare of electricity or the pestilent flame of gas, and all night long there was April moonlight outside, in the old garden, whence the smell of the box, and the myrtle, and of violets, was borne in fitfully through the open windows with each breath of moving air.

There was also, that night, a general feeling of being at home and in a measure free from the oppression of social tyranny, and from the disturbing presence of the rich social recruit, who was sown in wealth, so 'to say, in the middle of the century, and who is now plentifully reaped in vulgarity.

"It is more like the old times than anything I remember for years," said Corona to Gianforte Campodonico, as they walked slowly through the rooms together.

"It must be the wax candles and the smell of the flowers from the garden," he answered, not exactly comprehending, for he was not a sensitive man, and was, moreover, considerably younger than Corona.

But Corona was silent, and wished that she were

walking with her husband, or sitting alone with him in some quiet corner, for something in the air reminded her of a ball in the Frangipani palace, many years ago, when Giovanni had spoken to her in a conservatory, and many things had happened in consequence. The wax candles and the smell of open-air flowers, and the glimpses of moonlight through vast windows may have had something to do with it; but surely there are times and hours, when love is in the air, when every sound is tuneful, and all silence is softly alive, when young voices seek each the other's tone caressingly, and the stealing hand steals nearer to the hand that waits.

There was no one to prevent Orsino Saracinesca from persuading Vittoria to go and sit down in one of the less frequented rooms, if he could do so. Her mother would be delighted, her brothers were not at the ball, and Orsino was responsible to no one for his actions. She had learned many things since she had come to Rome, but she did not understand more than half of them, and what she understood least of all was the absolute power which Orsino exerted over her when he was present. He haunted her thoughts at other times, too, and she had acquired a sort of conviction that she could not escape from him, which was greatly strengthened by the fact that she did not wish to be free.

On his part, his mind was less easy, for he was

well aware that he was making love to the girl with her mother's consent, whereas he was not by any means inclined to think that he wished to marry her. Such a position might not seem strange to a youth of Anglo-Saxon traditions; for there is a sort of tacit understanding among the English-speaking races to the effect that young people are never to count on each other till each has got the other up the steps of the altar, that there is nothing disgraceful in breaking an engagement, and that love-making at large, without any intention of marriage, is a harmless pastime especially designed for the very young. The Italian view is very different, however, and Orsino was well aware that unless he meant to make Vittoria d'Oriani his wife, he was doing wrong in his own eyes, and in the eyes of the world, in doing his best to be often with her.

One result of his conduct was that he frightened away other men. They took it for granted that he wished to marry her, dowerless as she was, and they kept out of his way. The girl was not neglected, however. San Giacinto had his own reasons for wishing to be on good terms with her brothers, and he made his wife introduce partners to Vittoria at dances, and send men to talk to her at parties. But as soon as Orsino came upon the scene, Vittoria's companion disappeared, whoever he happened to be at the time.

The Italian, even when very young, has a good deal of social philosophy when he is not under the influence of an emotion from which he cannot escape. He will avoid falling in love with the wrong person, if he can.

"For what?" he asks. "In order to be unhappy? Why?"

And he systematically keeps out of the way of temptation, well knowing his own weakness in love matters.

But Orsino was attracted by the girl and yielded to the attraction, though his manner of yielding was a domination over her whenever they met. His only actual experience of real love had been in his affair with the Countess del Ferice, before her second marriage. She was a mature woman of strong character and devoted nature, who had resisted him and had sacrificed herself for him, not to him. He had been accustomed to find that resistance in her. But Vittoria offered none at all, a fact which gave his rather despotic nature a sudden development, while the absence of opposition made him look upon his disinclination to decide the question of marriage as something he ought to have been ashamed of. At the same time, there was the fact that he had grown somewhat cynical and cold of late years, and if not positively selfish, at least negatively careless of others, when anything pleased him, which was not often. It is bad to have strength and not to use it, to possess power and not to exert it, to know that one is a personage without caring much what sort of person one may be. That had been Orsino's position for years, and it had not improved his character.

On this particular evening he was conscious of something much more like emotion than he had felt for a long time. San Giacinto had lain in wait for him near the door, and had told him that matters were settled at last and that they were to leave Rome within the week to take possession of the Corleone lands. The deeds had been signed and the money had been paid. There were no further formalities, and it was time to go to work. Orsino nodded, said he was ready, and went off to find Vittoria in the ballroom. But there was a little more colour than usual under his dark skin, and his eyes were restless and hungry.

He was passing his mother without seeing her, when she touched him on the sleeve, and dropped Campodonico's arm. He started a little impatiently, and then stood still, waiting for her to speak.

"Has anything happened?" she asked rather anxiously.

"No, mother, nothing — that is —" He hesitated, glancing at Campodonico. "I am going to Sicily with San Giacinto," he added in a low voice.

Corona could not have explained what she felt

just then, but she might have described it as a disagreeable chilliness creeping over her strong frame from head to foot. An hour later she remembered it, and the next day, and for many days afterwards, and she tried to account for it by telling herself that the journey was to make a great change in her son's life, or by arguing that she had half unconsciously supposed him about to engage himself to Vittoria. But neither explanation was at all satisfactory. She was not imaginative to that extent, as she well knew, and she at last made up her mind that it was an idle coincidence of the kind which some people call a warning, and remember afterwards when anything especial happens, though if nothing particular follows, they forget it altogether.

"Why are you going? Has it anything to do with the Corleone?" she asked, and she was surprised at the unsteadiness of her own voice.

"Yes. I will tell you some other time."

"Will you?"

"Yes, certainly."

She looked into his eyes a moment, and then took Campodonico's arm again. Orsino moved on quickly and disappeared in the ballroom they had left, wondering inwardly at his mother's manner as much as she was then wondering herself, and attributing it to her anxiety about his position with regard to Vittoria. Thinking of that, he stopped short in his walk just as he caught sight of the young girl in the distance, standing beside her mother. A man was before her, evidently just asking her to dance. Orsino watched them while he tried to get hold of himself and decide what he ought to do.

Vittoria came forward and swept out with her partner into the middle of the room. Orsino slipped back a little behind a group of people, so that she should not easily see him, but he watched her face keenly. Her eyes were restless, and she was evidently looking for him, and not thinking of her partner at all. As they came round to his side, Orsino felt the blood rise in his throat, and felt that his face was warm; and then, as they swung off to the other side of the big ballroom, he grew cool again, and asked himself what he should do, repeating the question rather helplessly. She came round once more, and just as he felt the same heat of the blood again, he saw that her eyes had caught his. In a flash her expression changed, and the colour blushed in her face. A moment later she stopped, and remained standing with her partner so that Orsino could see the back of her head. She half turned towards him two or three times, instinctively; but she would not turn quite round so as to look at him. She knew that she must finish the dance before he could come to her.

But he, deeply stirred, and, at the same time,

profoundly discontented with himself, suddenly left the room and went on till he stood all alone, out on one of the bridges which crossed the street to the garden at the back of the palace. The bridge was in the shadow, but the white moonlight fell full upon the fountain and the walks beyond; and moonlight has an extraordinary effect on people who do not habitually live in camps, or out of doors, at night. The sun shows us what is, but the moon makes us see what might be.

Orsino leaned against the stone parapet in the shadow, and made one of those attempts at self-examination which every honourable man has made at least once in his life, and which, with nine men out of ten, lead to no result, because at such times the mind is in no state to examine anything, least of all itself. Indeed, no healthy-minded man resorts to that sort of introspection unless he is in a most complicated situation, since such a man is normally always perfectly conscious of what is honourable and right, without any self-analysis, or picking to pieces of his own conscience.

But Orsino Saracinesca was in great difficulty. He did not question the fact that he was very much in love with Vittoria, and that this love for a young girl was something which he had never felt before. That was plain enough, by this time. The real question was, whether he should marry her, or whether he should go away to Sicily with San Giacinto and try to avoid her in future until he should have more or less forgotten her.

He was old enough and sensible enough to foresee the probable consequences of marrying into such a family, and they were such as to check him at the outset. He knew all about the Pagliuca people, as his father did, and the phrase 'the worst blood in Italy' was familiar to his thoughts. Vittoria's mother was, indeed, a harmless soul, provincial and of unusual manners, but not vulgar in the ordinary sense of the word. Vittoria's father was said to have been a very good kind of man, who had been outrageously treated by his elder brother. But the strain was bad. There were hideous stories of treachery, such as Giovanni had quoted to his wife, which were alone enough to make Orsino hesitate. And then, there were Vittoria's brothers, for whom he felt the strongest repulsion and distrust. In many ways it would have been wiser for him to marry a girl of the people, a child of Trastevere, rather than Vittoria d'Oriani.

He did not believe that any of the taint was on herself, that in her character there was the smallest shade of deceit or unfaithfulness. He found it hard to believe that she was really a Corleone at all. His arguments began from a premiss which assumed her practically perfect.

Had he been alone in the world, he would not have hesitated long, for he could have married her and taken her away for ever — he was enough in love for that.

But such a marriage meant that he should bring her brothers intimately into his father's house; that he and his own family must accept Tebaldo and Francesco Pagliuca, and possibly the third brother, whom he did not know, as near relations, to be called, by himself at least, 'thee' and 'thou,' and by their baptismal names. Lastly, it meant that Vittoria's mother and his own should come into close terms of intimacy, for Maria Carolina would make the most of the connexion with the Saracinesca. That thought was the most repugnant of all to the young man, who looked upon his mother as a being apart from the ordinary world and entitled to a sort of veneration. Maria Carolina would not venerate anybody, he thought.

On the other side, there was his honour. He did not care what the young men might think, but he had certainly led the girl herself to believe that he meant to marry her. And he was in love. Compared with giving up Vittoria, and with doing something which seemed dishonourable, the accumulated wickedness of generations of the Corleone shrank into insignificance. There was a sort of shock in his mind, as he brought up this side of the question.

Had there been any difficulty to be overcome in winning Vittoria's own consent, it would have been easier to decide. But he knew that he had but a word to say, and his future would be sealed irrevocably in a promise which he never would break. And in a day or two he was to leave Rome for a long time. It was clear that he ought to decide at once, this very night.

His nature rejected the idea of taking advice, and, generally, of confiding in anyone. Otherwise, he might have laid the matter before his mother, in the certainty that her counsel would be good and honourable. Or he might have told his favourite brother the whole story, and Ippolito would assuredly have told him what was right. But Orsino was not of those who get help from the judgment or the conscience of another.

It seemed to him that he stayed a long time on the bridge, thinking of all these things, for the necessity of finally weighing them had come upon him suddenly, since San Giacinto had given him warning to get ready for the journey. But presently he was aware that the distant music had changed, that the waltz during which he had watched Vittoria was over, and that a square dance had begun. He smiled rather grimly to himself as he reflected that he might stand there till morning, without getting any nearer to a conclusion. He turned his back on the moonlight impatiently and went back into the palace. In the distance, through an open door, he saw faces familiar to him all his life, moving to and fro rapidly in a quadrille. He watched them as he walked straight on towards the ballroom, through the rather dimly lighted chamber with which the bridge communicated.

He was startled by the sound of Vittoria d'Oriani's voice, close beside him, calling him softly but rather anxiously.

"Don Orsino! Don Orsino!"

She was all alone, pale, and standing half hidden by the heavy curtain on one side of the door opening to the ballroom. Orsino stood still a moment, in great surprise at seeing her thus left to herself in an empty room. Then he went close to her, holding out his hand.

"What is the matter?" he asked in a low voice, for several men were standing about on the other side of the open door, watching the dance.

"Nothing — nothing," she repeated nervously, as he drew her aside.

"Who left you here alone?" asked Orsino, in displeasure at some unknown person.

"I — I came here —" she faltered. "I slipped out — it was hot, in there."

Orsino laughed softly.

"You must not get isolated in this way," he said. "It is not done here, you know. People would think it strange. You are always supposed to be with someone — your partner, or your mother. But I am glad, since I have found you."

" Yes, I have found you," she said softly, repeating his words. " I mean — " she corrected herself hurriedly — " I mean you have found me."

Orsino looked down to her averted face, and in the dim light he saw the blush at her mistake — too great a mistake in speech not to have come from a strong impulse within. Yet he could hardly believe that she had seen him go out that way alone, and had followed in the hope of finding him.

They sat down together, not far from the door opening upon the bridge. The colour had faded again from Vittoria's face, and she was pale. During some moments neither spoke, and the music of the quadrille irritated Orsino as he listened to it. Seeing that he was silent, Vittoria looked up sideways and met his eyes.

" It was really very warm in the ballroom," she said, to say something.

" Yes," he answered absently, his eyes fixed on hers. " Yes — I daresay it was."

Again there was a pause.

" What is the matter ? " asked Vittoria at last, and her tone sank with each word.

" I am going away," said Orsino, slowly, with fixed eyes.

She did not start nor show any surprise, but the

colour began to leave her lips. The irritating quadrille went pounding on in the distance, through the hackneyed turns of the familiar figures, accompanied by the sound of many voices talking and of broken laughter now and then.

"You knew it?" asked Orsino. "How?"

"No one told me: but I knew it—I guessed it."

Orsino looked away, and then turned to her again, his glance drawn back to her by something he could not resist.

"Vittoria," he began in a very low tone.

He had never called her by that name before. The quadrille was very noisy, and she did not understand. She leaned forward anxiously towards him when she spoke.

"What did you say? I did not hear. The music makes such a noise!"

The man was more than ever irritated at the sound; and as she bent over to him, he could almost feel her breath on his cheek. The blood rose in him, and he sprang to his feet impatiently.

"Come!" he said. "Come outside! We cannot even hear each other here."

Vittoria rose, too, without a word, and went with him, walking close beside him, and glancing at his face. She was excessively pale now; and all the golden light seemed to have faded at once, even from her hair and eyes, till she looked delicate and almost fragile beside the big dark man.

"Out of doors?" she asked timidly, at the threshold.

"Yes—it is very warm," answered Orsino, in a voice that was a little hoarse.

Once out on the bridge, in the shadow, over the dark street, he stopped, and instantly his hand found hers and closed all round it, covering it altogether.

Vittoria could not have spoken just then, for she was trembling from head to foot. The air was full of strange sounds, and the trees were whirling round one another like mad black ghosts in the moonlight. When she looked up, she could see Orsino's eyes, bright in the shadow. She turned away, and came back to them more than once; then their glances did not part any more, and his face came nearer to hers.

"We love each other," he said; and his voice was warm and alive again.

She felt that she saw his soul in his face, but she could not speak. Her eyes looking up to his, she slowly bent her little head twice, while her lips parted like an opening flower, and faintly smiled at the sweetness of an unspoken word.

He bent nearer still, and she did not draw back. His blood was hot and singing in his ears. Then, all at once, something in her appealed to him, her young delicacy, her dawn-like purity, her exquisite fresh maidenhood. It seemed a crime to touch her lips as though she had been a mature woman. He dropped her hand, and his long arms brought her tenderly and softly up to his breast; and as her head fell back, and her lids drooped, he kissed her eyes with infinite gentleness, first the one and then the other, again and again, till she smiled in the dark, and hid her face against his coat, and he found only her silky hair to kiss again.

"I love you — say it, too," he whispered in her ear.

"Ah, yes! so much, so dearly!" came her low answer.

Then he took her hand again, and brought it up to his lips close to her face; and his lips pressed the small fingers passionately, almost roughly, very longingly.

"Come," he said. "We must be alone — come into the garden."

He led her across the bridge, and suddenly they were in the clear moonlight; but he went on quickly, lest they should be noticed through the open door from within. The air was warm and still and dry, as it often is in spring after the evening chill has passed.

"We could not go back into the ballroom, could we?" he asked, as he drew her away along a gravel walk between high box hedges.

"No. How could we — now?" Her hand tightened a little on his arm.

They stopped before a statue at the end of the walk, full in the light, a statue that had perhaps been a Daphne, injured ages ago, and stone-grey where it was not very white, with flying draperies broken off short in the folds, and a small, frightened face that seemed between laughing and crying. One fingerless hand pointed at the moon.

Orsino leaned back against the pedestal, and lovingly held Vittoria before him, and looked at her, and she smiled, her lips parting again, and just glistening darkly in the light as a dewy rose does in moonlight. The music was very far away now, but the plashing of the fountain was near.

"I love you!" said Orsino once more, as though no other words would do.

A deep sigh of happiness said more than the words could, and the stillness that followed meant most of all, while Vittoria gently took his two hands and nestled closer to him, fearlessly, like a child or a young animal.

"But you will not go away — now?" she asked pleadingly.

Orsino's face changed a little, as he remembered the rest of his life, and all he had undertaken to do. He had dreamily hoped that he might forget it.

"We will not talk of that," he answered.

"How can I help it, if it is true? You will not go — say you will not go!"

"I have promised. But there is time — or, at

least. I shall soon come back. It is not so far to Sicily —"

"Sicily? You are going to Sicily?" She seemed surprised.

"I thought you knew where I was going —" he began.

"No — I guessed; I was not sure. Tell me! Why must you go?"

"I must go because I have promised. San Giacinto would think it very strange if I changed my mind."

"It is stranger that you should go — and with him! Yes — I see — you are going to take possession of our old place —"

Her voice suddenly expressed the utmost anxiety, as she sprang from one conclusion to another without a mistake. She pressed his hands tightly, and her face grew pale again with fear for him.

"Oh please, please, stay here!" she cried. "If it were anywhere else — if it were to do anything else —"

"Why?" he asked, in surprise. "I thought you did not care much for the old place. If I had known that it would hurt you —"

"Me? No! It is not that — it is for you! They will kill you. Oh, do not go! Do not go!" She spoke in the greatest distress.

Orsino was suddenly inclined to laugh, but he saw how much in earnest she was.

"Who will kill me?" he asked, as though humouring her. "What do you mean?"

Vittoria was more than in earnest; she was almost in terror for him. Her small hands clung to his arm nervously, catching him and then loosing their hold. But she said nothing, though she seemed to be hesitating in some sort of struggle. Though she loved him with all the whole-hearted impulses of her nature, it was not easy to tell him what she meant. The Sicilian blood revolted at the thought of betraying her wild brother, who had joined the outlaws, and would be in waiting for Orsino and his cousin when they should try to take possession of the lands.

"You must not go!" she cried, suddenly throwing her arms round his neck as though she could keep him by force. "You shall not go — oh, no, no, no!"

"Vittoria — you have got some mad idea in your head — it is absurd — who should try to kill me? Why? I have no enemies. As for the brigands, everyone laughs at that sort of thing nowadays. They belong to the comic opera!" He let himself laugh a little at last, for the idea really amused him.

But Vittoria straightened herself beside him and grew calmer, for she was sensible and saw that he thought her foolishly afraid.

"In Rome the outlaws belong to the comic opera

— yes," she answered gravely. "But in Sicily they are a reality. I am a Sicilian, and I know. People are killed by them almost every day, and the mafia protects them. They are better armed than the soldiers, for they carry Winchester rifles — "

"What do you know about Winchester rifles?" asked Orsino, smiling.

"My brothers have them," she said quietly. "And the outlaws almost all have them."

"I daresay. But why should they wish to kill me? They do not know me."

Vittoria was silent a moment, making up her mind what she should tell him. She was not positively sure of anything, but she had heard Francesco say lately that Camaldoli was a place easier to buy than to hold while Ferdinando was alive, and she knew what that meant, when coupled with the occasional comments upon Ferdinando's mode of life, which escaped in Francesco's incautious conversation at home. To a Sicilian, the meaning of the whole situation was not hard to guess. At the same time Vittoria was both desperately anxious for Orsino and afraid that he might laugh at her fears, as he had done already.

"This is it," she said at last in a low and earnest voice. "It has nothing to do with you or your cousin, personally, nor with your taking possession of Camaldoli, so far as I am concerned. But it

is a wild and desolate place, and all through this
year a large band of outlaws have been in the
forests on the other side of the valley. They
would never have hurt my brothers, who are Sicilians and poor, and who did not trouble them
either. But you and your cousin are great people,
and rich, and not Sicilians, and the mafia will
be against you, and will support the brigands if
they prevent you from taking possession of Camaldoli. You would be opposed to the mafia; you
would bring soldiers there to fight the outlaws.
Therefore they will kill you. It is certain. No
one ever escapes them. Do you understand?
Now you will not go, of course, since I have explained it all."

Orsino was somewhat puzzled, though it all
seemed so clear to her.

"This mafia — what is it?" he asked. "We
hear it spoken of, but we do not any of us really
know who is the head of it, nor what it can do."

"It has no head," answered the young girl.
"Perhaps it is hard to explain, because you are
not a Sicilian. The mafia is not a band, nor anything of that sort. It is the resistance which the
whole Sicilian people opposes to all kinds of government and authority. It is, how shall I say?
A sentiment, a feeling, a sort of wild love of
our country, that is a secret, and will do anything. With us, everybody knows what it is, and

evil comes to everyone who opposes it — generally death."

" We are not much afraid of it, since we have the law on our side." said Orsino, rather incredulously.

" You are not afraid because you do not understand." answered Vittoria, her voice beginning to express her anxiety again. "If you knew what it is, as we know, you would be very much afraid."

She spoke so simply and naturally that it did not occur to Orsino to be offended at the slight upon his courage.

"We shall take an escort of soldiers, to please you," he said, smiling, and drawing her to him again, as though the discussion were over.

But her terror for him broke out again. She had not told him all she knew, still less all she suspected.

"But I am in earnest!" she cried, holding herself back from him so that he could see her eyes. "It is true earnest, deadly earnest. They mean to kill you — in the end, they will! Oh, tell me that you will not go!"

"San Giacinto has bought the place —"

"Let him go, and be killed, then, and perhaps they will be satisfied! What do I care for anyone but you? Is it nothing, that I love you so? That we have told each other? That you say you love me? Is it all nothing but words, mere words, empty words?"

"No, it is my whole life, dear—"

"Then your life is mine, and you have no right to throw it away, just to please your cousin. Let him get a regiment of soldiers sent there by the government to live in Santa Vittoria. Then after three or four years the brigands will be all gone."

"Three or four years!" Orsino laughed, in spite of himself.

"Ah, you do not know!" exclaimed Vittoria, sadly. "You do not know our country, nor our people! You think it is like Rome, all shop-keepers and policemen, and sixty noble families, with no mafia! You laugh now — but when they have killed you I shall not live to laugh again. Am I your life? Then you are mine. What will there be without you, when they have killed you? And the Winchester rifles shoot so far, and the outlaws aim so straight! How can you be saved? Do you think it is nothing that I should know that you are going to your death?"

"It is an exaggeration," said Orsino, trying to soothe her. "Such things are not done in a civilized country, in the nineteenth century."

"Such things? Ah, and worse, far worse! Last year they buried a man up to his neck in the earth, alive, and left him there to die, in the woods not far from Camaldoli, because they thought he was a spy! And one betrayed some of the band last summer, and they did not kill him at once, but caught him and tortured him, so that it took him three days to die. You do not know. You laugh, but you do not know what people there are in Sicily, nor what Sicilians will do when they are roused. Promise me that you will not go!"

"Even if all you tell me were true, I should go," answered Orsino.

"Will nothing keep you from going?" asked the girl, piteously.

"You will laugh at all this when I come back to you. You will wonder how you could have tried to frighten me with such tales."

She looked at him a long time in silence, and then her lip quivered, so that she quickly raised one hand to her mouth to hide it.

"It would have been better if I had never left the convent," she said in a broken voice. "When they have killed you, I shall go back and die there."

"When I come back, we shall be married, love — "

"Oh, no — not if you go to Camaldoli — we shall never be married in this world."

The slight and graceful girl shook all over for a moment, and then seemed to grow smaller, as though something crushed her. But there were no tears in her eyes, though she pressed her fingers on her lips as though to force back a sob.

"Let us go back," she said. "I want to go home — I can pray for you, if I cannot save you.

God will hear me, though you do not, and God knows that it will be your death."

He put his arm about her and tried to comfort her, but she would not again lift her face, and he kissed her hair once more, when they were again in the shadow on the bridge. Then they waited till no one was passing through the small room, and went in silently to find her mother. She stopped him at the door of the ballroom.

"Promise me that you will not speak to my mother, nor my brothers, about—about us," she said in a low voice.

"Very well. Not till I come back, if you wish it," he answered.

And they went in, amongst the people, unnoticed.

CHAPTER VIII

VITTORIA realized that it was beyond her power to keep Orsino in Rome, and she was in great trouble. She had begged him not to speak of their betrothal, scarcely knowing why she made the request, but she was afterwards very glad that she had done so. To her, he was a condemned man, and her betrothal was a solemn binding of herself to keep faith with a beloved being who must soon be dead. She did not believe that she could really outlive him, but if Heaven should be so unkind to her, she had already made up her mind to return to the convent where she had been educated, and to end her days as a nun. The acute melancholy which belongs to the people of the far south, as well as of the far north, of Norway and of Sicily or Egypt alike, at once asserted itself and took possession of her. The next time Orsino saw her he was amazed at the change. The colour was all gone from her face, her lips were tightly set, and her brown eyes followed him with a perpetual, mute anxiety. Her radiance was veiled, and her beauty was grievously diminished.

It was at a garden party, in a great, old villa beyond the walls, two days after the dance. Orsino had not been able to see her in the meantime, and had wisely abstained from visiting her mother, lest, in any way, he should betray their joint secret. She was already in the garden when he arrived with Corona, who caught sight of Vittoria from a distance and noted the change in her face.

"Vittoria d'Oriani looks ill," said the Princess, and she went towards her at once.

She was too tactful to ask the girl what was the matter, but she saw how Vittoria's eyes could not keep from Orsino, and she half guessed the truth, though her son's face was impenetrable just then. An old friend came up and spoke to her, and she left the two alone.

They quietly moved away from the more crowded part of the garden, walking silently side by side, till they came to a long walk covered by the interlacing branches of ilex trees. Another couple was walking at some distance before them. Orsino glanced down at Vittoria, and tried to say something, but it was not easy. He had not realized how the mere sight of her stirred him, until he found himself speechless when he wished to say many things.

"You are suffering," he said softly, at last. "What is it?"

"You know," she answered. "What is the use of talking about it? I have said all — but tell me only when you are going."

"To-morrow morning. I shall be back in a fortnight."

"You will never come back," said Vittoria, in a dull and hopeless tone.

She spoke with such conviction that Orsino was silent for a moment. He had not the smallest belief in any danger, but he did not know how to argue with her.

"I have thought it all over," she went on. "If you try to live there, you will certainly be killed. But if you only go once, there is a chance — a poor, miserable, little chance. Let them think that you are coming up from Piedimonte, by way of Randazzo. It is above Randazzo that the black lands begin, all lava and ashes, with deep furrows in which a man can lie hidden to shoot. That is where they will try to kill you. Go the other way, round by Catania; it is longer, but they will not expect you, and you can get a guide. They may not find out that you have changed your plan. If they should know it, they could kill you even more easily on that side, in the narrow valley; but they need not know it."

"Nothing will happen to me on either side," said Orsino, carelessly.

Vittoria bent her head and walked on in silence beside him.

"I did not wish to talk about all that," he continued. "There are much more important things. When I come back we must be married soon —"

"We shall never be married if you go to Sicily," answered Vittoria, in the same dull voice.

It was a fixed idea, and Orsino felt the hopelessness of trying to influence her, together with a pardonable impatience. The couple ahead of them reached the end of the walk, turned, met them, and passed them with a greeting, for they were acquaintances. Where the little avenue ended there was a great fountain of travertine stone, behind which, in the wide arch of the opening trees, they could see the Campagna and the Sabine mountains to the eastward.

Vittoria stopped when they reached the other side of the basin, which was moss-grown but full of clear water that trickled down an almost shapeless stone triton. The statue and the fountain hid them from anyone who might be coming up the walk, and at their feet lay the broad green Campagna. They were quite alone.

The young girl raised her eyes, and she looked already as though she had been in an illness.

"We cannot stay more than a moment," she said. "If people see us going off together, they will guess. I want it to be all my secret. I want to say goodbye to you — for the last time. I shall remember you always as you are now, with the light on your face.”

She looked at him long, and her eyes slowly filled with tears, which did not break nor run over, but little by little subsided again, taking her grief back to her heart. Orsino’s brows frowned with pain, for he saw how profoundly she believed that she was never to see him again, and it hurt him that for him she should be so hurt, most of all because he was convinced that there was no cause.

“We go to-morrow,” he said. “We shall be in Messina the next day. On the day after that go and see my mother, and she will tell you that she has had news of our safe arrival. What more can I say? I am sure of it.”

But Vittoria only looked long and earnestly into his face.

“I want to remember,” she said, in a low voice.

“For a fortnight?” Orsino smiled lovingly, and took her hand.

“For ever,” she answered very gravely, and her fingers clutched his suddenly and hard.

He still smiled, for he could find nothing to say against such possession of presentiment. Common sense never has anything effectual to oppose to conviction.

“Goodbye,” she said softly. “Goodbye, Orsino.”

She had not called him by his name yet, and it sounded like an enchantment to him, though it was a rough name in itself. The breeze stirred the ilex leaves overhead in the spring afternoon, and the water trickled down, with a pleasant murmur, into the big basin. It was all lovely and peaceful and soft, except the look in her despairing eyes. That disturbed him as he met it and saw no change in it, but always the same hopeless pain.

"Come," he said quietly, "this is not sensible. Do I look like a man who is going to be killed like a dog in the street, without doing something to help myself?"

Her eyes filled again.

"Oh, pray — please — do not speak like that! Say goodbye to me — I cannot bear it any longer — and yet it kills me to let you go!"

She turned from him and covered her eyes with her hands for a moment, while he put his arm round her reassuringly. Then, all at once, she looked up.

"I will be brave — goodbye!" she said quickly.

It was a silent leave-taking after that, for he could not say much. His only answer to her must be his safe return, but as they went back along the walk, she felt that she was with him for the last time. It was like going with him to execution.

Orsino walked back to the city alone, thinking over her words and her face, and wondering whether there could be anything in presentiments of evil. He had never had any himself, that he could remember, and he had never seen anybody so thoroughly under the influence of one as Vittoria seemed to be.

Before dinner he went to see San Giacinto, whom he found alone in his big study, sitting in his huge chair before his enormous table. He was so large that he had his own private furniture made to suit his own dimensions. The table was covered with note books and papers, very neatly arranged, and the grey-haired giant was writing a letter. He looked up as Orsino entered and uttered a sort of inarticulate exclamation of satisfaction. Then he went on writing, while Orsino sat down and watched him.

"Do you happen to have a gun license?" asked San Giacinto, without looking up.

"Of course."

"Put it in your pocket for the journey," was the answer, as the pen went on steadily.

"Is there any game about Camaldoli?" enquired Orsino, after a pause.

"Brigands," replied San Giacinto, laconically, and still writing.

He would have said 'woodcock' in the same tone, being a plain man and not given to dramatic emphasis. Orsino laughed a little incredulously, but said nothing, as he sat waiting for his kinsman to finish his letter. His eyes wandered about the room, and presently they fell on a stout sole-leather bag which stood by a chair near the window. On the chair itself lay two leathern gun-cases obviously containing modern rifles, as their shape and size showed. With a man's natural instinct for arms, Orsino rose and took one of the weapons out of its case, and examined it.

"Winchesters," said San Giacinto, still driving his pen.

"I see," answered Orsino, feeling the weight, and raising the rifle to his shoulder as though to try the length of the stock.

"Most people prefer them in Sicily," observed San Giacinto, who had signed his name and was folding his note carefully.

"What do you want them for?" asked the younger man, still incredulous.

"It is the custom of the country to carry them down there," said the other. "Besides, there are brigands about. I told you so, just now."

San Giacinto did not like to repeat explanations.

"I thought you were joking," remarked Orsino.

"I never did that. I suppose we shall not have the luck to fall in with any of those fellows, but there has been a good deal of trouble lately, and we shall not be particularly popular as Romans going to take possession of Sicilian lands. We should be worth a ransom too, and by this time the whole country knows that we are coming."

"Then we may really have some excitement," said Orsino, more surprised than he would show at his cousin's confirmation of much that Vittoria had said. "How about the mafia?" he asked by way of leading San Giacinto into conversation. "How will it look at us?"

"The mafia is not a man," answered San Giacinto, bluntly. "The mafia is the Sicilian character — Sicilian honour, Sicilian principles. It is an idea, not an institution. It is what makes it impossible to govern Sicily."

"Or to live there," suggested Orsino.

"Except with considerable tact. You will find out something about it very soon, if you try to manage that place. But if you are nervous, you had better not try."

"I am not nervous, I believe."

"No, it is of no use to be. It is better to be a fatalist. Fatalism gives you your own soul, and leaves your body to the chemistry of the universe, where it belongs. If your body comes into contact with something that does not agree with it, you die. That is all."

There was an admirable directness in San Giacinto's philosophy, as Orsino knew. They made a final agreement about meeting at the station on the following morning, and Orsino went home a good deal less inclined to treat Vittoria's presentiments lightly. It had been characteristic of San Giacinto that he had hitherto simply forgotten to mention that there might be real danger in the expedition to Camaldoli, and it was equally in accordance with Orsino's character to take the prospect of it simply and gravely. There was a strong resemblance between the two kinsmen, and Orsino understood his cousin better than his father or any of his brothers.

He had already explained to his mother what he was going to do, and she had been glad to learn that he had found something to interest him. Both Corona and Sant' Ilario had the prevailing impression that the Sicilian difficulties were more or less imaginary. That is what most Romans think, and the conviction is general in the north of Italy. As Orsino said nothing about his conversation with San Giacinto on that last evening, his father and mother had not the slightest idea that there was danger before him, and as they had both noticed his liking for Vittoria, they were very glad that he should go away just then, and forget her.

The old Prince bade him goodbye that night.

"Whatever you do, my boy," he said, shaking his snowy old head energetically, "do not marry a Sicilian girl."

The piece of advice was so unexpected that Orsino started slightly, and then laughed, as he took his grandfather's hand. It was oddly smooth, as the hands of very old men are, but it was warm still, and not so feeble as might have been expected.

"And if you should get into trouble down there," said the head of the house, who had known Sicily seventy years earlier, "shoot first. Never wait to be shot at."

"It is not likely that there will be much shooting nowadays," laughed Sant' Ilario.

"That does not make my advice bad, does it?" asked old Saracinesca, turning upon his son, for the least approach to contradiction still roused his anger instantly.

"Oh, no!" answered Giovanni. "It is very good advice."

"Of course it is," growled the old gentleman, discontentedly. "I never gave anyone bad advice in my life. But you boys are always contradicting me."

Giovanni smiled rather sadly. It was not in the nature of things that men over ninety years old should live much longer, but he felt what a break in the household's life the old man's death must one day make, when the vast vitality should be at last worn out.

CHAPTER IX

Orsino travelled down to Naples with San Giacinto in that peculiar state of mind in which an unsentimental but passionate man finds himself when he is leaving the woman he loves in order to go and do something which he knows must be done, which he wishes to do, and which involves danger and difficulty.

San Giacinto did not say much more about brigands, or the mafia, but he talked freely of the steps to be taken on arriving in Messina, in order to get a proper escort of soldiers from Piedimonte to Camaldoli, and it was perfectly clear that he anticipated trouble. Orsino was surprised to find that he expected to have four or five carabineers permanently quartered at Camaldoli, by way of protection, and that he had already applied in the proper quarter to have the men sent to meet him. Then he began to talk of the projected railway and of the questions of engineering involved.

Orsino felt lonely in his society, and it was a sensation to which he was not accustomed. It was long since he had known what it was to miss a woman's eyes and a woman's voice, and he had not thought that he should know it again.　As the train ran on, hour after hour, he grew more silent, not wondering at himself, but accepting quite simply the fact that it hurt him to leave Vittoria far behind, and that he longed for her presence more and more.　He could not help thinking how easy it would be for him to refuse to go on, and to take the next train back from Naples to Rome, and to see her to-morrow.　He would not have done such a thing for the world, but he could not escape from the rather contemptible pleasure of thinking about it.

Late in the afternoon the steamer that was to take them to Messina got under way, — an old-fashioned, uncomfortable boat, crowded with people of all kinds, for the vessel was to go on to Malta on the next day.　At the bad dinner in the dim cabin the tables were full, and many of the people were talking in the Maltese dialect, which is an astonishing compound of Italian and Arabic, perfectly incomprehensible both to Arabs and Italians.　They stared at San Giacinto because he was a giant, and evidently talked about him in their own language, which irritated Orsino, though the big man seemed perfectly indifferent.　Neither cared to speak, and they got through their abominable dinner in silence and went up to smoke on deck.

Orsino leaned upon the rail and gazed longingly

at the looming mountains, behind which the full moon was rising. He was not sentimental, for Italian men rarely are, but like all his fellow-countrymen he was alive to the sensuous suggestions of nature at certain times, and the shadowy land, the rising moon, the gleaming ripple of the water, and the evening breeze on his face, brought Vittoria more vividly than ever to his mind. He looked up at San Giacinto, and even the latter's massive and gloomy features seemed to be softened by the gentle light and the enchantment of the southern sea. Unconsciously he was more closely drawn to the man of his own blood, after being jostled in the crowd of doubtful passengers who filled the steamer.

It was not in his nature to make confidences, but he wished that his friend and kinsman knew that he was in love with Vittoria and meant to marry her. It would have made the journey less desolate and lonely. He was still young, as San Giacinto would have told him, with grim indifference, if Orsino had unburdened his heart at that moment. But he did not mean to do that. He leaned over the rail and smoked in silence, looking from the moon to the rippling water and back again, and wishing that the night were not before him, but that he were already in Messina with something active to do. To be doing the thing would be to get nearer to Vittoria, since he could return with a clear conscience as soon as it should be done. At last he spoke, in a careless tone.

"My grandfather gave me some advice last night," he said. "Never to marry a Sicilian girl, and always to shoot first if there were any shooting to be done."

"Provided that you do not marry the Corleone girl, I do not see why you should not take a Sicilian wife if you please," answered San Giacinto, calmly.

"Why should a man not marry Vittoria d'Oriani?" enquired Orsino, startled to find himself so suddenly speaking of what filled him.

"I did not say 'a man' in general. I meant you. It would be a bad match. It would draw you into relationship with the worst blood in the country, and that is a great objection to it. Then she is a niece, and her brothers are nephews, of that old villain Corleone who married one of the Campodonico women. She died of unhappiness, I believe, and I do not wonder. Have you noticed that none of the Campodonico will have anything to do with them? Even old Donna Francesca — you know? — the saint who lives in the Palazzetto Borgia — she told your mother that she hoped never to know a Corleone by sight again. They are disliked in Rome. But you would never be such an arrant fool as to go and fall in love with the girl, I suppose, though she is charming, and I can see that you admire her. Not very clever, I fancy, — brought up by a museum of old Sicilian ladies in a Palermo convent, —but very charming."

It was an unexpectedly long speech, on an unexpected theme, and it was fortunate that it contained nothing which could wound Orsino's feelings through Vittoria; for, in that case, he would have quarrelled with his cousin forthwith, not being of a patient disposition. As it was, the young man glanced up sharply from time to time, looking out for some depreciatory expression. He was glad when San Giacinto had finished speaking.

"If I wished to marry her," said Orsino, "I should not care who her relations might be."

"You would find yourself caring a great deal afterwards, if they made trouble with your own people. But I admit that the girl has charm and some beauty, and it is only fools who need clever wives to think for them. Good night. We may have a long day to-morrow, and we shall land about seven in the morning. I am going to bed."

Orsino watched the huge figure as it bent low and disappeared down the companion, and he was glad that San Giacinto had taken himself off without talking any more about Vittoria. He stayed on deck another hour, watching the light on the water, and then went below. He and his cousin had a cabin together, and he found the old giant asleep on the sofa, wrapped in a cloak, with his long legs resting on a portmanteau and extending half across the available space, while he had widened the transom for his vast shoulders by the help of a camp stool. He slept soundly, almost solemnly, under the small swinging oil-lamp, and there was something grand and soldier-like about his perfect indifference to discomfort. In a corner of the cabin, among a quantity of traps, the two rifles stood upright in their leathern cases. It was long before Orsino fell asleep.

He was glad when they got ashore at last in the early morning. Messina has the reputation of being the dirtiest city in all Italy, and it has the disagreeable peculiarity of not possessing a decent inn of any sort. San Giacinto and Orsino sat down in a shabby and dirty room to drink certain vile coffee which was brought up to them on little brass trays from a café at the corner of the street. San Giacinto produced a silver flask and poured a dose of spirits into his cup, and offered Orsino some; but the younger man had not been bred in the country and had never acquired the common Italian habit of strengthening bad coffee with alcohol. So he consoled his taste with cigarettes.

San Giacinto found that it would be impossible to proceed to Camaldoli till the following day, and the two men spent the morning and most of the afternoon in making the necessary arrangements. It was indispensable to see the officer in command of the carabineers and the prefect of the province, and San Giacinto knew that it would be wiser to send certain supplies up from Messina.

"I suppose that someone is there to hand the place over?" said Orsino.

"Tebaldo Pagliuca said that we should make enquiries of an old notary called Basili, in Randazzo, as his brother, being displeased with the sale, would probably refuse to meet us. Basili is to have the keys and will send a man with us. We shall have to rough it for a day or two."

"Do you mean to say that they have locked the place up and left it without even a servant in charge?" asked Orsino.

"Apparently. We shall know when we get there. I daresay that we may have to make our own coffee and cook our own food. It is rather a lonely neighbourhood, and the people whom Ferdinando Pagliuca employed have probably all left."

"It sounds a little vague," observed Orsino. "I suppose we shall find horses to take us up?"

"That is all arranged. We shall go up in a carriage, with four or five mounted carabineers, who will stay with us till they are relieved by others. They will all be waiting at the town of Piedimonte, above the station. I daresay that ruffian has carried off the furniture, too, and we may have to sleep on the floor in our cloaks."

"It would have been sensible to have brought a servant with us."

"No. Servants get into the way when there is trouble."

Orsino lighted another cigarette and said nothing. He was beginning to think that the whole thing sounded like an expedition into an enemy's country. They were dining in a queer little restaurant built over the water, at the end of the town towards the Faro. It was evidently the fashionable resort at that time of year, and Orsino studied the faces of the guests at the other tables. He thought that many of them were like Tebaldo Pagliuca, though with less malignity in their faces; but now and then he heard words spoken with the unmistakable Neapolitan accent, showing that all were not Sicilians.

"They killed a carabineer close to Camaldoli last week," said San Giacinto, thoughtfully dividing a large slice of sword-fish, which is the local delicacy. "One of them put on the dead soldier's uniform, passed himself off for a carabineer, and arrested the bailiff of the Duca di Fornasco that night, and marched him out of the village. They carried him off to the woods, and he has not been heard of since. He had given some information against them in the winter, so they will probably take some pains to kill him slowly, and send his head back to his relations in a basket of tomatoes in a day or two."

"Are those things positively true?" asked Orsino, incredulous even now.

"The story was in the paper this morning, and I asked the prefect. He said it was quite exact. You see the rifles may be useful, after all, and the carabineers are rather more indispensable than food and drink."

Again Orsino though of all Vittoria had told him, and he realized that whether the wild tales were literally true or not, she was not the only person who believed them. Just then a long fishing-boat ran past the little pier, close to the place where he was sitting at table. Six men were sending her along with her sharp stern foremost, as they generally do, standing to their long oars and throwing their whole strength into the work, for they were late, and the current would turn against them when the moon rose, as everyone knows who lives in Messina. Orsino did not remember that he had ever seen just such types of men, bare-headed, dark as Arabs, square-jawed, sinewy, fierce-eyed, with grave, thin lips, every one of them a fighting match for three or four Neapolitans. They were probably the first genuine Sicilians of the people whom he had ever seen, and they were not like any other

Italians. San Giacinto watched them too, and he smiled a little, as though the sight gave him satisfaction.

"That is the reason why there is no salt-tax in Sicily," he said. "That is also the reason why Italy is ruled by a single Sicilian, by Crispi. Good or bad, he is a man, at all events — and those fellows are men. I would rather have one of those fishermen at my elbow in danger, than twenty bragging Piedmontese, or a hundred civilized Tuscans."

"But they are treacherous," observed Orsino.

"No, they are not," answered the older man, thoughtfully. "They hate authority and rebel against it, and the mafia idea keeps them together like one man. Successful revolution is always called patriotism, and unsuccessful rebellion is always branded as treachery or treason. I have heard that somewhere, and it is true. But what we want in Italy is men, not ideas; action, not talk; honesty, not policy."

"We shall never get those things," said Orsino, who was naturally pessimistic. "Italian unity has come too late for a renascence, and too soon for a new birth."

San Giacinto smiled rather contemptuously.

"You are an aristocrat, my dear boy," he answered. "You want the clear wine without the filthy, fermenting must."

"I think we have the same name, you and I," observed Orsino.

"Yes, but I should be what I am, if I had been called Moscetti."

"And I?" enquired Orsino, his eyes kindling a little at the implied contrast of powers.

"If you had been plain Signor Moscetti, you would have been a very different kind of man. You would have worked hard at architecture, I suppose, and you would have acquired an individuality. As it is, you have not much more than the individuality of your class, and very little of your own. You are a product, whereas I was forced to become a producer when I was very young — a worker, in other words. Socially, I am a Saracinesca, like you; morally and actually, I have been a man of the people all my life, because I began among the people. I have made myself what I am. You were made what you are by somebody who lived in the twelfth century. I do not blame you, and I do not boast about myself. We like each other, but we are fundamentally different, and we emphatically do not like the same things. We are different kinds of animals that happen to be called by the same name."

"I tried to work once," said Orsino, thoughtfully.

"A man cannot do that sort of work against the odds of sixty-four quarterings and an unlimited fortune. But you had the instinct, just as I have it. You and I have more in common with those fishermen who just went by, than we have with most of our friends in Rome. We are men, at all events, as I said of Crispi."

Orsino was silent, for he was not in the humour to argue about anything, and he saw the truth of much that his cousin had said, and felt a hopelessness about doing anything in the world with which he had long been familiar.

The sun had gone down, leaving a deep glow on the Calabrian mountains, on the other side of the straits, and the water rippled with the current like purple silk. To the left, the heights above Scilla were soft and dreamy in a wine-coloured haze, and the great lighthouse shot out its white ray through the gathering dusk. To the right, the royal yards and top-gallant rigging of the vessels in the harbour made a dark lace against the high, white houses that caught the departing twilight. It was near moonrise, and the breeze had almost died away. The lights of the city began to shine out, one by one, then quickly, by scores, and under the little jetty, where the two men sat, the swirling water was all at once black and gleaming as flowing ink. Far off, a boat was moving, and the oars swung against the single tholes with an even, monotonous knocking that was pleasant to hear.

Orsino poured out another glass of the strong black wine and drank it, for the air was growing chilly. San Giacinto did the same and lighted a cigar. They sat almost an hour in silence, and then went slowly back to their squalid hotel on the quay.

CHAPTER X

On the following day Orsino and San Giacinto descended from the train at the little station of Piedimonte d'Etna, 'the foot of Mount Etna,' as it would be translated. It is a small, well-kept station near the sea, surrounded by gardens of oranges and lemons, and orchards of fruit trees, and gay with vines and flowers, penetrated by the intense southern light. The sky was perfectly cloudless, the sea of a gem-like blue, the peach blossoms were out by thousands, and the red pomegranate flowers had lately burst out of the bud, in splendid contrast with the deep, sheeny green of the smooth orange leaves. The trees had an air of belonging to pleasure gardens rather than to business-like orchards, and the whole colouring was almost artificially magnificent. It was late spring in the far south, and Orsino had never seen it. He had been on the Riviera, and in Sorrento, when the orange blossoms were all out, scenting the sea more than a mile from land, and he had seen the spring in England, which, once in every four or five years, is worth seeing; but he had not dreamt of such dazzling glories of colour as filled the earth and sky and sea of Sicily. It was not tropical, for there was nothing uncultivated nor unfruitful in sight; it seemed as though the little belt of gardens he saw around him must be the richest in the whole world, and as though neither man nor beast nor flower nor fruit could die in the fluid life of the fragrant air. It was very unexpected. San Giacinto was not the kind of man to give enthusiastic descriptions of views, and the conversation on the previous evening had prepared Orsino's mind for the wild hill country above, but not for the belt of glory which Sicily wears like a jewelled baldric round her breast, hidden here and there as it were, or obliterated, by great crags running far out into the sea, but coming into sight again instantly as each point is passed.

In the heap of traps and belongings that lay at his feet on the little platform, the two repeating rifles in their leathern cases were very good reminders of what the two men had before them on that day and for days and weeks afterwards.

"Winchesters," observed the porter who took the things to the carriage behind the station.

"How did you know that?" asked Orsino, surprised at the man's remark.

"As if they were the first I have carried!" exclaimed the man, with a grin. "Almost all the signori have them nowadays. People say they will kill at half a kilometre."

"Put them inside," said San Giacinto, as they were arranging the things. "Put them on the back seat with that case."

"Yes, the cartridges," said the porter, knowingly, as he felt the weight of the package.

"And God send you no need of them!" exclaimed the coachman, a big dark man with a stubbly chin, a broad hat, and a shabby velvet jacket.

"Amen!" ejaculated the porter.

"Are you going with us all the way?" asked San Giacinto of the coachman, looking at him keenly.

"No, signore. The master will drive you up from Piedimonte. He is known up there, but I am of Messina. It is always better to be known — or else it is much worse. But the master is a much respected man."

"Since he has come back," put in the porter, his shaven mouth stretching itself in a grim smile.

"Has he been in America?" asked Orsino, idly, knowing how many of the people made the journey to work, earn money, and return within a few years.

"He has been to the other America, which they call Ponza," answered the man.

The coachman scowled at him, and poked him in the back with the stock of his whip, but San

Giacinto laughed. Ponza is a small island off the Roman coast, used as a penitentiary and penal settlement.

"Did he kill his man?" enquired San Giacinto, coolly.

"No, signore," said the coachman, quickly. "He only gave him a salutation with the knife. It was a bad knife," he added, anxious for his employer's reputation. "But for that — the master is a good man! He only got the knife a little way into the other's throat — so much — " he marked the second joint of his middle finger with the end of his whip — "and then it would not cut," he concluded, with an apologetic air.

"The Romans always stab upwards under the ribs," said San Giacinto.

"One knows that!" answered the man. "So do we, of course. But it was only a pocket knife and would not have gone through the clothes, and the man was fat. That is why the master put it into his throat."

Orsino laughed, and San Giacinto smiled. Then they got into the carriage and settled themselves for the long drive. In twenty minutes they had left behind them the beautiful garden down by the sea, and the lumbering vehicle drawn by three skinny horses was crawling up a steep but well-built road, on which the yellow dust lay two inches thick. The coachman cracked his long whip of twisted cord with a noise like a quick succession of pistol shots, the lean animals kicked themselves uphill, as it were, the bells jingling spasmodically at each effort, and the dust rose in thick puffs in the windless air, under the blazing sun, uniting in a long low cloud over the road behind.

San Giacinto smoked in silence, and Orsino kept his mouth shut and his eyes half closed against the suffocating dust. After the first half-mile, the horses settled down to a straining walk, and the coachman stopped cracking his whip, sinking into himself, round-shouldered, as southern coachmen do when it is hot and a hill is steep. From time to time he swore at the skinny beasts in a sort of patient, half-contemptuous way.

"May they slay you!" he said. "May your vitals be torn out! May you be blinded! Curse you! Curse your fathers and mothers, and whoever made you! Curse the souls of your dead, your double-dead and your extra-dead, and the souls of all the horses that are yet to be born!"

There was a long pause between each imprecation, not as though the man were thinking over the next, but as if to give the poor beasts time to understand what he said. It was a kind of litany of southern abuse, but uttered in a perfunctory and indifferent manner, as many litanies are.

"Do you think your horses are Christians, that you revile them in that way?" asked Orsino, speaking from the back of the carriage, without moving.

The man's head turned upon his slouching shoulders, and he eyed Orsino with curiosity.

"We speak to them in this manner," he said. "They understand. In your country, how do you speak to them?"

"We feed them better, and they go faster."

"Every country has its customs," returned the man, stolidly. "It is true that these beasts are not mine. I should feed them better, if I had the money. But these animals consist of a little straw and water. This they eat, and this they are. How can they draw a heavy carriage uphill? It is a miracle. The Madonna attends to it. If I beat them, what do I beat? Bones and air. Why should I fatigue myself? There are their souls, so I speak to them, and they understand. Do you see? Now that I talk with you, they stop."

He turned as the carriage stood still, and addressed the spider-like animals again, in a dull, monotonous tone, that had something business-like in it.

"Ugly beasts! May you have apoplexy! May you be eaten alive!" And he went on with a whole string of similar expressions, till the unhappy brutes strained and threw themselves forward and began to kick themselves uphill again spasmodically, as before.

It seemed very long before they reached the town, dusty and white under the broad clear sun, and decidedly clean; spotless, indeed, compared with a Neapolitan or Calabrian village. Here and there among the whitewashed houses there were others built of almost black tufo, and some with old bits of effective carving in a bastard style of Norman-Saracen ornament.

The equine spiders entered the town at a jog-trot. Orsino fancied that but for the noise of the bells and the wheels he could have heard their bones rattle as their skeleton legs swung under them. They turned two or three corners and stopped suddenly before their stable.

"This is the master," said the coachman as he got down, indicating a square-built, bony man of medium height who stood before the door, dressed in a clean white shirt and a decent brown velveteen jacket. He had a dark red carnation in his button-hole and wore his soft black hat a little on one side.

In the shadow of the street near the door stood five carabineers in their oddly old-fashioned yet oddly imposing uniforms and cocked hats, each with a big army revolver and a cartridge case at his belt, and a heavy cavalry sabre by his side. They were tall, quiet-eyed, sober-looking men, and they saluted San Giacinto and Orsino gravely, while one, who was the sergeant, came forward, holding out a note, which San Giacinto read, and put into his pocket.

"I am San Giacinto," he said, "and this gentleman is my cousin, Don Orsino Saracinesca, who goes with us."

"Shall we saddle at once, Signor Marchese?" asked the sergeant, and as San Giacinto assented, he turned to his men and gave the necessary order in a low voice.

The phantom horses were taken out of the carriage, and the two gentlemen got out to stretch their legs while the others were put in. The carabineers had all disappeared, their quarters and stables being close by; so near, indeed, that the clattering of their big chargers' hoofs and the clanking of accoutrements could be plainly heard.

"The master is to drive us up to Camaldoli," observed Orsino, lighting a cigarette.

"Yes," replied his companion. "He is a smart-looking fellow, but for my part I prefer the other man's face. Stupidity is always a necessary quality in servants. The master looks to me like a type of a 'maffeuso.'"

"With five carabineers at our heels, I imagine that we are pretty safe."

"For to-day, of course. I was thinking of our future relations. This is the only man who can furnish carriages between Camaldoli and the station. One is in his power."

"Why should we not have carriages and horses of our own?" asked Orsino.

"It is a useless expense at present," answered San Giacinto, who never wasted money, though he never spared it. "We shall see. In a day or two we shall find out whether you can have them at all. If it turns out to be possible, it will be because you find yourself on good terms with the people of the neighbourhood."

"And turn 'maffeuso' myself," suggested Orsino, with a laugh.

"Not exactly, but the people may tolerate you. That is the most you can expect, and it is much."

"And if not, I am never to move without a squad of carabineers to take care of me, I suppose."

"You had better go armed, at all events," said San Giacinto, quietly. "Have your revolver always in your pocket and take a rifle when you go out of the house. The sight of firearms has a salutary effect upon all these people."

The fresh horses had been put in, very different from the wretched creatures that had dragged the carriage up from the station, for they were lean indeed, but young and active. San Giacinto looked at them and remarked upon the fact as he got in.

"Of course!" answered the philosophical coachman; "the road is long and you must drive up as high as paradise. Those old pianos could never get any higher than purgatory."

"Pianos?"

"Eh — they have but three legs each, and they are of wood, like a piano," answered the man, without a smile. "You also heard the music they made with their bones, as we came along."

The master mounted to his seat, and at the same moment the carabineers came round the corner, already in the saddle, each with his canvas bread-bag over his shoulder and his rifle slung by his stirrup. They were mounted on powerful black chargers, well-fed, good-tempered animals, extremely well kept, and evidently accustomed to long marches. The carabineers, foot and horse, are by far the finest corps in the Italian army, and are, indeed, one of the finest and best equipped bodies of men in the world. They are selected with the greatest care, and every man has to prove that neither he nor his father has ever been in jail, even for the slightest misdemeanour. The troopers and the men of the foot corps rank as corporals of the regular army, and many of them have been sergeants. In the same way each degree of rank is reckoned as equal to the next higher in the army, and the whole corps is commanded by a colonel. There are now about twenty-five thousand in the whole country, quartered in every town and village in squads from four or five, to twenty or thirty strong. The whole of Italy is patrolled by them, day and night, both by high roads and bridle-paths, and on the mainland they have effectually stamped out brigandage and highway robbery. But in Sicily they are pitted against very different odds.

The road rises rapidly beyond Piedimonte, winding up through endless vinelands to the enormous yoke which unites Etna with the inland mountains. Orsino leaned back silently in his place, gazing at the snow-covered dome of the volcano, from the summit of which rose a thin wreath of perfectly white smoke. From time to time San Giacinto pointed out to his companion the proposed direction of his light railway, which was to follow the same general direction as the carriage road. The country, though still cultivated, was lonely, and the barren heights of Etna, visible always, gave the landscape a singular character. To the westward rose the wooded hills, stretching far away inland, dark and mysterious.

They halted again in the high street of a long, clean village, called Linguaglossa, and some of the carabineers dismounted and drank from a fountain, being half choked with the dust. The master of the vehicle got down and dived into a quiet-looking house, returning presently with a big, painted earthenware jug full of wine, and a couple of solid glasses, which he filled and held out, without a word, to San Giacinto and Orsino. The wine was almost black, very heavy and strong. They quenched their thirst, and then the man swallowed two glasses in succession. San Giacinto held out some small change to him to pay for the drink. But he laughed a little.

"One does not pay for wine in our country," he said. "They sell a pitcher like this for three sous at the wineshops, but this is the house of a very rich signore, who makes at least a thousand barrels every year. What should one pay? One sou? That is as much as it is worth. A man can get drunk for five sous here."

"I should think so! It is as strong as spirits," said Orsino.

"But the people are very sober," answered San Giacinto. "They have strong heads, too."

They were soon off again, along the endless road. Gradually, the vinelands began to be broken by patches of arid ground, where dark stone cropped up, and the dry soil seemed to produce nothing but the poisonous yellow spurge.

It was long past noon when the dark walls and the cathedral spire of Randazzo came into sight. They found Basili's house, and the notary, whose daughter was already famous in Rome, was at work in his dingy study, with a sheet of governmental stamped paper before him. He was a curious compound of a provincial and a man of law, with regular features and extremely black eyebrows, the rest of his hair being white. Orsino thought that he must have been handsome in his youth.

Everything was prepared according to the orders San Giacinto had written. Basili handed over a big bunch of keys, most of which were rusty, while two of them were bright, as though they had been recently much used. He hardly spoke at all, but looked at his visitors attentively, and with evident curiosity. He called a man who was in readiness to go with them.

"Shall we find anybody at the house?" enquired Orsino.

"Not unless someone has been locked in," was the answer. "Nevertheless, it might be safer not to go straight to the door, but to get under the wall, and come up to it in that way. One never knows what may be behind a door until it is open."

San Giacinto laughed rather dryly, and Orsino looked hard at Basili to discover a smile.

"But, indeed," continued the notary, "there are too many bushes about the house. If I might be so bold as to offer my advice, I should say that you had better cut down the bushes at once. You will have time to begin this evening, for the days are long."

"Are they unhealthy?" enquired Orsino, not understanding in the least.

"Unhealthy? Oh, no. But they are convenient for hiding, and there are people of bad intentions everywhere. I do not speak of Don Ferdinando Pagliuca, believe me. But there are persons of no conscience, who do not esteem life as anything. But I do not mean to signify Don Ferdinando Pagliuca, I assure you. Gentlemen, I wish you a pleasant journey, and every satisfaction, and the fulfilment of your desires."

He bowed them out, being evidently not inclined to continue the conversation, and they drove on again, the man whom he had sent with them being beside the padrone on the box. He had a long old-fashioned gun slung over his shoulder, evidently loaded, for there was a percussion cap on the nipple of the lock.

Orsino thought Randazzo a grim and gloomy town in spite of its beautiful carved stone balconies and gates, and its Saracen-Norman cathedral, and he was glad when they were out in the country again, winding up through the beginning of the black lands. San Giacinto looked about him, and then began to get out one of the Winchesters, without making any remark. Orsino watched him as he dropped the cartridges one by one into the repeater and then examined the action again, to see that all was in working order.

"You understand them, I suppose?" he asked of Orsino.

"Yes, of course."

"Then you had better load the other," said the big man, quietly.

"As you please," answered Orsino, evidently considering the precaution superfluous, and he got out the other rifle with great deliberation.

They were going slowly up a steep hill, and the carabineers were riding close behind them at a foot pace. The two gentlemen could, of course, not see the road in front. The padrone and Basili's man were talking in a low tone in the Sicilian dialect.

Suddenly, with a clanging and clattering, two of the troopers passed the carriage at a full gallop up the hill. The sergeant trotted up to San Giacinto's side, looking sharply ahead of him. Basili's man slipped the sling of his gun over his head in an instant, and laid the weapon across his knees, and Orsino distinctly heard him cock the old-fashioned hammer. San Giacinto still had his rifle in his hand, and he leaned out over the carriage to see what was ahead.

There was nothing to be seen but the two carabineers charging up the steep road at a gallop.

"There was a man on horseback waiting at the crest of the hill," said the sergeant. "As soon as he saw us he wheeled and galloped on. He is out of sight now. They will not catch him, for he had a good horse."

"Have you had much trouble lately?" asked San Giacinto.

"They killed one of my men last week and used his uniform for a disguise," answered the soldier, gravely. "That fellow was waiting there to warn somebody that we were coming."

The troopers halted when they reached the top of the hill, looked about, and made a sign to the sergeant, signifying that they could not catch the man. The sergeant answered by a gesture which bade them wait.

"Touch your horses, Tatò," he said to the padrone, who had neither moved nor looked round during the excitement, but who immediately obeyed.

The carriage moved quickly up the hill, till it overtook the carabineers. Then San Giacinto saw that the road descended rapidly by a sharp curve to the left, following a spur of the mountain. No one was in sight, nor was there any sound of hoofs in the distance. To the right, below the road, the land was much broken, and there was shelter from sight for a man and his horse almost anywhere for a mile ahead.

When Orsino had finished loading the rifle, he looked about him, and saw for the first time the black lands of which Vittoria had spoken, realizing the truth of what she had said about the possibility of a man hiding himself in the fissures of the lava, to fire upon a traveller in perfect security. With such an escort he and his companion were perfectly safe, of course, but he began to understand what was meant by the common practice of carrying firearms.

It is impossible to imagine anything more hideously desolate and sombrely wild than the high ground behind Mount Etna. The huge eruptions of former and recent times have for ages sent down rivers of liquid stone and immeasurable clouds of fine black ashes, which have all hardened roughly into a conformation which is rugged but not wholly irregular, for the fissures mostly follow the downward direction of the slope, westward from the volcano. All over the broad black surface the spurge grows in patches during the spring, and somehow the vivid yellow of the flowers makes the dark stone and hardened ash look still darker and more desolate. Here and there, every two or three miles, there are groups of deserted huts built of black tufo, doorless and windowless, and almost always on the edge of some bit of arable land that stretches westward between two old lava beds. The distances are so great that the peasants move out in a body to cultivate these outlying fields at certain times of the year, and sleep in the improvised villages until the work is done, when they go back to the towns, leaving the crops to take care of themselves until harvest time. In the guerilla warfare which breaks out periodically between the carabineers and the outlaws, the stone huts are important points of vantage, and once or twice have been the scene of hard-fought battles. Being of stone, though roughly built, and being pierced with mere holes for windows, they are easily defended from within by men armed with repeaters and plentiful ammunition.

After the little excitement caused by the pursuit of the unknown rider, two of the troopers rode before the carriage, and three followed it, while all got their rifles across their saddle-bows, ready for action. They knew well enough that as long as they kept together, even a large band of brigands would not attack them on the open road, but there were plenty of narrow places where the earth was high on each side, and where a single well-directed volley might easily have killed many of the party. Since the outlaws' latest invention of shooting the carabineers in order to disguise themselves in their uniforms, the troopers were more than ever cautious and on the alert against a surprise.

But nothing happened. The single horseman had disappeared altogether, having probably taken to the broken land for greater safety, and the carriage jogged steadily on across the high land, towards its destination, with a regular jingling of harness bells, and an equally rhythmic clanking of sabres.

"A little quicker, Tatò," said the sergeant to the

padrone, from time to time, but no one else said
anything.

Both San Giacinto and Orsino were weary of the
long drive when, at an abrupt curve of the road,
the horses slackened speed, to turn out of the highway, to the right.

"There is Camaldoli," said Tatò, turning round
to speak to them for the first time since they had
started. "You can see the Druse's tower above
the trees, and the river is below."

So far as the two gentlemen could see there was
not another habitation in sight, though it was no
very great distance to the village of Santa Vittoria,
beyond the next spur of Etna. The ancient building, of which only the top of one square black tower
appeared, was concealed by a dense mass of foliage
of every kind. Below, to the right and towards the
mountain stream which Tatò called a river, the land
was covered with wild pear trees, their white blossoms all out and reflecting the lowering sun. Nearer
the building, the pink bloom of the flowering
peaches formed a low cloud of exquisite colour, and
the fresh green of the taller trees of all kinds made
a feathery screen above and a compact mass of
dark shadow lower down. The narrow drive was
thickly hedged with quantities of sweetbrier and
sweet hawthorn, which increased as the road
descended, till it filled everything up to a man's
height and higher. The way was so narrow that

when the carabineers tried to ride on each side of the carriage, they found it impossible to do so without being driven into the tangle of thorns at every step. The whole party moved forward at a quick trot, and Orsino understood what Basili the notary had said about the bushes, so that even he laid his rifle across his knees and peered into the brambles from time to time, half expecting to see the muzzle of a gun sticking through the green leaves and white flowers.

The avenue seemed to be about half a mile long. In the middle of it the trees were so thick as to make it almost gloomy, even in the broad afternoon daylight. The road was rough and stony.

Suddenly the horse of one of the carabineers ahead stumbled and fell heavily, and the other trooper threw his horse back on its haunches with an exclamation. Almost at the same instant, the sharp crack of a rifle rang through the trees on the right; and the bullet, singing overhead, cut through the branches just above the carriage, so that a twig with its leaves dropped upon Orsino's knees. Another shot, fired very low down, struck a spoke of one of the carriage wheels, and sent the splinters flying, burying itself somewhere in the body of the vehicle. Another and another followed, all fired either far too high or much too low to strike any of the party. As the shots all came from the same side, however, the sergeant of carabineers sprang to the ground and plunged into the brush on that side, his rifle in his hand, calling to his men to follow him. San Giacinto stood up and knelt on the cushion of the carriage, though he knew that he could not fire in the direction taken by the carabineers, lest he should hit one of them by accident.

"Keep a lookout on your side, too!" he cried to Orsino. "Shoot anybody you see, and do not miss. They may be on both sides, but I think not."

Strangely enough, from the moment the soldiers entered the brush, not another shot was fired. Clearly the assailants were beating a hasty retreat.

At that moment something black stirred in the bushes on Orsino's side. Instantly his rifle was at his shoulder, and he fired. San Giacinto started and turned round, bringing up his own weapon at the same time.

"I believe I heard something fall," said Orsino, opening the door of the carriage. Tatò had disappeared. Basili's man had followed the soldiers into the brush.

In an instant both the gentlemen were in the thicket, Orsino leading, as he followed the direction of his shot.

CHAPTER XI

Orsino's gloved hand trembled violently as he pushed aside the tangle of sweetbrier, trying to reach the place where the man upon whom he had fired had fallen.

"Let me go first," said San Giacinto. "I am bigger and my gloves are thicker."

But Orsino pushed on, his heart beating so hard that he felt the pulse in his throat and his eyes. He had been cool enough when the bullets had been flying across the carriage, and his hand had been quite steady when he had aimed at the black something moving stealthily in the bushes. But the sensation of having killed a man, and in such a way, was horrible to him. He pushed on, scratching his face and his wrists above his gloves, in the sharp thorns. The bushes were more than breast high, even to his tall figure, but San Giacinto could see over his head.

"There!" exclaimed the giant, suddenly. "There he is—to your right—I can see him!"

Orsino pushed on, and in another moment his foot struck something hard that moved a little, but was not a stone. It was the dead man's foot in a heavy shooting-boot.

They found him quite dead, not fallen to the ground, but half sitting and half lying in the thorns. He had fallen straight backwards, shot through the temples. The eyes were wide open, but without light, the handsome face perfectly colourless, and the silky, brown moustache hid the relaxed mouth. His rifle stood upright in the bush as it had fallen from his hand. His soft hat was still firmly planted on the back of his head.

Orsino was stupefied with horror and stood quite still, gazing at the dead man's face. San Giacinto looked down over his shoulders.

"He looks like a gentleman," he said, in a low voice.

The chill of a terrible presentiment froze about Orsino's heart. As he looked, the handsome features became familiar, all at once, as though he had often seen them before.

"We had better get him out to the road," said San Giacinto. "The carabineers may identify him. The sooner, the better, though you were perfectly justified in shooting him."

He laid his hand upon Orsino's shoulder to make him move a little, and the young man started. Then he bit his trembling lip and stooped to try and lift the body. As he touched the velveteen coat, the head fell suddenly to one side, and

Orsino uttered an involuntary exclamation. He had never moved a dead man before.

"It is nothing," said San Giacinto, quietly. "He is quite dead. Take his feet."

He pushed past Orsino and lifted the head and shoulders, beginning to move towards the road at once, walking backwards and breaking down the bushes with his big shoulders. They got him out upon the road. The carriage horses were standing quite still, with their heads hanging down, as though nothing had happened. They had plunged a little at first. In the road before them stood the trooper who had been thrown, holding his own and another charger by the bridle. The cause of the accident was clear enough. A pit had been treacherously dug across the road and covered with sticks and wood, so as to be invisible. Fortunately the horse had escaped injury. The others were tethered by their bridles to the back of the carriage. In the brush, far to the right, the tall bushes were moving, showing where the other four carabineers were searching for the outlaws who had fired, if, indeed, there had been more than one.

They laid the dead man in the middle of the road, on the other side of the ditch, out of reach of the horses' feet, and the trooper watched them without speaking, though with a satisfied look of approval.

"Do you know him?" asked San Giacinto, addressing the soldier.

"No, Signor Marchese. But I have not been long on this station. The brigadiere will know him, and will be glad. I came to take the place of the man they killed last week."

Orsino looked curiously at the young carabineer, who took matters so quietly, when he himself was struggling hard to seem calm. He would not have believed that he could ever have felt such inward weakness and horror as filled him, and he could not trust himself to speak, yet he had no reason to doubt that he had saved his own life or San Giacinto's by firing in time.

"I see why the other ones fired so wildly," said San Giacinto. "They were afraid of hitting their friend, who was to do the real work alone, while they led the carabineers off on a false scent on the other side. This fellow felt quite safe. He thought he could creep up to the carriage and make sure of us at close quarters. He did not expect that one of us would be on the lookout."

"That is a common trick," said the soldier. "I have seen it done at Noto. It must have been a single person that fired, and this man was also alone. If he had been with a companion, the gentleman's shot would have been answered, and one of you would have been killed."

"Then it was the other man who was waiting

on horseback in the road to warn this one of our coming?"

"Evidently, Signor Marchese."

Still Orsino stood quite still, gazing down into the dead man's face, and feeling very unsteady. Just then nothing else seemed to have any existence for him, and he was unaware of all outward things excepting that one thing that lay there, limp and helpless, killed by his hand in the flash of an instant. And as he gazed, he fancied that the young features in their death pallor grew more and more familiar, and at his own heart there was a freezing and a stiffening, as though he were turning into ice from within.

The sergeant and the troopers came back, covered with brambles, hot and grim, and empty-handed.

"Did any of you fire that other shot?" he asked, as soon as he was in the road.

"I did," said Orsino. "I killed this man."

The sergeant sprang forward, and his men pressed after him to see. The sergeant bent down and examined the dead face attentively. Then he looked-up.

"You have killed rather an important person," he said gravely. "This is Ferdinando Pagliuca. We knew that he was on good terms with the outlaws, but we could not prove it against him."

"Oh, yes," said Tatò, the padrone, suddenly appearing again. "That is Don Ferdinando. I know him very well, for I have often driven him. Who would have thought it?"

Orsino had heard nothing after the sergeant had pronounced the name. He almost reeled against San Giacinto, and gripped the latter's arm desperately, his face almost as white as the dead man's. Even San Giacinto started in surprise. Then Orsino made a great effort and straightened himself, and walked away a few paces.

"This is a bad business," said San Giacinto, in a preoccupied tone. "We shall have the whole mafia against us for this. Has the other man escaped?"

"Clean gone," said the sergeant. "You had better luck than we, for we never saw him. He must have fired his shots from his horse and bolted instantly. We could not have got through the brush with our horses."

Orsino went and leaned against the carriage, shading his eyes with his hands, while San Giacinto and the soldiers talked over what had happened. The sergeant set a couple of men to work on the brambles with their sabres, to cut a way for the carriage on one side of the pitfall that covered the road.

"Put the body into the carriage," said San Giacinto. "We can walk. It is not far." He roused Orsino, who seemed to be half stunned.

"Come, my boy!" he said, drawing him away

from the carriage as the soldiers were about to lay the body in it. "Of course it is not pleasant, but it cannot be helped, and you have rendered the government a service, though you have got us into an awkward position with the Corleone."

"Awkward!" Orsino's voice was hoarse and broken. "You do not know!" he added.

San Giacinto did not understand, but made him fall back behind the carriage, which jolted horribly with its dead occupant, as Tatò forced his horses to drag it round the end of the ditch. The carabineers, still distrustful of the thick trees and the underbrush, carried their rifles and led their horses, and the whole party proceeded slowly along the drive towards the ancient house. It might have been a quarter of a mile distant. Orsino walked the whole way in silence, with bent head and set lips.

They emerged upon a wide open space, overgrown with grass, wild flowers, and rank weeds, through which a narrow path led straight up to the main door. There had been a carriage road once, following a wide curve, but it had long been disused, and even the path was not much trodden, and the grass was beginning to grow in it.

The front of the house presented a broad, rough-plastered surface, broken by but few windows, all of which were high above the ground. The tower was not visible from this side. From the back, the sound of water came up with a steady, low roar. The door was, in fact, a great oak gate, studded with big rusty nails, paintless, grey, and weather-beaten. Regardless of old Basili's advice, San Giacinto walked straight up to it, followed by the notary's man with the bunch of keys.

The loneliness of it all was beyond description, and was, if possible, enhanced by the roar of the water. The air was damp, too, from the torrent bed, and near one end of the house there were great patches of moss. At the other side, towards the sun, the remains of what had been a vegetable garden were visible, rank broccoli and cabbages thrusting up their bunches of pale green leaves, broken trellises of cane, half fallen in, and over-grown with tomato vines and wild creeping plants. A breath of air brought a smell of rotting vege-tables and damp earth to San Giacinto's nostrils, as he tried one key after another in the lock.

They got in at last, and entered under a gloomy archway, beyond which there was a broad court-yard, where the grass grew between the flagstones. In the middle was an ancient well, on the right a magnificently carved doorway led into the old chapel of the monastery. On the left, opposite the chapel, a long row of windows, with closed shutters in fairly good condition, showed the posi-tion of the habitable rooms.

"Is that a church?" asked San Giacinto of

Basili's man. "Take the dead man in and leave him there," he added, as the man nodded and began to look for the key on the bunch.

They took Ferdinando Pagliuca's body from the carriage, which stood in the middle of the court-yard, and carried it in and laid it down on the uppermost step of one of the side altars, of which there were three. Orsino followed them.

It was a very dilapidated place. There had once been a few frescoes, which were falling from the walls with age and dampness. High up, through the open windows from which the glass had long since disappeared, the swallows shot in and out, bringing a dark gleam of sunshine on their sharp, black wings. Although the outer air had free access, there was a heavy, death-like smell of mould in the place. The altars were dismantled and the grey dust lay thick upon them, with fragments of plaster here and there. Only on the high altar a half-broken wooden candle-stick, once silvered, stood bending over, and a little glazed frame still contained a mouldering printed copy of the Canon of the Mass. In the middle of the floor a round slab of marble, with two greenish bolts of brass, bore the inscription, 'Ossa R R. P P.' covering the pit wherein lay the bones of the departed monks who had once dwelt in the monastery.

The troopers laid Ferdinando's body upon the

stone steps in silence, and then went away, for there was much to be done. Orsino stayed behind, alone, for his cousin had not even entered the church. He knelt down for a few moments on the lowest step. It seemed a sort of act of reverence to the man whom he had killed. Mechanically he said a prayer for the dead.

But his thoughts were of the living. The man who lay there was Vittoria d'Oriani's brother, the brother of his future wife, of the being he held most dear in the world. Between him and her there was her own blood, shed by his hand. The shot had done more than kill Ferdinando Pagliuca; it had mortally wounded his own life.

He asked himself whether Vittoria, or any woman, could marry the man who had killed her brother. In time, she might forgive, indeed, but she could not forget. No one could. And there were her other brothers, and her mother, and they were Sicilians, revengeful and long pursuing in their revenge. Never, under any imaginable circumstances, would they give their consent to his marriage with Vittoria, even supposing that she herself, in the course of years, could blot out the memory of the dead. He might as well make up his mind that she was lost to him.

But that was hard to do, for the roots of growing love had struck deep and burrowed themselves in under his heart almost unawares, from week to week since he had known her, and to tear them up was to tear out the heart itself.

He went to the other side of the dim chapel and rested his dark forehead against the mouldering walls. It was as though he were going mad then and there. He drew himself up and said, almost aloud, that he was a man and must act like a man. No one had ever accused him of being unmanly, and he could not tamely bear the accusation from himself.

All the old hackneyed phrases of cynical people he had known came back to him. 'Only one woman, and the world was full of them'—and much to that same effect. And all the time he knew that such words could never fit his lips, and that though the world was full of women, there was only one for him, and between her and him lay the barrier of her own brother's blood.

He turned as he stood, and saw the straight, dark figure, with its folded hands, lying on the steps of the altar opposite—the outward fact, as his love for Vittoria was the inward truth.

The horror of it all came over him again like a surging wave, roaring in his ears and deafening him. It could have been but one degree worse if Vittoria's brother had been his friend, instead of his enemy, and if he had killed him in anger.

He remembered that he had expected to send his

mother a long and reassuring telegram on this day, and that he had told Vittoria that she should go to the Palazzo Saracinesca and hear news of him. There was a telegraph station at Santa Vittoria, three-quarters of a mile from Camaldoli, but he was confronted by the difficulty of sending any clear message which should not contain an allusion to Ferdinando Pagliuca's death, since the carabineers would be obliged to report the fact at once, and it would be in the Roman papers on the following morning.

That was a new and terrible thought. There would be the short telegraphic account of how Don Orsino Saracinesca had been attacked by brigands in a narrow road and had shot one of the number, who turned out to be Ferdinando Corleone. Her mother, who always read the papers, would read that, too. Then her brothers — then Vittoria. And his own mother would see it — his head seemed bursting. And there lay the fact, the source of these inevitable things, cold and calm, with the death smile already stealing over its white face.

San Giacinto stalked in, looking about him, and the sound of his tread roused Orsino.

"Come," he said, rather sternly. "There is much to be done. I could not find you. The man is dead; you did right in killing him, and we must think of our own safety."

“What do you mean?” asked Orsino, in a dull voice. “We are safe enough, it seems to me.”

“The sergeant does not seem to think so,” answered San Giacinto. “Before night it will be known that Ferdinando Pagliuca is dead, and we may have half the population of Santa Vittoria about our ears. Fortunately this place will stand a siege. Two of the troopers have gone to the village to try and get a reinforcement, and to bring the doctor to report the death, so that we can bury the man. Come — come with me! We will shut the church up till the doctor comes, and think no more about it.”

He saw that Orsino was strangely moved by what had happened, and he drew him out into the air. The carriage was being unloaded by Tatò and the notary’s man, and the horses had all disappeared. The sergeant and the two remaining troopers were busy clearing out a big room which opened upon the court, with the intention of turning it into a guardroom. Orsino looked at them indifferently. A renewed danger would have roused him, but nothing else could. San Giacinto led him away to show him the buildings.

“Your nerves have been shaken,” said the older man. “But you will soon get over that. I remember once upon a time being a good deal upset myself, when a man whom I had caught·in mischief suddenly killed himself almost in my hands.”

"I shall get over it, as you say," answered Orsino. "Give me one of those strong cigars of yours, will you?"

He would have given a good deal to have been able to confide in San Giacinto and tell him the real trouble. Had he been sure that any immediate good could come of it, he would have spoken; but it seemed to him, on the contrary, that to speak of Vittoria might make matters worse. They wandered over the dark old place for half an hour. At the back, over the torrent, there was one long wall with a rampart, terminating in the evil-looking Druse's tower. The trees grew thick over the stream, and there was only one opening in the wall, closed by double low doors with heavy bolts. The whole building was, in reality, a tolerably strong fortress, built round the four sides of a single great courtyard, to which there was but one entrance,—besides the little postern over the river.

"I should like to send a telegram to Rome," said Orsino, suddenly. "It is not too late for them to get it to-night."

"You can send it to Santa Vittoria by the doctor, when he goes back."

Orsino went down into the court and got a writing-case out of his bag. It seemed convenient to write on the seat of the carriage, but just as he was going to place his writing things there, he saw that there were dark wet spots on the cushions. He shuddered and turned away in disgust, and wrote his message, leaning on the stone brink of the well.

He telegraphed that San Giacinto and he had arrived and were well, that they had met with an attack, and that he himself had killed a man. But he did not write Ferdinando's name. That seemed useless.

The doctor arrived, and the carabineers brought a couple of men of the foot brigade to strengthen the little garrison. As they entered, San Giacinto saw that four rough-looking peasants were standing outside the gate, conversing and looking up to the windows; grim, clean-shaven, black-browed men of the poorer class, for they had no guns and wore battered hats and threadbare blue cloaks. San Giacinto handed the doctor over to the sergeant and went outside at once. The men stared in silence at the gigantic figure that faced them. In his rough dark clothes and big soft hat, San Giacinto looked more vast than ever, and his bold and sombre features and stern black eyes completed the impression he made on the hill men. He looked as though he might have been the chief of all the outlaws in Sicily.

"Listen!" he said, stepping up to them. "This place is mine now, for I have bought it and paid for it, and I mean to keep it. Your friend Ferdinando Pagliuca is dead. After consenting to the sale, he dug a pitfall in the carriage road to stop us, and he and a friend of his attacked us. We shot him, and you can go and look at his body in the chapel, in there, if you have curiosity about him. There are eleven men of us here, seven being carabineers, and we have plenty of ammunition, so that it will not be well for anyone who troubles us. Tell your friends so. This is going to be a barrack, and there will be a company of infantry here before long, and there will be a railway before two years. Tell your friends that also. I suppose you are men from the Camaldoli farms."

Two of the peasants nodded, but said nothing.

"If you want work, begin and clear away those bushes. You will know where there are tools. Here is money, if you will begin at once. If you do not want money, say what you do want. But if you want nothing, go, or I shall shoot you."

He suddenly had a big army revolver in one hand, and he pulled out a loose bank note with the other.

"But I prefer that we should be good friends," he concluded, "for I have much work for everybody, and plenty of money to pay for it."

The men were not cowards, but they were taken unawares by San Giacinto's singular speech. They looked at each other, and at the bushes. One of them threw his head back a little, thrusting out his chin, which signifies a negation. The shortest of the four, a broad-shouldered, tough-looking fellow stepped before the rest.

"We will work for you, but we will not cut down the bushes. We will do any other work than that. You will not find anybody here who will cut down the bushes."

"Why not?" asked San Giacinto.

"Eh — it is so," said the man, with a peculiar expression.

The other three shrugged their shoulders and nodded silently, but kept their eyes on San Giacinto's revolver.

"We are good people," continued the man. "We wish to be friends with everyone, and since you have bought the estate, and own the land on which we live, we shall pay our rent, when we have anything wherewith to pay, and when we have not, God will provide. But as for the bushes, we cannot cut them down. We wish to be friends with everyone. But as for that, signore, if you have no axes nor hedging knives, we have them. We will bring them, and then we will go away and do any other work for you. Thus we shall not cut down the bushes, but perhaps the bushes will be cut down."

San Giacinto laughed a little, and the big revolver went back into his pocket.

"I see that we shall be friends, then," he said. "When you have brought the hatchets, then you can come inside and help to clean the house. Then I will give you this money for your work this evening and to-morrow."

The men spoke rapidly together in dialect, so that San Giacinto could not understand them. Then the spokesman addressed him again.

"Signore," he said, "we will bring the hatchets to the door, but it is late to clean the house this evening. We do not want the money to-night. We will return in the morning and work for you."

"There are three hours of daylight yet," observed San Giacinto. "You could do something in that time, I should think."

"An hour and a half," replied the man. "It is late," he added. "It is very late."

The other three nodded. San Giacinto understood perfectly that there was some other reason, but did not insist. He fancied that they were suspicious of his own intentions with regard to them, and he let them go without further words.

As he turned back, the village doctor appeared under the arch, leading his mule. He was a pale young fellow from Messina, who had been three or four years at Santa Vittoria. San Giacinto offered him an escort back to the village, but he refused.

"If I could not go about alone, my usefulness

would be over," he said. "It is quite safe now. They will probably kill me the next time there is a cholera season."

"Why?"

"They are convinced that the government sends them the cholera through the doctors, to thin the population," answered the young man, with a dreary smile.

"What a country! It is worse than Naples."

"In some ways, far worse. In others, much better."

"In what way is it better?" asked San Giacinto, with some curiosity.

"They are terrible enemies," said the doctor, "but they can be very devoted friends, too."

"Oh — we have had a taste of their enmity first. I hope we may see something of their friendship before long."

"I doubt it, Signor Marchese. You will have the people against you from first to last, and your position is dangerous. Ferdinando Corleone was popular, and he had the outlaws on his side. I have no doubt that many of the band have been hidden here. It is a lonely and desolate house, full of queer hiding-places. By the bye, are you going to bury that poor man here? Shall I send people down from Santa Vittoria with a coffin, to carry him up to the cemetery?"

"You know the country. What should you

advise me to do? We must give him Christian burial, I suppose."

"I should be inclined to lift up the slab in the church and quietly drop him down among the monks," said the doctor. "That would be Christian burial enough for him. But you had better consult the sergeant about it. If he is taken up to Santa Vittoria, there will be a great public funeral, and all the population will follow, as though he were a martyr. If you bury him without a priest, they will say that you not only murdered him treacherously, but got rid of his body by stealth. Consult the sergeant, Signor Marchese. That is best."

The doctor mounted his mule and rode away. San Giacinto closed and barred the great gate himself before he went back into the court. He found Orsino in the midst of a discussion with the sergeant, regarding the same question of the disposal of the body.

"I know his family," Orsino was saying. "Some of them are friends of mine. He must be decently buried by a priest. I insist upon it."

The sergeant repeated what the doctor had said, namely, that a public funeral would produce something like a popular demonstration.

"I should not care if it produced a revolution," answered Orsino. "I killed the man like a dog, not knowing who he was, but I will not have him buried like one. If you are afraid of the village, let them send their priest down here, dig a grave under the floor of the church, and bury him there. But he shall not be dropped into a hole like a dead rat without a blessing. Besides, it is not legal — there are all sorts of severe regulations — "

"There is one against burying anyone within a church," observed the sergeant. "But the worst that could happen would be that you might have to pay a fine. It shall be as you please, signore. In the morning we will get a priest and a coffin, and bury him under the church. I have the doctor's certificate in my pocket."

Orsino was satisfied, and went away to be alone again, not caring where. But San Giacinto and the carabineers proceeded to turn the great court into something like a camp. There were all sorts of offices, kitchens, bake-houses, oil-presses, and storerooms, which opened directly upon the paved space. The men collected old wood and kindling stuff to make a fire, and prepared to cook some of the provisions which San Giacinto had brought for the night, while he and the sergeant determined on the best positions for sentries.

Orsino wandered about the great rooms upstairs. They were half dismantled and much dilapidated, but not altogether unfurnished. Ferdinando had retired some days previously to the village and had taken what he needed for his own use, but had left the rest. There was a tolerably furnished room immediately above the great gate. Orsino opened the window wide, and leaned out, breathing the outer air with a certain sense of relief from oppression. Watching the swallows that darted down from under the eaves to the weed-grown lawn, and up again with meteor speed, and catching in his face the last reflexions of the sun, which was sinking fast between two distant hills, he could almost believe that it had all been a bad dream. He could at least try to believe it for a little while.

But the sun went down quickly, though it still blazed full on the enormous snowy dome of Etna, opposite the window; and the chill of evening came on while it was yet day, and with it came back the memory of the coldly smiling, handsome face of dead Ferdinando Pagliuca, and the terrible suggestion of a likeness to Vittoria, which had struck at Orsino's heart when he had found him in the bushes, shot through the head. It all came back with a sudden, drowning rush that was overwhelming. He turned from the window, and, to occupy himself, he went and got his belongings and tried to make the room habitable. He knew that it was in a good position for the night, since it was not likely that he should sleep much, and he could watch the gate from the window, for his share of the defence.

CHAPTER XII

As was perhaps to be expected, considering the precautions taken, the friends of Ferdinando Pagliuca gave no sign during the night. The carabineers, when they are actually present anywhere, impose respect, though their existence is forgotten as soon as they are obliged to move on.

Orsino lay down upon a dusty mattress in the room he had chosen. He had been down to the court again, where San Giacinto ate his supper from the soldiers' improvised kitchen, by the light of a fire of brush and scraps of broken wood, which one of the men replenished from time to time. But Orsino was not hungry, and presently he had gone upstairs again. About the middle of the night, San Giacinto, carrying a lantern, opened his door, and found him reading by the light of a solitary candle.

"Has all been quiet on this side?" asked the big man.

"All quiet," answered Orsino.

San Giacinto nodded, shut the door, and went off, knowing that the young man would rather be alone. An hour later, Orsino's book dropped from his hand, and he dozed a little, in a broken way. Outside, the waning moon had risen high above the shoulders of Etna, not a breath was stirring, and only the distant roar of the water came steadily up from the other side of the old monastery. Orsino dreamed strange, shapeless dreams of vast desolateness and empty darkness, in which he had no perception by sight, and heard only the unbroken rush of water far away. Then, in the extreme blackness of nothing, a dead face appeared, with wide and sightless eyes that stared at him, and he woke and turned upon his side with a shudder, to doze again, and dream again, and wake again. It was a horrible night.

Towards morning the dream changed. In the darkness, together with the sub-bass of the torrent, a voice came to him, in a low, long-drawn lamentation. It was Vittoria's voice, and yet unlike hers. He could hear the words:

"Me l' hanno ammazzato! Me l' hanno ammazzato!"

It was Vittoria d'Oriani wailing over her brother's body. Orsino heard the words and the voice distinctly. She was outside his door. She had dragged the corpse up from the church in the dark, all the long, winding way, to bring it to him and reproach him, and to weep over it. He refused to allow himself to awake, as one sometimes can in a dream, for he knew, somehow, that he was not altogether dreaming. There was an element of reality in the two sounds of the river and the voice, interfering with each other, and the voice came irregularly, always repeating the same words, but the river roared on without a break. Then there was a sound of moaning without words, and then the words began again, always the same.

Orsino started and sat up, wide awake. He was sure that he was awake now, for he could see that the light outside the window was grey. The dawn was beginning to drink the moonlight out of the air. He heard the voice distinctly.

"Me l' hanno ammazzato!" it moaned, but much less loudly than he had heard it in his dream. "They have killed him for me," is the meaning of the words.

Orsino sprang from the bed, and opened the door, which was opposite the window. The long corridor was dark and quiet, and he turned back and opened the casement, and looked out.

The words were half spoken again, but suddenly ceased as he threw the window open. In the dim grey dawn he saw a muffled figure crouching on the stones by the gate, slowly swaying forwards and backwards. The wail began again, very soft and low, and as though the woman half feared to be heard and yet could not control herself.

Orsino watched her intently for a few moments, and then understood. It was some woman who had loved Ferdinando Pagliuca, and who came in the simple old way to mourn at the door of the house wherein he lay dead. Her head was covered with a black shawl, and her skirts were black, too, but her hands were clasped about her knees, and visible, and looked white in the dawn.

The young man drew back softly from the window, and sat down upon the edge of the bed. He, of all men, had no right to silence the woman. She did no harm, wailing for the dead man out there in the cold dawn. She was not the only one who was to mourn him on that day. In a few hours his sister would know, his mother, his brothers, and all the world besides, though the rest of the world mattered little enough to Orsino. But this woman's grief was a sort of foretaste of Vittoria's. She was but a peasant woman, perhaps, or at most a girl of the small farmers' class, but she had loved him, and would hate for ever the man who had killed him. How much more should the slayer be hated by the dead man's own flesh and blood!

The light grew less grey by quick degrees, and there were heavy footsteps in the corridor. Then came a knock at the door, and a trooper appeared in his forage cap.

"We have made the coffee, signore," he said, on the threshold.

He held out a bright tin pannikin from which

the steam rose in fragrant clouds. The physical impression of the aromatic smell was the first pleasant sensation which Orsino had experienced since he had pulled the trigger of his rifle on the previous afternoon. If we could but look at things as they are, we should see that there is neither love nor hate, neither joy nor grief, nor hope nor fear, that will not at last efface itself for a moment before hunger and thirst; so effectually can this dying body mask and screen the undying essence.

Orsino drank the hot coffee with keen physical delight. though the woman's wailing came up to his ears through the open window, and though he had known a moment earlier that the stealing dawn was the beginning of a day which might end in a broken heart.

But the trooper heard the voice, and went to the window and looked out, while Orsino drank.

"Ho, there!" he cried roughly. "Will you go or not?" He turned to Orsino. "She has been there since two o'clock," he explained. "We heard her through the closed gate."

"Let her alone," said Orsino, authoritatively. "She is only a woman, and can do no harm; and she has a right to her mourning, God knows."

"There will be a hundred before the sun has been up an hour, signore," answered the soldier. "The people will collect about her, for they will come out of curiosity, from many miles away. It will be better to get rid of them as fast as they come."

"You might let that poor woman in," suggested Orsino. "After all, I have killed her lover—she has a right to see his body."

"As you wish, signore," answered the trooper, taking the empty pannikin.

Orsino got up and looked out again, as the man went away. The girl had risen to her feet, and stood looking up to the window. Her shawl had fallen back upon her shoulders, and disclosed a young and dishevelled but beautiful head, of the Greek type, though the eyes were somewhat long and almond-shaped. There was no colour in the olive-pale cheeks, and little in the parted lips; and the hand that gathered the shawl to the bosom was singularly white. The regular features were set in a tragic mask of grief, such as one very rarely sees in the modern world.

When she saw Orsino, she suddenly raised both hands to him, like a suppliant of old.

"They have killed him!" she cried. "They have killed my bridegroom! Let me see him! let me kiss him! Are they Christians, and will not let me see him?"

"You shall see him," answered Orsino. "I will let you in myself."

"God will render it to you, signore. And God will render also to his murderer a bad death."

She sat down upon the stones, thinking, perhaps, that it would be long before the gate was opened; and she began her low moan again.

"They have killed him! They have murdered him!"

But Orsino had already left the window and the room. He had understood clearly from her words and face that she was no light creature, for whom Ferdinando had conceived a passing fancy. He had meant to marry her, perhaps within a few days. There was in her face the high stamp of innocence, and her voice rang fearless and true. Ferdinando had never been like his brothers. He had meant to marry this girl, doubtless a small farmer's daughter, from her dress; and he would have lived happily with her, sinking, perhaps, to a lower social level, but morally rising far higher than his scheming brothers. Orsino had guessed from his dead face, and from what he had heard, that Ferdinando had been the best of the family; and in a semi-barbarous country like the interior of Sicily, the young Roman did not blame him overmuch for having tried to resist the new owners of his father's house when they came to take possession.

San Giacinto and the sergeant objected on principle to admitting the girl, but Orsino insisted, and at last opened the gate himself. She had covered her head and face again, and followed him swiftly

and noiselessly across the court to the door of the
church.   As though by instinct she turned directly
to her lover's body, where it lay before the side
altar, and with a low wail like a wounded animal,
she fell beside it, with clasped hands.   Orsino left
her there alone, closing the door softly, and came
out into the court, where it was almost broad daylight.   The men had drunk their coffee and were
grooming their black chargers tethered to rusty
rings in the wall.   The old stables were between
the court and the rampart.   The two foot-cara-
bineers were despatched to Santa Vittoria to get a
coffin for the dead man and a priest to come and
bury him.

From the church came every now and then the
piteous echo of the girl's lamentations.   Then
there was a knocking at the gate, and someone
called from without.   One of the troopers looked
out through the narrow slit in the stone, made
just wide enough to let the barrel of a gun pass.
Half a dozen peasants were outside, and the soldiers could see two more coming down the drive
towards the house.   He asked what they wanted.

" We wish to speak with the master," said one,
and two or three repeated the words.

They were the men who had brought the tools
on the previous evening, with a number of others,
the small tenants of the little estate.   San Giacinto
went and spoke with them, assuring them that he

would be a better landlord than they had ever had, if they would treat him well, but that if he met with any treachery, he would send every man of them to the galleys for life. It was his way of making acquaintance, and they seemed to understand it.

While he was speaking a number of men and women appeared in the drive, headed by the two soldiers who had gone to the village. Close behind them, swaying with the walk of the woman who carried the load upon her head, a white deal coffin caught the morning light. Then more people, and always more, came in sight, up the drive. Amongst them walked a young priest in his short white 'cotta' over his shabby cassock, and beside him came a big boy bearing a silver basin with holy water, and the little broom for sprinkling it. The two trudged along in a business-like way, and all the people were talking loudly. It seemed to San Giacinto that half the population of the village must have turned out. He stepped back and called to the troopers to keep the gate, and prevent the crowd from entering. Then he waited outside. The people became silent as they came near, and he looked at them, scrutinizing their faces. Some of the men had their guns slung over their shoulders, but many were only labourers and had none.

Many scowling glances were turned on San Giacinto as the crowd came up to the gate, and he began to anticipate trouble of some sort. The troopers had their rifles in their hands as they formed up behind him. The tenants of Camaldoli mixed with the crowd, evidently not wishing to identify themselves with their new landlord.

"What do you want?" asked San Giacinto, in a harsh, commanding voice.

The priest came close to him, and bowed and smiled, as though the occasion of meeting were a pleasant one. Then he stood aside a little, and a strapping woman who carried the coffin on her head marched in under the gate between the soldiers, who made way for her. And behind her came her husband, a crooked little carpenter, carrying a leathern bag from which protruded the worn and blackened handle of a big hammer. The third comer was stopped by the sergeant. He was a ghastly pale old man, with a three-days beard on his pointed chin, and he was dressed in dingy black.

"Who are you?" asked the sergeant, sharply.

"I am one without whom people are not buried," answered the old man, in a cracked voice. "You have a carpenter and a priest, but there is a third —I am he, the servant of the dead, who give no orders."

The sergeant understood that the man was the parish undertaker, and let him pass also. Meanwhile San Giacinto repeated his question.

" What do you all want?" he asked in a thundering tone, for he was annoyed.

" If it please you, Signor Marchese," said the priest, " these, my parishioners, desire the body of Don Ferdinando Corleone, in order to bury it in holy ground, for he was beloved of many. Pray do not be angry, Excellency, for they come in peace, having heard that Don Ferdinando had been killed by an accident. Grant their request, which is a proper one, and they shall depart quickly. I answer for them."

As he spoke the last words in a tone which all could hear, he turned to the crowd, as though for their assent.

" He answers for us," said many of them, in a breath. " Good, Don Niccola! You answer for us. We are Christians. We wish to bury Don Ferdinando properly."

" I have not the slightest objection," said San Giacinto. " On the contrary, I respect your wish, and I only regret that I have not the means of doing more honour to your friend. You must attend to that. Be kind enough to wait here while the priest blesses the body."

The priest and the boy with the holy water passed in, and the gate closed upon the crowd. While they had been talking, the carpenter and his wife had entered the court. Basili's man led them to the door of the church and opened it. The woman marched in with her swinging stride, and one hand on her hips, while the other steadied the deal coffin.

"Where is he?" she asked in a loud, good-natured voice, for the church seemed very dark after the morning light outside.

She was answered by a low cry from the steps of the side altar, where the unhappy girl lay half across her lover's body, looking round towards the door, in a new horror.

The woman uttered an exclamation of surprise, and then slowly swung her burden round so that she could see her husband.

"Help me, Ciccio," she said, in a matter-of-fact way. "They are always inconvenient things."

The man held up his hands and took the foot, while his wife raised her hands also and shifted the weight towards him little by little, until she got hold of the head. The loose lid rattled as they set the thing down on the floor. Then the woman took the rolled towel on which she had carried the weight, from her head, undid it, wiped her brow with it, and looked at the girl in some perplexity.

"It is the apothecary's Concetta," she said, suddenly recognizing the white features in the gloom. "Oh, poor child! Poor child!" she cried, going forward quickly, while her husband took the lid from the coffin and began to fumble in his leathern bag for his nails.

As the woman approached the step, Concetta threw her arms wildly over her head, stiffened her limbs straight out, and rolled over and over upon the damp pavement, in one of those strange fainting fits which sometimes seize women in moments of intense grief. The carpenter's wife tried to lift her, and to bend her arms, so as to get hold of her; but the girl was as rigid as though she were in a cataleptic trance.

"Poor child! Poor Concetta!" exclaimed the carpenter's wife, softly.

Then, bending her broad back, she raised the girl up by main strength. getting first one arm round her and then the other, till she got her weight up and could carry her. Her crooked little husband paid no attention to her. Women were women's business at such times. The big woman got the girl out into the morning sunshine in the court, meeting the eccentric undertaker and the priest, who were talking together outside. San Giacinto came forward instantly, followed by Orsino, who had been wandering about the rampart over the river when the crowd had come. San Giacinto took the unconscious girl's body from the woman, with ease.

"Come," he said, carrying her before him on his arms. "Get some water."

He entered the room where the men had slept on some straw and laid Concetta down, her arms still stiffened above her head. One of the troopers brought water in a pannikin. San Giacinto dashed the cold drops upon the white face, and the features quivered nervously.

"Take care of her," he said to the woman. "Who is she?"

"She is Concetta, the daughter of Don Atanasio, the apothecary. She was to marry Don Ferdinando next week. But now that they have killed him, she will marry someone else."

"Poor girl!" exclaimed San Giacinto, compassionately, and he turned and went out.

Orsino was standing by the door, looking in, and he had heard what the woman had said. It confirmed what he had guessed from the girl's own words. He wondered how it was possible that the action of one second could really cause such terrible trouble in the world.

From the open door of the church came the sound of the regular blows of a hammer. The work had been quickly done, and the carpenter was nailing down the lid of the coffin. The priest, who had stayed in the early sunshine for warmth, hung a shabby little stole round his neck, and took the holy water basin and the little broom from the boy, and entered the church to bless the body before it was taken away.

As it was not advisable to let in the crowd, the six soldiers lifted the coffin and bore it out of the gate. Then the peasants laid it on a bier which had been brought after them and covered it with a rusty black pall. The priest walked before it, and began to recite the psalms for the dead. The women covered their heads, and some of the men uncovered theirs, and a few joined in the priest's monotonous recitations. A quarter of an hour later, San Giacinto, watching from the gate, saw the last of the people disappear up the drive. But the carpenter's wife had stayed with Concetta.

"It is a bad business," said the old giant to himself, as he turned and went in.

CHAPTER XIII

The taking possession of Camaldoli had turned
out much more difficult and dangerous than even
San Giacinto had anticipated, for the catastrophe
of Ferdinando Pagliuca's death had at once aroused
the anger and revengeful resentment of the whole
neighbourhood. He made up his mind that it
would be necessary for himself or Orsino to return
to Rome at once, both in order to see the Minister
of the Interior, with a view to obtaining special
protection from the government, and to see the
Pagliuca family, in the hope of pacifying them.

The latter mission would not be an easy nor an
agreeable one, and San Giacinto would gladly have
undertaken it himself. On the other hand, he did
not trust Orsino's wisdom in managing matters
in Sicily. The young man was courageous and
determined, but he had not the knowledge of
the southern character which was indispensable.
Moreover, he was not the real owner of the lands,
and would not feel that he had authority to act
independently in all cases. It was, therefore, decided that Orsino should go back to Rome at

once, while San Giacinto remained at Camaldoli to get matters into a better shape.

It was a dreary journey for Orsino. He telegraphed that he was coming, found that there was no steamer from Messina, crossed to Reggio, and travelled all night and all the next day by the railway, reaching Rome at night, jaded and worn.

He found, as he had expected, that all Rome was talking of his adventure with the brigands, and of the death of Ferdinando Pagliuca, and of the probable consequences. But he learned to his surprise how Tebaldo had been heard to say at the club on the previous afternoon that Ferdinando was no relation of his, and that it was a mere coincidence of names.

"Nevertheless," said Sant' Ilario, "we all believe that you have killed his brother. Tebaldo Pagliuca has no mind to have it said that his brother was a brigand and died like a dog. He says he is not in Sicily, but left some time ago. As no one in Rome ever saw him, most people will accept the statement for the girl's sake, if not for the rest of the family."

Orsino looked down thoughtfully while his father was speaking. He understood at once that the story being passably discreditable to the d'Oriani, he had better seem to fall in with their view of the case, by holding his peace when he could. His father and mother, as well as the old Prince, insisted upon hearing a detailed account of the affair in the woods, however, and he was obliged to tell them all that had happened, though he said nothing about the fancied resemblance of Ferdinando to Vittoria, and as little as possible about the way in which the people had carried off the man's body with a public demonstration of sorrow. After all, no one had told him that Ferdinando was the brother of Tebaldo. He had taken it for granted, and it was barely possible that he might have been mistaken.

"There may be others of the name," he said, as he concluded his story.

His mother looked at him keenly. Half an hour later he was alone with her in her own sitting-room.

"Why did you say that there might be others of the name?" she asked gravely. "Why did you wish to imply that the unfortunate man may not have been the brother of Don Tebaldo and Donna Vittoria?"

Orsino was silent for a moment. There was reproach in Corona's tone, for she herself had not the slightest doubt in the matter. He came and stood before her, for he was a truthful man.

"It seemed to me," he said, "that I might let him have the benefit of any doubt there may be, though I have none myself. The story will be a terrible injury to the family."

"You are certainly not called upon to tell it to

everyone," said Corona. "I only wished to know what you really thought."

"I am sorry to say that I feel sure of the man's identity, mother. And I want you to help me," he added suddenly. "I wish to see Donna Vittoria alone. You can manage it."

Corona did not answer at once, but looked long and earnestly at her eldest son.

"What is it, mother?" he asked, at last.

"It is a very terrible thing," she answered slowly. "You love the girl, you wish to marry her, and you have killed her brother. Is not that the truth?"

"Yes, that is the truth," said Orsino. "Help me to see her. No one else can."

"Does anyone know? Did you speak about it to her mother, or her brothers, before you left? Does Ippolito know?"

"No one knows. Will you help me, mother?"

"I will do my best," said Corona, thoughtfully. "Not that I wish you to marry into that family," she added. "They have a bad name."

"But she is not like them. It is not her fault."

"No, it is not her fault, and she has not their faults. But for her brothers — well, we need not talk of that. For the sake of what there has been between you two, already, you have a sort of right to see Vittoria."

"I must see her."

"I went there yesterday, after we read the news in the papers," said Corona. "Her mother was ill. Later your father came in and said he had seen Don Tebaldo at the club. You heard what he said. They mean to deny the relationship. In fact, they have done so. I can therefore propose to take Vittoria to drive to-morrow afternoon, and I can bring her here to tea, in my own sitting-room. Then you may come here and see her, and I will leave you alone for a little while. Yes—you have a right to see her and to defend yourself to her, and explain to her how you killed that poor man, not knowing who he was."

"Thank you—you are very good to me. Mother—" he hesitated a moment—"if my father had killed your brother by accident, would you have married him?"

He fixed his eyes on Corona's. She was silent for a moment.

"Yes," she answered presently. "The love of an honest woman for an honest man can go farther than that."

She turned her beautiful face from Orsino as she spoke, and her splendid eyes grew dreamy and soft, as she leaned back in her chair beside her writing-table. He watched her, and a wave of hope rose slowly to his heart. But all women were not like his mother.

Early on the following morning she wrote a note

to Vittoria. The answer came back after a long time, and the man sent up word that he had been kept waiting three-quarters of an hour for it. It was written in a tremulous hand, and badly worded, but it said that Vittoria would be ready at the appointed time. Her mother, she added, was ill, but wished her to accept the Princess's invitation.

Vittoria had grown thin and pale, and there was a sort of haunted look in her young eyes as she sat beside Corona in the big carriage. Corona herself hesitated as to what she should say, for the girl was evidently in a condition to faint, or break down with tears, at any sudden shock. Yet it was necessary to tell her that Orsino was waiting for her, and it might be necessary also to use some persuasion in inducing her to meet him.

"My dear," said Corona, after a little while, "I want you to come home with me when we have had a little drive. Do you mind? We will have tea together in my little room."

"Yes — of course — I should like it very much," answered Vittoria.

"We shall not be quite alone," Corona continued. "I hope you will not mind."

Corona Saracinesca had many good qualities, but she was not remarkably clever, and when she wished to be tactful she often found herself in conflict with the singular directness of her own character. At the same time, she feared to let the girl at her side see how much she knew. Vittoria looked so pale and nervous that she might faint. Corona had never fainted. The girl naturally supposed that Orsino was still in Sicily.

They were near the Porta Salaria, and there was a long stretch of lonely road between high walls, just beyond it. Corona waited till they had passed the gate.

"My dear," she began again, taking Vittoria's hand kindly, "do not be surprised at what I am going to tell you. My son Orsino—"

Vittoria started, and her hand shook in her companion's hold.

"Yes—my son Orsino has come back unexpectedly and wishes very much to see you."

Vittoria leaned back suddenly and closed her eyes. Corona thought that the fainting fit had certainly come, and tried to put her arm round the slight young figure. But as she looked into Vittoria's face, she saw that the soft colour was suddenly blushing in her cheeks. In a moment her eyes opened again, and there was light in them for a moment.

"I did not know how you would take it," said Corona, simply, "but I see that you are glad."

"For him—that he is safe," answered the young girl, in a low voice. "But—"

She stopped, and gradually the colour sank away from her face again, and her eyes grew heavy once more. The trouble was greater than the gladness.

" Will you see him, in my own room ? " asked the elder woman, after a pause.

" Oh, yes — yes! Indeed I will — I must see him. How kind you are!"

Corona leaned forward and spoke to the footman at once, and the carriage turned back towards the city. She knew well enough how desperately hard it would be for Vittoria to wait for the meeting. She knew also, not by instinct of tact, but by a woman's inborn charity, that it would be kind of her to speak of other things, now that she had said what was necessary, and not to force upon Vittoria the fact that Orsino had revealed his secret, still less to ask her any questions about her true relationship to Ferdinando Pagliuca, which might put her in the awkward position of contradicting Tebaldo's public statement. But as they swept down the crowded streets, amongst the many carriages, Vittoria looked round into Corona's face almost shyly, for she was very grateful.

" How good you are to me!" she exclaimed softly. "I shall not forget it."

Corona smiled, but said nothing, and ten minutes later the carriage thundered under the archway of the gate. Corona took Vittoria through the state apartments, where they were sure of meeting no one at that time, and into her bedroom by a door

she seldom used. Then she pointed to another at
the other side.

"That is the way to my sitting-room, my dear,"
she said. "Orsino is there alone."

With a sudden impulse, she kissed her on both
cheeks and pushed her towards the door.

CHAPTER XIV

Orsino heard the door of his mother's bedroom open, and rose to his feet, expecting to see Corona. He started as Vittoria entered, and he touched the writing-table with his hand as though he were unsteady. The young girl came forward towards him quickly, and the colour rose visibly in her face while she crossed the little room. Orsino was white and did not hold out his hand, not knowing what to expect, for it was the hand that had killed her brother but two days ago.

Vittoria had not thought of what she should do or say, for it had been impossible to think. But as she came near, both her hands went out instinctively, to touch him. Almost instinctively, too, he drew back from her touch a little. But she did not see the movement, and her eyes sought his, as she laid her fingers lightly upon his shoulders and looked up to him. Then the sadness in his face, that had been almost like fear of her, relaxed toward a change, and his eyes opened wide in a sort of hesitating surprise. Two words, low and earnest, trembled upon Vittoria's lips.

"Thank God!"

In an instant he knew that she loved him in spite of all. Yet, arguing against his senses that it was impossible, he would not take her at her word. He took both her hands from his shoulders and held them, so that they crossed.

"Was he really your brother?" he asked slowly.

"Yes," she answered faintly, and looked down.

Perhaps it seemed to her that she should be ashamed of forgiving, before he had said one word of defence or uttered one expression of sorrow for what he had done. But she loved him, and since she had been a little child she had not seen her brother Ferdinando half a dozen times. It was true that when she had seen him she had been drawn to him, as she was not drawn to the two that were left, for he had not been like the others. She knew that she should have trusted Ferdinando if she had known him better.

Orsino began his defence.

"We were fired upon several times," he said. Her hands started in his, as she thought of his danger. "I saw a man's coat moving in the brush," he continued, "and I aimed at it. I never saw the man's face till we found him lying dead. It was not an accident, for bullets cut the trees overhead and struck the carriage." Again her hands quivered. "It was a fight, and I meant to kill the man. But I could not see his face."

She did not speak for a moment. Then, for the first time, she shrank a little, and withdrew her hands from his.

"I know — yes — it is terrible," she said in broken tones; and she glanced at him, and looked down again. "Do not speak of it," she added suddenly, and she was surprised at her own words.

It was the woman's impulse to dissociate the man she loved from the deed, for which she could not but feel horror. She would have given the world to sit down beside him and talk of other things. But he wished the situation to be cleared for ever, as any courageous man would.

"I must speak of it," he answered. "Perhaps we shall never have the chance again — "

"Never? What do you mean?" she asked quickly. "Why not?"

"You may forgive me," he answered earnestly. "You know that I would have let him shoot me ten times over rather than have hurt you — "

"Orsino — " She touched his arm nervously, trying to stop him.

"Yes — I wish I were in his grave to-day! You may forgive, but you cannot forget — how can you?"

"How? If — if you still love me, I can forget — "

Orsino's eyes were suddenly moist. It seemed as though something broke, and let in the light.

"I shall always love you," he said simply; as

men sometimes do when they are very much in earnest.

"And I—"

She did not finish the sentence in words, but her hand and face said the rest.

"Sit down," she said, after a little silence.

They went to a little sofa and sat down together, opposite the window.

"Do you think that anything you could do could make me not love you?" she asked, looking into his face. "Are you surprised? Did you think that I should turn upon you and accuse you of my brother's death, and say that I hated you? You should not have judged me so — it was unkind!"

"It has all been so horrible that I did not know what to expect," he said. "I have not been able to think sensibly until now. And even now — no, I have not judged you, as you call it, dear. But I expected that you would judge me, as God knows you have the right."

"Why should I judge you?" asked Vittoria, softly and lovingly. "If you had lain in wait for him and killed him treacherously, as he meant to kill you, it would have been different. If he had killed you, as he was there to kill you — as he might have killed you if you had not been first — I — well, I am only a girl, but even these little hands would have had some strength! But as it

is, God willed it. Whom shall I judge? God?
That would be wrong. God protected you, and
my brother died in his treachery. Do you think
that if I had been there, and had been a man, and
the guns firing, and the bullets flying, I should not
have done as you did, and shot my own brother?
It would have been much more horrible even than
it is, but of course I should have done it. Then
why are you in such distress? Why did you think
that I should not love you any more?"

"I did not dare to think it," answered Orsino.

"You see, as I said, God willed it — not you.
You were but the instrument, unconscious and
innocent. It is only a little child that will strike
the senseless thing that hurts it."

"You are eloquent, darling. You will make me
think as you do."

"I wish you would, indeed I wish you would!
I am sorry, I am grieved, I shall mourn poor Ferdinando, though I scarcely knew him. But you —
I shall love you always, and for me, as I see it, you
were no more the willing cause of his death than
the senseless gun you held in your hand. Do you
believe me?"

She took his hand again, as though to feel that
he understood. And understanding, he drew her
close to him and kissed her young eyes, as he had
done that first time, out on the bridge over the
street.

"You have my life," he said tenderly. "I give you my life and soul, dear."

She put up her face suddenly, and kissed his cheek, and instantly the colour filled her own, and she shrank back, and spoke in a different tone.

"We will put away that dreadful thing," she said, drawing a little towards her own end of the sofa. "We will never speak of it again, for you understand."

"But your mother, your brothers," answered Orsino. "What of them? I hear that they do not acknowledge — " he stopped, puzzled as to how he should speak.

"My mother is ill with grief, for Ferdinando was her favourite. But Tebaldo and Francesco have determined that they will act as though he were no relation of ours. They say that it would ruin us all to have it said that our brother had been with the brigands. That is true, is it not?"

"It would be a great injury to you," answered Orsino.

"Yes. That is what they say. And Tebaldo will not let us wear mourning, for fear that people should not believe what he says. This morning when the Princess's note came, Tebaldo insisted that I should accept, but my mother said that I should not come to the house. They had a long discussion, and she submitted at last. What can she do? He rules everybody — and he is bad, bad in his heart, bad in his soul! Francesco is only weak, but Tebaldo is bad. Beware of him, for though he says that Ferdinando was not his brother, he will not forgive you. But you will not go back to Sicily?"

"Yes, I must go. I cannot leave San Giacinto alone, since I have created so much trouble."

"Since poor Ferdinando is dead, you will be safer—I mean—" she hesitated. "Orsino!" she suddenly exclaimed, "I knew that he would try to kill you—that is why I wanted to keep you here. I did not dare tell you—but I begged so hard—I thought that for my sake, perhaps, you would not go. Tebaldo would kill me if he knew that I were telling you the truth now. He knew that Ferdinando had friends among the outlaws, and that he sometimes lived with them for weeks. And Ferdinando wrote to Tebaldo, and warned him that although he had signed the deed, no one should ever enter the gate of Camaldoli while he was alive. And no one did, for he died. But the Romans would think that he was a common brigand; and I suppose that Tebaldo is right, for it would injure us very much. But between you and me there must be nothing but the truth, so I have told you all. And now beware of Tebaldo; for, in spite of what he says, he will some day try to avenge his brother."

"I understand it all much better now," said

Orsino, thoughtfully. "I am glad you have told me. But the question is, whether your mother and your brothers will ever consent to our marriage, Vittoria. That is what I want to know."

"My mother — never! Tebaldo might, for interest. He is very scheming. But my mother will never consent. She will never see you again, if she can help it."

"What are we to do?" asked Orsino, speaking rather to himself than to Vittoria.

"I do not know," she answered, in a tone of perplexity. "We must wait, I suppose. Perhaps she will change, and see it all differently. We can afford to wait — we are young. We love each other, and we can meet. Is it so hard to wait awhile before being married?"

"Yes," said Orsino. "It is hard to wait for you."

"I will do anything you like," answered Vittoria. "Only wait a little while, and see whether my mother does not change. Only a little while!"

"We must, I suppose," said Orsino, reluctantly. "But I do not see why your mother should not always think of me as she does to-day. I can do nothing to improve matters."

"Let us be satisfied with to-day," replied Vittoria, rather anxiously, and as though to break off the conversation. "I was miserably unhappy this evening, and I thought you were in Sicily; and

instead, we have met. It is enough for one day —
it is a thousand times more than I had hoped."

"Or I," said Orsino, bending down and kissing
her hand more than once.

The handle of Corona's door turned very audibly
just then, and a moment later the Princess entered
the room. Without seeming to scrutinize the faces
of the two, she understood at a glance that Vittoria
had accepted the tragic situation, as she herself
would have done; and that if there had been any
discussion, it was over.

Vittoria coloured a little, when she met Corona's
eyes, realizing how the older woman had, as it
were, arranged a lovers' meeting for her. But
Corona herself did not know whether to be glad
or sorry for what had happened.

Nor was it easy for anyone to foresee the consequences of the present situation. It was only too
clear that the young people loved each other with
all their hearts; and Corona herself was very fond
of Vittoria, and believed her to be quite unlike her
family. Yet at best she was an exception in a
race that had a bad name; and Corona knew how
her husband and his father would oppose the marriage, even though she herself should consent to
it. She guessed, too, that Vittoria's mother would
refuse to hear of it. Altogether Orsino had fallen
in love very unfortunately, and Corona could see
no possible happy termination to the affair.

Therefore, against her own nature and her affection for her son, she was conscious of a certain disappointment when she saw that the love between the two was undiminished, even by the terrible catastrophe of Ferdinando's death. It would have been so much simpler if Vittoria had bidden goodbye for ever to the man who had killed her brother.

CHAPTER XV

Ippolito Saracinesca was, perhaps, of all the household the most glad to see his favourite brother at home again so soon. He missed the companionship which had always been a large element in his life.

"I shall go with you when you return," he said, sitting on the edge of Orsino's table, and swinging his priestly legs in an undignified fashion.

"Are you in earnest?" asked Orsino, with a laugh.

"Yes. Why not? You say that there is a church on the place, or a chapel. I will say mass there for the household on Sundays, and keep you company on week-days. You will be .lonely when San Giacinto comes back. Besides, after what has happened, I hate to think that you are down there alone among strangers."

"Have you nothing to keep you in Rome?" asked Orsino, much tempted by the offer.

"Nothing in the world."

"There will be no piano at Camaldoli."

"I suppose there is an organ in your church, is there not?"

"No. There is probably one in the church of Santa Vittoria. You could go and play on it."

"How far is it?"

"Three-quarters of a mile, I was told."

"As far as from the Piazza di Venezia to the Piazza del Popolo."

"Less. That is a mile, they always used to say, when the loose horses ran the race in carnival."

"It would be just a pleasant walk, then," said Ippolito, already planning his future occupations at Camaldoli. "I could go over in the afternoon, when the church is closed, and play on the organ an hour or two whenever I pleased."

"I have no idea what sort of thing the Santa Vittoria organ will turn out to be," answered Orsino. "It is probably falling to pieces, and has not been tuned since the beginning of the century."

"I will mend it and tune it," said Ippolito, confidently.

"You?" Orsino looked at his brother's delicate hands and laughed.

"Of course. Every musician knows something about the instruments he plays. I know how an organ is tuned, and I understand the mechanism. The old-fashioned ones are simple things enough.

When a note goes wrong you can generally mend
the tracker with a bit of wire, or a stick, as the
case may be — or if it is the wind chest — ”

“ It is not of the slightest use to talk to me
about that sort of thing,” interrupted Orsino, “ for
I understand nothing about organs, nor about
music either, for that matter.”

“ I will take some tools with me, and some kid,
and a supply of fine glue,” said Ippolito, still full
of his idea. “ How about the rooms ? Is there
any decent furniture ? ”

Orsino gave him a general idea of the state of
Camaldoli, not calculated to encourage him in his
intention, but the young priest was both very fond
of his brother, and he was in love with the novelty
of his idea.

“ I daresay that they have not too many priests
in that part of the country,” he said. “ I may be
of some use.”

“ We got one without difficulty to bury that poor
man,” answered Orsino. “ But you may be right.
You may be the means of redeeming Sicily.” He
laughed.

He was, indeed, inclined to laugh rather unexpectedly, since his interview with Vittoria. He
was far too manly and strong to be saddened for
any length of time by the fact of having taken
the life of a man who had, undoubtedly, attempted
to murder him by stealth. He had been op-

pressed by the certainty that the deed had raised an insurmountable barrier between Vittoria and himself. Since he had found that he had been mistaken, he was frankly glad that he had killed Ferdinando Pagliuca, for the very plain reason that if he had not done so, Ferdinando Pagliuca would have certainly killed him, or San Giacinto, or both. He had no more mawkish sentiment about the horror of shedding human blood than had embarrassed his own forefathers in wilder times. If men turned brigands and dug pitfalls, and tried to murder honest folk by treachery, they deserved to be killed; and though the first impression he had received, when he had been sure that he had killed his man, had been painful, because he was young and inexperienced in actual fighting, he now realized that but for the relationship of the dead man, it had been not only excusable, but wise, to shoot him like a wild beast. His own people thought so too.

It was natural, therefore, that his spirits should rise after his interview with Vittoria. On that day he had already been busy in carrying out San Giacinto's directions, and on the following morning he went to work with increased energy.

Corona watched him when they met, and the presentiment of evil which had seized her when he had first spoken of going to Sicily became more oppressive. She told herself that the worst had happened which could happen, but she answered herself with old tales of Sicilian revenge after long-nourished hatred. She was shocked when Ippolito announced his intention of accompanying his brother. Ippolito was almost indispensable to her. The old Prince used to tell her that her priest son answered the purpose of a daughter with none of the latter's disadvantages, at which Ippolito himself was the first to laugh good-naturedly, being well aware that he had as good stuff in him as his rough-cast brothers. But Corona really loved him more as a daughter than a son, and because he was less strong than the others, she was not so easily persuaded that he was safe when he was away from her, and she half resented the old gentleman's jest. She especially dreaded anything like physical exposure or physical danger for him. She was a brave and strong woman in almost every way, and would have sent her other three sons out to fight for their country or their honour without fear or hesitation. But Ippolito was different. Orsino might face the brigands if he chose. She could be momentarily anxious about him, but the belief prevailed with her that he could help himself and would come back safe and sound. One of the reasons, an unacknowledged one, why she had been so ready to let Ippolito follow his inclination for the church, was that priests are less exposed to all sorts of danger than other men. San Giacinto's Sicilian schemes suddenly seemed to her quite mad since Ippolito wished to accompany his brother and share in any danger which might present itself.

But Ippolito was one of those gently obstinate persons whom it is hard to move and almost impossible to stop when they are moving. He had made up his mind that he would go to Camaldoli, and he met his mother's objections with gentle but quite unanswerable arguments.

Had there ever been an instance of a priest being attacked by brigands? Corona was obliged to admit that she could remember none. Was he, Ippolito, accomplishing anything in the world, so long as he stayed quietly in Rome? Might he not do some good in the half-civilized country about Camaldoli and Santa Vittoria? He could at least try, and would. There was no answer to this either. Was not Orsino, who was melancholic by nature, sure to be wretchedly lonely down there after San Giacinto left? This was undoubtedly true.

"But the malaria," Corona objected at last. "There is the fever there, all summer, I am sure. You are not so strong as Orsino. You will catch it."

"I am much stronger than anybody supposes," answered Ippolito. "And if I were not, it is not always the strong people that escape the fever. Besides, there can be none before June or July, and Orsino does not expect to stay all summer."

He had his way, of course, and made his preparations. Orsino was glad for his own sake, and he also believed that the change of existence would do his brother good. He himself was not present when these discussions took place. Ippolito told him about them.

Orsino wished to see Vittoria again before leaving Rome, but Corona refused to help him any further.

"I cannot," she said. "You had a right to see her that once. At least, I thought so. It seemed to be a sort of moral right. But I cannot arrange meetings for you. I cannot put myself in such a position towards that family. One may do in a desperate situation what one would absolutely refuse to do every day and in ordinary circumstances."

"Going away, not knowing when I may come back, does not strike me as an ordinary circumstance," said Orsino, discontentedly.

"You must see that for me to cheat Vittoria's mother and brothers by bringing her here to see you secretly, is to sacrifice all idea of dignity," answered Corona.

"I had not looked at it in that light, nor called it by that name."

"But I had, and I do. I am perfectly frank with you, and I always have been. I like the girl very much, but I do not wish you to marry her, on account of her family. It is one thing to object to a marriage on the score of birth or fortune. You know that I should not, though I hope you will marry in your own class. Happiness is, perhaps, independent of the details of taste which make up daily life, but it runs on them, as a train runs on rails — and if a bad jolting is not unhappiness, it is certainly discomfort."

"You are wise, mother. I never doubted that. But this is different —"

"Very different. That is what I meant to say. There would, perhaps, be no question of that sort of moral discomfort with Vittoria; she has been well brought up in a convent of ladies, like most of the young girls you meet in the world, like me, like all the rest of us. It is different. It is her family — they are impossible, not socially, for they are as good as anybody in the way of descent. Bianca Campodonico married Vittoria's uncle, and no one thought it a bad match until it turned out badly. But that is just it. They are all people who turn out badly. Tebaldo Pagliuca has the face of a criminal, and his brother makes one think of a satyr. Their mother is a nonentity and does not count. Vittoria is charming. I suppose she is like someone on her mother's side, for she has not the smallest resemblance to any of the others. But all the charm in the world will not compensate you for the rest of them. And now you have had the frightful misfortune to kill their brother. Did you never hear of a vendetta? The southern people are revengeful. The Corleone will never acknowledge to the world that Ferdinando was one of them, but they will not forget it, against you and yours, and your children. I meet those young men in the street, and they bow as though nothing had happened, but I know well enough that if they could destroy every one of us, they would. Can I put myself in the position of cheating such people by bringing Vittoria here to see you secretly? It is impossible. You must see it yourself."

"Yes," answered Orsino. "I suppose I must admit it. It would be undignified."

"Yes, very. The word is not strong enough. You must help yourself. I do not propose any solution of the difficulty. You love the girl. Heaven forbid that I should stand in the way of honest love between honest man and woman. But frankly, I wish that you did not love her, and that she did not love you. And I cannot help you any more, because I will not humiliate myself to deceive people who hate me, and you, and all of us, even to our name."

"Do you think they do? Would they not be

glad to see Vittoria married to me? After all, I am a great match for a ruined family's only daughter, and if Tebaldo Pagliuca is anything, he is grasping, I am sure."

"Yes, but he is more revengeful than grasping, and more cunning than revengeful — a dangerous enemy. That is why I hate to see Ippolito go with you to the south. Some harm will come to him, I am sure. The Corleone have the whole country with them."

"I will answer for him," said Orsino, smiling. "Nothing shall happen to him."

"How can you answer for him? How can you pledge yourself that he shall be safe? It is impossible. You cannot spend your life in protecting him."

"I can provide people who will," answered the young man. "But you are wrong to be so timid about him. No one ever touches a priest, in the first place, and before he has been there a fortnight, all the people will like him, as everybody always does. It is impossible not to like Ippolito. Besides, Tebaldo Pagliuca has no reason for going to Sicily now that the place is sold. Why in the world should he go? Little by little we shall gain influence there, and before long we shall be much more popular than the Corleone ever were. San Giacinto has written to me already. He says that everything is perfectly quiet already, — that was twenty-four hours after I left, — that he had twenty men from the village at work on the house, making repairs, and that they worked cheerfully and seemed to like his way of doing things. Since Ferdinando is dead there is no one to lead an opposition. They are all very poor and very glad to earn money."

"It may be as you say," said Corona, only partially reassured. "I do not understand the condition of life there, of course, and I know that when you promise to answer for Ippolito you are in earnest, and will keep your word. But I am anxious — very anxious."

"I am sorry, mother," replied Orsino. "I am very sorry. But you will soon see that you have no reason to be anxious. That is all I can say. I will answer for him with my life."

"That is a mere phrase, Orsino," said Corona, gravely, "like a great many things one says when one is very much in earnest. If anything happened to him, your life would be still more precious to me than it is, if that were possible. You all think that because I am often anxious about him, he is my favourite. You do not understand me, any of you. I love you all equally, but I am not equally anxious about you all, and my love shows itself most for the one who seems the least strong and able to fight the world."

"For that matter, mother, Ippolito is as able to

fight his own battles as the strongest of us. He
is obstinate to a degree hardly anyone can understand. He has the quiet, sound, uncompromising
obstinacy of the Christian martyrs. People who
have that sort of character are not weak, and they
are generally very well able to take care of themselves."

" Yes, I know he is obstinate. That is, when he
insists upon going with you."

Corona was very far from being satisfied, and
Orsino felt that in spite of what she had said she
was in reality laying upon him the responsibility
for his brother's safety. He himself felt no anxiety on that score, however. In Rome, many hundreds of miles away from Camaldoli, even the
things which had really happened during his brief
stay in Sicily got an air of improbability and distance which made further complications of the
same sort seem almost impossible. Besides, he
had the promise of the Minister of the Interior
that a company of infantry should shortly be
quartered at Santa Vittoria, which would materially increase the safety of the whole neighbourhood.

Orsino's principal preoccupation was to see Vittoria again, alone, before he left. In the hope of
meeting her he went to a garden party, and in the
evening to two houses where she had gone frequently during the winter with her mother. But

she did not appear. Her mother was ill, and Vittoria stayed at home with her. Her brothers, on the contrary, were everywhere, always smiling and apparently well satisfied with the world.

It was said that Tebaldo was trying to marry an American heiress, and Orsino twice saw him talking with the young stranger, who was reported to have untold millions, and was travelling with an aunt, who seemed to have as many more of her own. He looked at the girl without much curiosity, for the type has become familiar in Europe of late years.

Miss Lizzie Slayback — for that was her name — was undeniably pretty, though emphatically not beautiful. She was refined in appearance, too, but not distinguished. One could not have said that she was 'nobody,' as the phrase goes, yet no one would have said, at first sight, that she was 'somebody.' Yet she had an individuality of her own, which was particularly apparent in her present surroundings, a sort of national individuality, which contrasted with the extremely de-nationalized appearance and manner of Roman society. For the Romans of the great houses have for generations intermarried with foreigners from all parts of Europe, until such strongly Latin types as the Saracinesca are rare.

Miss Slayback was neither tall nor short, and she had that sort of generally satisfactory figure which has no particular faults and which is extremely easy to dress well. Her feet were exquisite, her hands small, but not pretty. She had beautiful teeth, but all her features lacked modelling, though they were all in very good proportion. Her head was of a good shape, and her hair was of a glossy brown, and either waved naturally or was made to wave by some very skilful hand. She had dark blue eyes with strong dark lashes, which atoned in a measure for a certain uninteresting flatness and absence of character about the brows and temples, and especially below the eyes themselves and at the angles, where lies a principal seat of facial expression. She spoke French fluently but with a limited and uninteresting vocabulary, so that she often made exactly the same remarks about very different subjects. Yet her point of view being quite different from that of Romans, they listened to what she said with surprise, and sometimes with interest.

Her aunt was not really her aunt, but her uncle's wife, Mrs. Benjamin Slayback, whose maiden name had been Charlotte Lauderdale — a fact which meant a great deal in New York and nothing at all in Rome. She was an ambitious woman, well born and well educated, and her husband had been a member of Congress and was now a senator for Nevada. He was fabulously rich, and his wife, who had married him for his money, having been brought up poor, had lately inherited a vast fortune of her own. Miss Lizzie Slayback was the only daughter of Senator Slayback's elder brother.

Orsino was told a great many of these facts, and they did not interest him in the least, for he had never thought of marrying a foreign heiress. But he was quite sure from the first that Tebaldo had made up his mind to get the girl if he could. The Slaybacks had been in Rome about a month, but Orsino had not chanced to see them, and did not know how long Tebaldo might have known them. It was said that they did not mean to stay much longer, and Tebaldo was doing his best to make good his running in the short time that remained.

It chanced that the first time Orsino came face to face with Tebaldo was when the latter had just been talking with Miss Slayback and was flattering himself that he had made an unusually good impression upon her. He was, therefore, in a singularly good humour, for a man whose temper was rarely good and was often very bad indeed. The two men met in a crowded room. Without hesitation Tebaldo held out his hand cordially to Orsino.

"I am very glad to see you safely back," he said, with a great appearance of frankness. "You are the hero of the hour, you know."

For a moment even Orsino was confused by

the man's easy manner. Even the eyes did not
betray resentment. He said something by way of
greeting.

"I have had some difficulty in making out who
the brigand was whom you shot," continued
Tebaldo. "It is an odd coincidence. We think
it must have been one of the Pagliuca di Bauso.
There is a distant branch of the family — rather
down in the world, I believe — it must have been
one of them."

"I am glad it was no nearer relation," answered
Orsino, not knowing what to say.

"No near relative of mine would have been
likely to be in such company," answered the Sicilian, rather stiffly, for he was a good actor when
not angry.

"No — of course not — I did not mean to suggest such a thing. It was an odd coincidence, of
course." Orsino tried not to look incredulous.

Tebaldo was about to pass on, when an idea
presented itself to Orsino's mind, of which he had
not thought before now. Slow men sometimes
make up their minds suddenly, and not having
the experience of habitually acting upon impulses,
they are much more apt to make mistakes, on the
rare occasions when they are carried away by an
idea, and do so. It seemed to him that if he were
ever to speak to either of Vittoria's brothers about
marrying her, this was the moment to do so. It

would be impossible for Tebaldo, in an instant, to deny what he had just now said, and it would be hard for him to find a pretext for refusing to give his sister to such a man. The whole thing might be carried through by a surprise, and Orsino would take the consequences afterwards, and laugh at them, if he were once safely married.

Tebaldo had already turned away to speak to someone else, and Orsino went after him and called him back.

"There is a matter about which I should like to speak to you, Don Tebaldo," he said. "Can we get out of this crowd?"

Tebaldo looked at him quickly and sharply, before he answered by a nod. The two men moved away together to the outer rooms, of which there were three or four, stiffly furnished with pier tables and high-backed gilt chairs, as in most old Roman houses. When they were alone, Orsino stopped.

"It is an important matter," he said slowly. "I wish to speak with you, as being the head of your family."

"Yes," answered Tebaldo, and the lids drooped, vulture-like, at the corners of his eyes, as he met Orsino's look steadily. "By all means. We shall not be interrupted here. I am at your service."

"I wish to marry your sister, and I desire your consent," said Orsino. "That is the whole matter."

It would have been impossible to guess from the Sicilian's face whether he had ever anticipated such a proposition or not. There was absolutely no change in his expression.

"My sister is a very charming and desirable young girl," he said rather formally. "As there seems to be a good deal of liberty allowed to young girls in Rome, as compared with Sicily, you will certainly pardon me if I ask whether you have good reason to suppose that she prefers you in any way."

"I have good reason for supposing so," answered Orsino, but he felt the blood rising to his face as he spoke, for he did not like to answer such a question.

"I congratulate you," said Tebaldo, smiling a little, but not pleasantly. "Personally, I should also congratulate myself on the prospect of having such a brother-in-law. I presume you are aware that my sister has no dowry. We were ruined by my uncle Corleone."

"It is a matter of perfect indifference," replied Orsino.

"You are generous. I presume that you have inherited some private fortune of your own, have you not?"

"No. I am dependent on my father."

"Then — pardon my practical way of looking at the affair," said Tebaldo, accentuating his smile a little, "but. as a mere formality, I think that there must be some proposal from the head of your house. You see, you and Vittoria will be dependent on an allowance from your father, who, again, is doubtless dependent on your grandfather, Prince Saracinesca. As my poor sister has nothing, there must necessarily be some understanding about such an allowance."

"It is just," answered Orsino, but he bit his lip. "My father has an independent estate," he added, by way of correction. "And my mother has all the Astrardente property."

"There is no lack of fortune on your side, my dear Don Orsino. You are, of course, sure of your father's consent, so that an interview with him will be a mere formality. For myself, I give you my hand heartily and wish you well. I shall be happy to meet the Prince of Sant' Ilario at any time which may be agreeable to him."

Orsino felt that the man had got the better of him, but he had to take the proffered hand. Mentally he wondered what strange monster this Tebaldo Pagliuca could be within himself, to grasp the hand that had killed his brother less than a week ago, welcoming its owner as his brother-in-law. But he saw that the very simple and natural request for an interview with his father would probably prove a source of almost insurmountable difficulty.

"I had hoped," he said, "to have had the pleasure of seeing Donna Vittoria here this evening. I shall be obliged to return to Sicily in a day or two. May I see her at your house before I go?"

Tebaldo hesitated a moment.

"You will find her at home with my mother to-morrow afternoon," he answered almost immediately. "I see no reason why you should not call."

"But your mother—" Orsino stopped short.

"What were you going to say?" enquired Tebaldo, blandly.

"You will be kind enough to tell her that I am coming, will you not?" Orsino saw that he was getting into a terribly difficult situation.

"Oh, yes," Tebaldo answered. "I shall take great pleasure in announcing you. She is better, I am glad to say, and I have no doubt that this good news will completely restore her."

Orsino felt a vague danger circling about his heart, as a hawk sails in huge curves that narrow one by one until he strikes his prey. The man was subtle and ready to take advantage of the smallest circumstance with unerring foresight while wholly concealing his real intention.

"Come at three o'clock, if it is convenient," concluded Tebaldo. "And now—" he looked at his watch—"you will forgive me if I leave you. I have an engagement which I must keep."

He shook hands again with great cordiality, and they parted. Tebaldo went out directly, without returning to the inner rooms, but Orsino went back to stay half an hour longer. Out of curiosity he got a friend to introduce him to Miss Lizzie Slayback.

The girl looked up with a bright smile when she heard the great name.

"I have so much wanted to meet you," she said quickly. "You are the man who killed the brigand, are you not? Do tell me all about it!"

He was annoyed, for he could not escape, but he resigned himself and told the story in the fewest possible words.

"How interesting!" exclaimed Miss Slayback. "And we all thought he was the brother of Don Tebaldo. You know Don Tebaldo, of course? I think he is a perfect beauty, and so kind."

Orsino had never thought of Tebaldo Pagliuca as either kind or beautiful, and he said something that meant nothing, in reply.

"Oh, you are jealous of him!" cried the girl, laughing. "Of course! All the men are."

Orsino got away as soon as he could. As a necessary formality he was introduced to Mrs. Slayback. He asked her an idle question about how she liked Rome, such as all Romans ask all foreigners about whom they know nothing.

"How late is it safe to stay here?" she asked, with singular directness, by way of an answer.

"Rome becomes unhealthy in August," said Orsino. "The first rains bring the fever. Until then it is perfectly safe, and one can return in October without danger. The bad time lasts for six weeks to two months, at most."

"Thank you," answered Mrs. Slayback, with a little laugh. "We shall not stay till August, I think. It would be too hot. I suppose that it is hot in June."

"Yes," said Orsino, absently. "I suppose that you would find it hot in June."

He wanted to be alone, and he left her as soon as he could. He walked home in the warm night and reviewed his position, which had suddenly become complicated. It was clear that he must now speak to his father, since he had committed the folly of making his proposal to Tebaldo. It was almost certain that his father would refuse to hear of the marriage, on any consideration, and he knew that his mother disapproved of it. It was clear also that he could not avoid going to call upon Vittoria and her mother on the following afternoon, but he could not understand why Tebaldo had pretended to be so sure that he should be received, when he himself was tolerably certain that Maria Carolina would refuse to see him. That, however, was a simple matter. He should ask for her, and on being told that she could not receive, he should leave his card and go away. But that would not help him to see Vittoria, and it was in order to see her alone before he left that he had suddenly determined to make his proposal to Tebaldo.

He had got himself into a rather serious scrape, and he was not gifted with more tact than the rest of his bold but tactless race. He therefore decided upon the only course which is open to such a man, which was to take his difficulties, one by one, in their natural order and deal with each as best he could.

He had nothing more to hope from his mother's intervention. He knew her unchangeable nature and was well aware that she would now hold her position to the last. She would not oppose his wishes, and that was a great deal gained, but she would not help him either.

Early on the following morning he went to Sant' Ilario's own room, feeling that he had a struggle before him in which he was sure to be defeated, but which he could not possibly avoid. His father was reading the paper over his coffee by the open window, a square, iron-grey figure clad in a loose grey jacket. The room smelt of coffee and cigarettes. Sant' Ilario's perfect contentment and happiness in his surroundings made him a particularly difficult person to approach suddenly with a crucial question. His serene felicity made a sort of resisting shell around him, through which it was necessary to break before he himself could be reached.

He looked up and nodded as Orsino entered. Such visits from his sons were of daily occurrence, and he expected nothing unusual. It was of no use to beat about the bush, and Orsino attacked the main question at once.

"I wish to speak to you about a serious matter, father," he said, sitting down opposite Sant' Ilario.

"I wish Sicily were in China, and San Giacinto in Peru," was the answer.

"It has nothing to do with San Giacinto," said Orsino. "I want to be married."

Sant' Ilario looked up sharply, in surprise. His eldest son's marriage was certainly a serious matter.

"To whom?" he enquired.

"To Vittoria d'Oriani," said Orsino, squaring his naturally square jaw, in anticipation of trouble.

Sant' Ilario dropped the paper, took his cigarette from his lips, and crossed one leg over the other angrily.

"I was afraid so," he said. "You are a fool. Go back to Sicily and do not talk nonsense."

The Saracinesca men had never minced matters in telling each other what they thought.

"I expected that you would say something like that," answered Orsino.

“Then why the devil did you come to me at all?” enquired his father, his grey hair bristling and his eyebrows meeting.

But Orsino was not like him, being colder and slower in every way, and less inclined to anger.

“I came to you because I had no choice but to come,” he answered quietly. “I love her, she loves me, and we are engaged to be married. It was absolutely necessary that I should speak to you.”

“I do not see the necessity, since you knew very well that I should not consent.”

“You must consent in the end, father—”

“I will not. That ends it. It is the worst blood in Italy, and some of the worst blood in Europe. Corleone was a scoundrel, his father was a traitor—”

“That does not affect Donna Vittoria so far as I can see,” said Orsino, stubbornly.

“It affects the whole family. Besides, if they are decent people, they will not consent either. It is not a week since you killed Ferdinando Pagliuca —Vittoria’s brother—”

“They deny it.”

“They lie, I believe.”

“That is their affair,” said Orsino.

“The fact does not beautify their family character, either,” retorted Sant’ Ilario. “With the whole of Europe to choose from, excepting a dozen royalties, you must needs fall in love with the sister of a brigand, the niece of a scoundrel, the granddaughter of — ”

“Yes — you have said all that. But I have promised to marry her, and that is a side of the question of which you cannot get rid so easily.”

“You did not promise her my consent, I suppose. I will not give it. If you choose to marry without it, I cannot hinder you. You can take her and live on her dowry, if she has one.”

“She has nothing.”

“Then you may live by your wits. You shall have nothing more from me.”

“If the wits of the family had ever been worth mentioning, I should ask nothing more,” observed Orsino, coldly. “Unfortunately they are not a sufficient provision. You are forcing me into the position of breaking my word to a woman.”

“If neither her parents nor yours will consent to your marriage, you are not breaking your engagement. They will not give her to you if you cannot support her. Of course, you can wait until I die. Judging from my father, and from my own state of health at present, it will be a long engagement.”

Orsino was silent for a moment. He did not lose his temper even now, but he tried to devise some means of moving Sant’ Ilario.

“I spoke to Tebaldo Pagliuca last night,” he said, after a pause. “In spite of what you seem to expect, he accepted my proposition, so far as he could.”

“Then he is an even greater villain than I had supposed him to be,” returned Sant’ Ilario.

“That is no reason why you should force me to humiliate myself to him —”

“Send him to me, if you are afraid to face him. I will explain the situation — I will —”

“You will simply quarrel with him, father. You would insult him in the first three words you spoke.”

“That is very probable,” said Sant’ Ilario. “I should like to. He has been scheming to catch you for his sister ever since the evening they first dined here. But I did not think you were such a childish idiot as to be caught so easily.”

“No one has caught me, as you call it. I love Vittoria d’Oriani, and she loves me. You have no right to keep us apart because you did not approve of her grandfather and uncle.”

“No right? I have no right, you say? Then who has?”

“No one,” answered Orsino, simply.

“I have the power, at all events,” retorted his father. “I would not have you marry her — would not? I will not. It is materially impossible for you to marry with no money at all, and you shall have none. Talk no more about it, or I shall positively lose my temper.”

It occurred to Orsino that it was positively lost already, but as he kept his own, he did not say so. He rose from his seat and calmly lighted a cigarette.

“Then there is nothing more to be said, I suppose,” he observed.

“Nothing more on that subject,” answered Sant’ Ilario. “Not that I have the least objection to saying over again all I have said,” he added.

“At all events, you do not pretend that you have any objection to Donna Vittoria herself, do you?”

“No — except that she has made a fool of you. Most women make fools of men, sooner or later.”

“Perhaps, but you should be the last person to say so, I think.”

“I married with my father’s consent,” replied Sant’ Ilario, as though the fact were an unanswerable argument. “If I had made to him such a proposition as you are making to me, he would have answered in a very different way, my boy, I can tell you!”

“In what way?” asked Orsino.

“In what way? Why, he would have been furiously angry! He would have called me a fool and an idiot, and would have told me to go to the devil.”

Orsino laughed in spite of himself.

“What are you laughing at?” enquired Sant’ Ilario, sharply, growing hot again in a moment.

“Those are exactly the words you have been saying to me,” answered Orsino.

“I? Have I? Well—that only proves that I am like my father, then. And a very good thing, too. It is a pity that you are not more like me than you are. We should understand each other better.”

“We may yet understand each other,” said Orsino, lingering in the vain hope of finding some new argument.

“No doubt. But not about this matter.”

Seeing that it was useless to prolong the discussion, Orsino went away to think matters over. He had been quite sure of his father’s answer, of course, but that did not improve the situation at all. It had been a necessity of conscience and honour to go to him, after speaking to Tebaldo on the previous evening, because it was not possible to take his answer for granted. But now it became equally a duty of honour and self-respect to communicate to Tebaldo what Sant’ Ilario had said, and to do so was a most unpleasant humiliation. He cared nothing for the fact that his father’s refusal might almost seem like an insult to Tebaldo Pagliuca, though he could not quite see how he could make the communication without giving offence. The real trouble was that he should be practically obliged to take back what he had said, and to say that after all, in the face of his family's objections, he could not marry Vittoria at present, and saw no prospect of being able to marry her in the future.

At the same time he wondered how much Tebaldo had told his mother. She also, according to Vittoria's statement, would oppose their marriage with all her power. Yet Tebaldo had professed himself quite certain that she would receive Orsino when he called. There was something mysterious about that.

Orsino made up his mind that he would ask for Tebaldo a quarter of an hour before the time named by the latter, and get over the disagreeable interview before making an attempt to have a word with Vittoria alone.

CHAPTER XVI

Orsino reached the Corleone's house before three o'clock on that afternoon. They lived on the second floor of a large new building in the Via Venti Settembre, 'Twentieth of September Street,' as it would be in English, so named to commemorate the taking of Rome on that day in 1870.

A porter in livery asked Orsino whom he wished to see, rang an electric bell, spoke through a speaking-tube, took off his cocked hat in order to listen for the answer, and finally told Orsino that he would be received. There is always something mysterious to the looker-on about any such means of communication at a distance, when he does not hear the voice speaking from the other end.

It would not have surprised Orsino, if he had heard, as the porter did, that the answer came back in Tebaldo Pagliuca's voice; but he would then not have been so much surprised, either, at being admitted so readily. Tebaldo, in fact, had told the porter to send the visitor up, for he had been waiting for the porter's bell; but he then told his servant that a gentleman was coming upstairs to see him, who was to be shown into the drawing-room at once, whither Tebaldo himself would presently come.

Tebaldo had been quite sure that his mother and sister would be at home at that hour, since the former was not yet well enough to go out; he had been equally sure that his mother would refuse to receive Orsino; he had, therefore, so arranged matters that Orsino should be ushered into her presence unexpectedly, and to accomplish this he had lain in wait in the neighbourhood of the speaking-tube, which came up into the hall of his apartment just inside the door opening upon the stairs.

So far the explanation of what happened is quite simple. It would be a different thing to unravel the complicated and passionate workings of Tebaldo's intricate thoughts. In the first place, in spite of his behaviour in public, he hated Orsino with all his heart for having unwittingly killed his brother, and important as the advantages would be, if Vittoria married the heir of the great house, they by no means outweighed his desire for revenge.

Tebaldo was not an inhuman monster, though a specialist might have said that he had a strong tendency to criminality. He was capable of affection in a certain degree, apart from mere passion. He was unscrupulous, treacherous, tortuous in his reasonings; but he was above all tenacious, and he was endowed with much boldness and daring, of the kind which cast a romantic glamour over crimes of violence.

It had been one thing to threaten Ferdinando with the law, if he refused to sign the deed by which Camaldoli was to be sold. It was quite another matter to give his sister to the man who had shot Ferdinando like a wild animal. There the man's humanity had revolted, though Orsino had not guessed it, when they had met and talked together at the party on the previous evening.

On the other hand, his cunning bade him not to put himself in the position of refusing Orsino's request, seeing that he denied his own relationship with his dead brother. It was easy enough for him to bring Orsino and his mother unexpectedly face to face, and to let the young man hear from her lips what she thought of such a union, if indeed the interview should ever get so far as that. Tebaldo could then calmly intrench himself behind his mother's refusal, and yet maintain outward relations with Orsino, while waiting for an opportunity to avenge his brother, which was sure to present itself sooner or later.

Orsino mounted the stairs resolutely, squaring himself to meet Tebaldo and tell him of Sant' Ilario's refusal as briefly and courteously as he could. At the same time he was half painfully and half happily conscious of Vittoria's presence in the house. The pain and the pleasure were intermittent and uncertain.

A servant was waiting and holding the door ajar.

" Don Tebaldo said that he would see me," said Orsino, mechanically.

The man bowed in silence, shut the door upon the landing, and then led the way through the little hall and the antechamber beyond, opened a door, and stood aside to let Orsino pass.

As the door closed behind him, he heard a short and sharp cry in the room, like the warning note of certain fierce wild animals. It was followed instantly by an exclamation of terror in another voice. At the same instant he was aware that there were two women in the room, — Maria Carolina d'Oriani and her daughter.

The mother had been lying on a couch, and on seeing him had started up, supporting herself on her hand. The room was half darkened by the partly closed blinds.

Maria Carolina was dressed in a loose black gown with wide sleeves that showed her thin, bare arms, for the weather was warm. Her white face was thin and ghastly, and her dark eyes gleamed as they caught a little of the light from the window. Orsino stood still two paces from the door.

" Assassin ! "

The one word — a word of the people, hissed

from her dry lips with such horror and hatred as Orsino had never heard. There was silence then. Vittoria, as white as her mother, and in an agony of terror, had risen, shrinking and convulsed, grasping with one hand the heavy inner curtain of the window.

Slowly the lean, dark woman left her seat, raising one thin arm, and pointing straight at Orsino's face, her head thrown back, her parched lips parted and showing her teeth.

"Murderer!" she cried. "You dare to show me your face — you dare to show me the hands that killed my son! You dare to stand there before God and me — to hear God's curse on you and mine — to answer for blood — "

Her lips and throat were dry, so that she could not speak, but choked, and swallowed convulsively, and her eyes grew visibly red. Orsino was riveted to the spot and speechless. For a moment he did not even think of Vittoria, cowering back against the curtain. The woman's worn face was changed in her immense wrath, and he could not take his eyes from her. She found her voice again, painfully, fighting against the fiery dryness that choked her.

"With his innocent blood on your hands, you come here — you come to face his very mother in her sacred grief — to see my tears, to tear out the last shreds of my heart, to revile my mother's soul

—to poison the air that breathes sorrow! But you think that I am weak, that I am only a woman. You think, perhaps, that I shall lose my senses and faint. It would be no shame, but I am not of such women."

Her voice gathered fulness but sank in tone as she went on. Still Orsino said nothing, for it was impossible to interrupt her. She must say her say, and curse her curse out, and he must listen, for he would not turn and go.

"You have come," she said, speaking quickly and with still rising fury. "I am here to meet you. I am here to demand blood of you for blood. I am here to curse you, and your name, and your race, your soul and their souls, dead and living, in the name of God, who made my son, of Christ, who died for him, of the Holy Saints, who could not save him from the devil you are — in the name of God, and of man, and of the whole world, I curse you! May your life be a century of cruel deaths, and when you die at last with a hundred years of agony in you, may your immortal soul be damned everlastingly a thousand fold! May you pray and not be heard, may you repent and not be forgiven, may you receive the Holy Sacraments to your damnation and the last Unction with fire in hell! May every living creature that bears your name come to an evil before your eyes, your father — your mother — the men and women of your house, and your unborn children! Blood — I would have blood! May your blood pay for mine, and your soul for my son's soul, who died unconfessed in his sins! Go, assassin! go, murderer of the innocent! go out into the world with my mother's curse on you, and may every evil thing in earth and hell be everlastingly with you and yours, living and dead! Blood! — blood! — blood!"

Her voice was suddenly and horribly extinguished in the last word, as an instrument that is strained too far cracks in a last discordant note and is silent. She stood one moment more, with outstretched hand and fingers that would still make the sign of one more unspoken curse, and then, without warning, she fell back in a heap towards the couch.

Simultaneously, Vittoria and Orsino sprang forward to catch her, but even before Vittoria could reach her she lay motionless on the floor, her head on the edge of the sofa, her hands stretched out on each side of her, her thin fingers twitching desperately at the carpet. A moment later, they were still, too, and she was unconscious, as the two began to lift her up.

For an instant neither looked at the other, but as Orsino laid the fainting woman upon the couch, he raised his eyes to Vittoria's. The girl was still overcome with fear at the whole situation, and trembling with horror at her mother's frightful outbreak of rage and hate. She shook her head in a frightened, hopeless way, as she bent down again and arranged a cushion for Maria Carolina.

"Why did you come — why did you come?" she almost moaned. "I told you—"

Orsino saw that if there was to be any explanation, he must seize the opportunity at once.

"I felt that I must see you before leaving," he answered. "Last night I told your brother Tebaldo that we were engaged to each other. He asked me to come at three o'clock, and said that your mother would receive me — I sent up word to ask — I was told to come up."

"We knew nothing of your coming. It must have been the servant's fault." She did not suspect her brother of having purposely brought about the meeting. "Now go!" she added quickly. "Go, before she comes to herself. Do not let her see you again. Go — please go!"

"Yes — I had better go," he answered. "Can I not see you again? Vittoria — I cannot go away like this —"

As he realized that it might be long before he saw her again, his voice trembled a little, and there was a pleading accent in his words which she had never heard.

"Yes — no — how can I see you?" she faltered. "There is no way — no place — when must you leave?" Maria Carolina stirred, and seemed about to open her eyes. "Go — please go!" repeated

Vittoria, desperately. "She will open her eyes and see you, and it will begin again! Oh, for Heaven's sake—"

Orsino kissed her suddenly while she was speaking, once, sharply, with all his heart breaking. Then he swiftly left the room without looking back, almost trying not to think of what he was doing.

He closed the door behind him. As he turned to look for the way out, in his confusion of mind, the door opposite, which was ajar, opened wide, and he was confronted by Tebaldo, who smiled sadly and apologetically. Orsino stared at him.

"I am afraid you have had an unpleasant scene," said the Sicilian, quickly. "It was a most unfortunate accident—a mistake of the servant, who took you for the doctor. The fact is, my mother seems to be out of her mind, and she will not be persuaded that Ferdinando is alive and well, till she sees him. She was so violent an hour ago that I sent for a doctor—a specialist for insanity. I am afraid I forgot that you were coming, in my anxiety about her. I hope you will forgive me. Of course, you have seen for yourself how she feels towards you at present, and in any case—at such a time—"

He had spoken so rapidly and plausibly that Orsino had not been able to put in a word. Now he paused as if expecting an answer.

"I regret to have been the cause of further disturbing your mother, who indeed seems to be very ill," said Orsino, gravely. "I hope that she will soon recover."

He moved towards the outer hall, and Tebaldo accompanied him to the door of the apartment.

"You will, of course, understand that at such a time it will be wiser not to broach so serious a matter as my sister's marriage," said Tebaldo. "Pray accept again my excuses for having accidentally brought you into so unpleasant a situation."

He timed his words so that he uttered the last when he was already holding the door open with one hand and stretching out the other to Orsino, who had no choice but to take it, as he said goodbye. Tebaldo closed the door and stood still a moment in thought before he went back. As he turned to go in, Vittoria came quickly towards him.

"How did it happen that Don Orsino was brought into the drawing-room?" she asked, still very pale and excited.

"I suppose the servant took him for the doctor," said Tebaldo, coolly, for he knew that she would not stoop to ask questions of the footman. "I am very sorry," he added.

He was going to pass on, but she stopped him.

"Tebaldo — I must speak to you — it will do as well here as anywhere. The nurse is with her," she said, looking towards the drawing-room. "She fainted. Don Orsino told me in two words, before he went away, that he had spoken to you last night, and that you had told him to come here to-day."

"That is perfectly exact, my dear. I have no doubt you have found out that your admirer, our brother's assassin, is a strictly truthful person. He insisted upon seeing you; it was impossible to talk at ease at a party, and I told him to come here, intending to see him myself. I told him to come at three o'clock — I daresay you know that, too?"

" Yes — he said it was to be at three o'clock." Tebaldo took out his watch and looked at it.

"It is now only four minutes to three," he observed, "and he is already gone. He came a good deal before his time, or I should have been in the antechamber to receive him and take him into my room, out of harm's way, where I could have explained matters to him. As it is, I was obliged to show him out with some apology for the mistake."

"How false you are!" exclaimed Vittoria, her nostrils quivering.

"Because I refuse to ruin you, and our own future position here? I think I am wise, not false. Yes, I myself assured him last night that he did not kill our brother, but one of the Pagliuca di Bauso. I took the hand that did it, and shook it — to save your position in Roman society. You seem to forget that poor Ferdinando had turned himself into an outlaw — in plain language, he was a brigand."

"He was worth a score of his brothers," said Vittoria, who was not afraid of him. "You talk of saving my position. It is far more in order to save your own chance of marrying the American girl with her fortune."

"Oh, yes," answered Tebaldo, with perfect calm. "I include that in the general advantages to be got by what I say. I do not see that it is so very false. On the one hand, Ferdinando was my brother. I shall not forget that. On the other, to speak plainly, he was a criminal. You see I am perfectly logical. No one is obliged to acknowledge that he is related to a criminal — "

"No one is obliged to lie publicly, as you do," broke in Vittoria, rather irrelevantly. "As you make me lie — rather than let people know what kind of men my surviving brothers are."

"You are not obliged to say anything. You do not go out into the world just now, because you have to stay with our mother. I will wager that you have not once told the lie you think so degrading."

"No — I have not, so far. No one has forced me to."

"You need only hold your tongue, and leave the rest to me."

"You make me act a lie — even in not wearing mourning — "

"Of course, if you make morality and honesty depend upon the colour of your clothes," said Tebaldo, scornfully, "I have nothing more to say about it. But it is a great pity that you have fallen in love with that black Saracinesca, the assassin. It will be a source of considerable annoyance and even suffering to you, I daresay. It even annoyed me. It would have been hard to refuse so advantageous an offer without accusing him of Ferdinando's death, which is precisely what I will not do, for the sake of all of us. But you shall certainly not marry him, though you are inhuman enough to love him — a murderer — stained with your own blood."

"He is not a murderer, for it was an accident — and you know it. I am not ashamed of loving him — though I cared for Ferdinando more than any of you. And if you talk in that way — if you come between us — " she stopped.

"What will you do?" he asked contemptuously.

"I will tell the truth about Ferdinando," she said, fixing her eyes upon him.

"To whom, pray ?"

"To Miss Slayback and her aunt," answered Vittoria, her gentle face growing fierce.

"Look here, Vittoria," said Tebaldo, more suavely. "Do you know that Orsino Saracinesca is going back to Camaldoli? Yes. And you know that Ferdinando had many friends there, and I have some in the neighbourhood. A letter from me may have a good deal to do with his safety or danger, as the case may be. It would be very thoughtless of you to irritate me by interfering with my plans. It might bring your own to a sudden and rather sad conclusion."

Vittoria turned pale again, for she believed him. He was playing on her fears for Orsino and on her ignorance of the real state of things at Camaldoli. But for the moment his words had the effect he desired. He instantly followed up his advantage.

"You can never marry him," he said. "But if you will not interfere with my own prospects of marriage, nothing shall happen to Saracinesca. Otherwise —" he stopped and waited significantly.

Exaggerating his power, she believed that it extended to giving warrant of death or safety for Orsino, and her imagination left her little choice. At all events, she would not have dared to risk her lover's life by crossing Tebaldo's schemes for himself.

"I am sorry for the American girl," she said. "I like her for her own sake, and I would gladly save her from being married to such a man as you. But if you threaten to murder Don Orsino if I tell her the truth, you have me in your power on that side."

"On all sides," said Tebaldo, scornfully, as he saw how deep an impression he had made on the girl. "I hold his life in my hand, so long as he is at Camaldoli, and while he is there you will obey me. After that, we shall see."

Vittoria met his eyes fiercely for an instant, and then, thinking of Orsino, she bent her head and went away, going back to her mother.

She found her conscious again, but exhausted, lying down on the couch and tended by the nurse, who had been in the house since the news of her son's death had prostrated Maria Carolina. She looked at Vittoria with a vague stare, not exactly recollecting whether the girl had been in the room during her outburst of rage against Orsino or not. Vittoria had been behind her all the time.

"Is he gone?" asked Maria Carolina, in a faint and hollow voice. "I am sorry — I could have cursed him much more —"

"Mother!" exclaimed Vittoria, softly and imploringly, and she glanced at the nurse. "You may go, now," she said to the latter, fearing a fresh outburst. "I will stay with my mother."

The nurse left the room, and the mother and daughter were alone together. They were almost strangers, as has been explained, Vittoria having been left for years at the convent in Palermo, unvisited by any of her family, until her uncle's death had changed their fortunes. It was impossible that there should be much sympathy between them.

There was, on the other hand, a sort of natural feeling of alliance between the two women of the household as against the two men. Maria Carolina was mentally degraded by many years of a semi-barbarous life at Camaldoli, which had destroyed some of her finer instincts altogether, and had almost effaced the effect of early education. She looked up to Vittoria as to a superior being, brought up by noble ladies, in considerable simplicity of life, but in the most extreme refinement of feeling on all essential points, and in an atmosphere of general cultivation and artistic taste, which had not been dreamed of in her mother's youth, though it might seem old-fashioned in some more modern countries. The girl had received an education which had been good of its kind, and very complete, and she was therefore intellectually her mother's superior by many degrees. She knew it, too, and would have despised her mother if she had been like her brothers. As it was, she pitied her, and suffered keenly when Maria Carolina did or said anything in public which showed more than usual ignorance or provinciality.

They had one chief characteristic in common,

and Ferdinando had possessed it also. They were naturally as frank and outspoken as the other two brothers were deceitful and treacherous. As often happens, two of the brothers had inherited more of their character from their father, while the third had been most like his mother. She, poor woman, felt that her daughter was the only one of the family whom she could trust, and looking up to her as she did, she constantly turned to her for help and comfort at home, and for advice as to her conduct in the world.

But since Ferdinando's death her mind, though not affected to the extent described by Tebaldo in speaking with Orsino, had been unbalanced. Nothing which Vittoria could say could make her understand how the catastrophe had happened, and though she had formerly liked Orsino, she was now persuaded that he had lain in wait for her son and had treacherously murdered him. Vittoria had soon found that the only possible means of keeping her quiet was to avoid the subject altogether, and to lead her away from it whenever she approached it. It would be harder than ever to accomplish this since she had seen Orsino.

She lay on her couch, moaning softly to herself, and now and then speaking articulate words.

"My son, my son! My handsome boy!" she cried, in a low voice. "Who will give him back to me? Who will find me one like him?"

Her lamentations were like the mourning of a woman of the people. Vittoria tried to soothe her. Suddenly she sat up and grasped the girl's arm, staring into her face.

"To think that we once thought he might marry you!" she cried wildly. "Curse him, Vittoria! Let me hear you curse him, too! Curse him for your soul's sake! That will do me good."

"Mother! mother!" cried the girl, softly pressing the hand that gripped her arm so roughly.

"What is the matter with you?" asked the half-mad creature fiercely, as her strength came back. "Why will you not curse him? Go down on your knees and pray that all the saints will curse him as I do!"

"For Heaven's sake, mother! Do not begin again!"

"Begin? Ah, I have not ended — I shall not end when I die, but always while he is alive my soul shall pursue him, day and night, and I will — " she broke off. "But you, too — you must wish him evil — you, all of us — then the evil will go with him always, if many of us cast it on him!"

She was like a terrible witch, with her pale face and dishevelled hair, and gaunt arms that made violent gestures.

"Speak, child!" she cried again. "Curse him for your dead brother!"

"No. I will never do that," said Vittoria.

A new light came into the raving woman's eyes.

"You love him!" she exclaimed, half choking. "I know you love him—"

With a violent movement she pushed Vittoria away from her, almost throwing her to the ground. Then she fell back on the couch, and slowly turned her face away, covering her eyes with both her hands. Her whole body quivered, and then was still, then shook more violently, and then, all at once, she broke into a terrible sobbing, that went on and on as though it would never stop while she had breath and tears left.

Vittoria came back to her seat and waited patiently, for there was nothing else to be done. And the sound of the woman's weeping was so monotonous and regular that the girl did not always hear it, but looked across at the half-closed blinds of the window and thought of her own life, and wondered at all its tragedy, being herself half stunned and dazed.

It was bad enough, as it appeared to her, but could she have known it all as it was to be, and all that she did not yet know of her brother Tebaldo's evil nature, she might, perhaps, have done like her mother, and covered her eyes with her hands, and sobbed aloud in terror and pain.

That might be said of very many lives, perhaps. And yet men do their best to tear the veil of the future, and to look through it into the darkened theatre which is each to-morrow. And many, if they knew the price and the struggle, would give up the prize beyond; but not knowing, and being in the fight, they go on to the end. And some of them win.

CHAPTER XVII

TTEBALDO's own affairs were by no means simple. He had made up his mind to get Miss Lizzie Slayback for his wife, and her fortune for himself; but he could not make up his mind to forget the beautiful Aliandra Basili. The consequence was that he was in constant fear lest either should hear of his devotion to the other, seeing that his brother Francesco was quite as much in love with the singer as he was himself, and but for native cowardice, as ready for any act of treachery which could secure his own ends. By that weakness Tebaldo held him, for the present, in actual bodily fear, which is more often an element even in modern life than is generally supposed. But how long that might be possible Tebaldo could not foresee. At any moment, by a turn of events, Francesco might get out of his power.

Aliandra's season in Rome had been a great success, and her career seemed secured, though she had not succeeded in obtaining an immediate engagement for the London season, which had been the height of her ambition. She had made her appearance too late for that, but the possibility of such a piece of good fortune was quite within her reach for the ensuing year. Being in reality a sensible and conscientious artist, therefore, and having at the same time always before her the rather vague hope of marrying one of the brothers, she had made up her mind to stay in Rome until July to study certain new parts with an excellent master she had found there. She therefore remained where she was, after giving a few performances in the short season after Lent, and she continued to live very quietly with her old aunt in the little apartment they had hired. A certain number of singers and other musicians, with whom she had been brought into more or less close acquaintance in her profession, came to see her constantly, but she absolutely refused to know any of the young men of society who had admired her and sent her flowers during the opera season. With all her beauty and youth and talent, she possessed a very fair share of her father's profound common sense.

Of the two, she very much preferred Francesco, who was gentler, gayer, and altogether a more pleasant companion; but she clearly saw the advantage of marrying the elder brother, who had a very genuine old title for which she could provide a fortune by her voice. There were two or three instances of such marriages which had turned out admirably, though several others had been failures.

She saw no reason why she should not succeed as well as anyone.

Tebaldo, on his part, had never had the smallest intention of marrying her, though he had hinted to her more than once, in moments of passion, that he might do so. Aliandra was as obstinate as he, and, as has been said, possessed the tenacious instinct of self-preservation and the keen appreciation of danger which especially characterize the young girl of the south. She was by no means a piece of perfection in all ways, and was quite capable of setting aside most scruples in the accomplishment of her end. But that desired end was marriage, and there was no probability at all that she should ever lose her head and commit an irrevocable mistake for either of the brothers.

She saw clearly that Tebaldo was in love with her, as he understood love. She could see how his eyes lighted up and how the warm blood mantled under his sallow brown skin when he was with her, and how his hand moved nervously when it held hers. She could not have mistaken those signs, even if her aunt, the excellent Signora Barbuzzi, had not taken a lively interest in the prospects of her niece's marriage, watching Tebaldo's face as an old sailor ashore watches the signs of the weather and names the strength of the wind, from a studding-sail breeze to a gale.

What most disturbed Aliandra's hopes was that

Tebaldo was cautious even in his passion, and seemed as well able to keep his head as she herself. His brother often told her that Tebaldo sometimes, though rarely, altogether lost control of himself for a moment, and became like a dangerous wild animal. But she did not believe the younger man, who was always doing his best to influence her against Tebaldo, and whom she rightly guessed to be a far more dangerous person where a woman was concerned.

Francesco had once frightened her, and she was really afraid to be alone with him. There was sometimes an expression which she dreaded in his satyr-like eyes and a smile on his red lips that chilled her. Once, and she could never forget it, he had managed to find her alone in her room at the theatre, and without warning he had seized her rudely and kissed her so cruelly while she struggled in his arms that her lips had been swollen and had hurt her all the next day. Her maid had opened the door suddenly, and he had disappeared at once without another word. She had never told Tebaldo of that.

Since then she had been very careful. Yet in reality she liked him better, for he could be very gentle and sympathetic, and he understood her moods and wishes as Tebaldo never did, for he was a woman's man, while Tebaldo was eminently what is called a man's man.

Aliandra was, as yet, in ignorance of Miss Slayback's existence, but she saw well enough that Tebaldo was concealing something from her. A woman's faculty for finding out that a man has a secret of some sort is generally far beyond her capacity for discovering what that secret is. He appeared to have engagements at unusual times, and there was a slight shade of preoccupation in his face when she least expected it. On the other hand, he seemed even more anxious to please her than formerly, when he was with her, and she even fancied that his manner expressed a sort of relief when he knew that he could spend an hour in her company uninterrupted.

When she questioned him, he said that he was in some anxiety about his affairs, and his engagements, according to his own account, were with men of business. But he never told what he was really doing. He had not even thought it necessary to inform her of the sale of Camaldoli. Though she was a native of the country, he told her precisely what he told everyone in regard to Ferdinando Pagliuca's death.

"Eh — you say so," she answered. "But as for me, I do not believe you. There never was but one Ferdinando Pagliuca, he was your brother, and he was a friend of all the brigands in Sicily. You may tell these Romans about the Pagliuca di Bauso, but I know better. Do you take me for a Roman? We of Randazzo know what a brigand is!"

"You should, at all events," answered Tebaldo, laughing, "for you are all related. It is one family. If you knew how many brigands have been called Basili, like you!"

"Then you and I are also related!" she laughed, too, though she watched his face. "But as for your brother, may the Lord have him in peace! He is dead, and Saracinesca killed him."

Tebaldo shrugged his shoulders, but showed no annoyance.

"As much as you please," he answered. "But my brother Ferdinando is alive and well in Palermo."

"So much the better, my dear friend. You need not wear mourning for him, as so many people are doing at Santa Vittoria."

"What do you mean?" asked Tebaldo, uneasily.

"Did you ever hear of Concetta, the beautiful daughter of Don Atanasio, the apothecary?" asked Aliandra, quietly smiling.

Tebaldo affected surprise and ignorance.

"It is strange," continued the singer, "for you admire beauty, and she is called everywhere the Fata del' Etna, — the Fairy of Etna, — and she is one of the most beautiful girls in the whole world. My father knows her father a little — of course, he is only an apothecary — " she shrugged her shoulders apologetically — "but in the country one knows everybody. So I have seen her sometimes, as at the fair of Randazzo, when she and her father have had a biscuit and a glass of wine at our house. But we could not ask them to dinner, because the mayor and his wife were coming, and the lieutenant of carabineers — an apothecary! You understand?"

"I understand nothing beyond what you say," said Tebaldo. "You did not consider the apothecary of Santa Vittoria good enough to be asked to meet the mayor of Randazzo. How does that affect me?"

"Oh, not at all!" laughed Aliandra. "But everything is known, sooner or later. Ferdinando, your brother, was at the fair, too — I remember what a beautiful black horse he had, as he rode by our house. But he did not come in, for he did not know us. Now, when Don Atanasio and Concetta went out, he was waiting a little way down the street, standing and holding his horse's bridle. I saw, for I looked through the chinks of the blinds to see which way Concetta and her father would go. And your brother bowed to the ground when they came near him. Fancy! To an apothecary's daughter! Just as I have seen you bow to the Princess of Sant' Ilario in the Villa Borghese. She is Saracinesca's mother, is she not? Very well. I tell you the truth when I tell

you that Don Ferdinando took the two to dine
with him in the best room at the inn. They say
he thought nothing good enough for the apothecary's daughter, though he was of the blood of
princes! But now Concetta wears mourning.
Perhaps it is not for him? Eh?"

Aliandra had learned Italian very well when a
child, and was even taking lessons in French, in
order to be able to sing in Paris. But as she talked
with Tebaldo she fell back into her natural dialect,
which was as familiar to him as to herself. He
loved the sound of it, though he took the greatest
pains to overcome his own Sicilian accent in order
not to seem provincial in Rome. But it was
pleasant to hear it now and then in the midst of
a life of which the restraints were all disagreeable
to him, while many of them were almost intoler-
ably irksome.

"How much better our language is than this
stilted Roman!" he exclaimed, by way of suddenly
turning the conversation. "I often wish you could
sing your operas in Sicilian."

"I often sing you Sicilian songs," she answered.
"But it is strange that Concetta should wear mourning, is it not?"

"Leave Concetta alone, and talk to me about
yourself. I have never seen her—"

"Do not say such things!" laughed Aliandra.
"I do not believe much that you say, but you will

soon not let me believe anything at all. Everyone has seen Concetta. They sing songs about her even in Palermo — La Fata del' Etna —"

"Oh, I have heard of her, of course, by that name, but I never remember seeing her. At all events, you are ten times more beautiful than she —"

"I wish I were!" exclaimed the artist, simply. "But if you think so, that is much."

"It would be just the same if you were ugly," said Tebaldo, magnanimously. "I should love you just as I do — to distraction."

"To distraction?" she laughed again.

"You know it," he answered, with an air of conviction. "I love you, and everything that belongs to you — your lovely face, your angelic voice, your words, your silence — too much."

"Why too much?"

"Because I suffer."

"There is a remedy for that, my dear Tebaldo."

"Tell me!"

"Marry me. It is simple enough! Why should you suffer?"

Her laughter was musical and sunny, but there was a little irony in its readiness to follow the words.

"You know that we have often spoken of that," he answered, being taken unawares. "There are difficulties."

"So you always say. But then it would be wiser of you not to love me any more, but to marry where you do not find those difficulties. Surely it should be easy!"

She spoke now with a little scorn, while watching him; and as she saw the vulture-like droop of his eyelids she knew that she had touched him, though she could not quite tell how. She had never spoken so frankly to him before.

"Not so easy as you think," he replied, with a rather artificial laugh.

"Then you have tried?" she asked. "I had thought so! And you have failed? My condolences!"

"I? Tried to marry?" he cried, realizing how far she was leading him. "What are you making me say?"

"I am trying to make you tell the truth," she answered, with a change of tone. "But it is not easy, for you are clever at deceiving me, and I wonder that you cannot deceive the woman you wish to marry."

"I do not wish to marry anyone," he protested.

"No — not even me. Me, least of all, because I am not good enough to marry you, though you are good enough to pursue me with what you call your love. I am only an artist, and you must have a princess, of course. I have only my voice, and you want a solid fortune. I have only my honour, but you want honours through your wife for yourself, and you would tear mine to rags if I yielded a hair's-breadth. You make a mistake, Don Tebaldo Pagliuca. I am a Sicilian girl and I came of honest people. You may suffer as much as you please, but unless you will marry me, you may go on suffering, for you shall not ruin me."

She spoke strongly, with a strange mixture of theatrical and commonplace expressions; but she was in earnest, and he knew it, and in her momentary anger she was particularly fascinating to him. Yet her speech made no real impression upon his mind. He tried to take her hand, but she drew it away sharply.

"No," she said. "I have had enough of this love-making, this hand-taking, and this faith-breaking. You sometimes speak of marrying me, and then you bring up those terrible, unknown difficulties, which you never define. Yes, you are a prince — but there are hundreds of them in our Italy. Yes, I am only an artist, but some people say that I am a great artist — and there are very few in Italy, or anywhere else. If it is beneath your dignity to marry a singer, Signor Principe di Corleone, then go and take a wife of your own class. If you love me, Tebaldo Pagliuca, as an honest man loves an honest woman — and God knows I am that — then marry me, and I, with my voice, will make you a fortune and buy back your estates, besides being a faithful wife to you. But if you will not do that, go. You shall not harm my good name by being perpetually about me, and you shall not touch the tips of my fingers with your lips until you are my lawful husband. There, I have spoken. You shall know that a Sicilian girl is as good as a Roman lady — better, perhaps."

Tebaldo looked at her in some surprise, and his mind worked rapidly, remembering all she had said during the preceding quarter of an hour. She spoke with a good deal of natural dignity and force, and he was ready to admit that she was altogether in earnest. But his quick senses missed a certain note which should have been in her tones if this had been a perfectly spontaneous outburst. It was clear, as it always had been, that she wished to marry him. It was not at all clear that she loved him in the least. It struck him instantly that she must have heard something of his attention to the foreign heiress, and that she had planned this scene in order to bring matters to a crisis. He was too sensible not to understand that he himself was absurdly in love with her, in his own way, and that she knew it, as women generally do, and could exasperate him, perhaps, into some folly of which he might repent, by simply treating him coldly, as she threatened.

During the silence which followed, she sat with folded arms and half-closed eyes, looking at him defiantly from under her lids.

"You do me a great injustice," he said at last.

"I am sorry," she answered. "I have no choice. I value my good name as a woman, besides my reputation as an artist. You do not justify yourself in the only way in your power, by explaining clearly what the insuperable difficulties are in the way of our marriage."

The notary's daughter did not lack logic.

"I never said that they were insuperable —"

"Then overcome them, if you want me," answered Aliandra, implacably.

"I said that there were difficulties, and there are great ones. You speak of making a fortune by your voice, my dear Aliandra," he continued, his tones sweetening. "But you must understand that a man who is a gentleman does not like to be dependent on his wife's profession for his support."

"I do not see that it is more dignified to depend on his wife's money, because she has not earned it by hard work," retorted the singer, scornfully. "It is honestly earned."

"The honour is entirely yours," said Tebaldo. "The world would grant me no share in it. Then there are my mother's objections, which are strong ones," he went on quickly. "She has, of course, a right to be consulted, and she does not even know you." ·

"It is in your power to introduce me to your mother whenever you please."

"She is too ill to see anyone —"

"She has not always been ill. You have either been afraid to bring an artist to your mother's house, which is not flattering to me, or else you never had the slightest intention of marrying me, in spite of much that you have said. Though I have heard you call your brother Francesco a coward, I think he is braver than you, for he would marry me to-morrow, if I would have him."

"And live on what you earn," retorted Tebaldo, with ready scorn.

"He has as much as you have," observed Aliandra. "Your uncle left no will, and you all shared the property equally —"

"You are not a notary's daughter for nothing," laughed Tebaldo. "That is true. But there was very little to share. Do you know what was left when the debts were paid? A bit of land here in Rome — that was all, besides Camaldoli. Both have been sold advantageously, and we have just enough to live decently all together. We should be paupers if we tried to separate."

"You are nothing if not plausible. But you will forgive me if I say that this difficulty has the air of being really insuperable. You absolutely refuse to share what I earn, and you are absolutely incapable of earning anything yourself. That being the case, the sooner you go away the better, for you can never marry me, on your own showing, and you are injuring my reputation in the meantime."

"I am engaged in speculations, in which I hope to make money," said Tebaldo. "I often tell you that I have appointments with men of business — "

"Yes, you often tell me so," interrupted Aliandra, incredulously.

"You are cold, and you are calculating," retorted Tebaldo, with a sudden change of manner, as though taking offence at last.

"It is fortunate for me that I am not hot-headed and foolish," replied Aliandra, coolly.

They parted on these terms. She believed that her coldness would bring him to her feet if anything could; but he was persuaded that his brother had betrayed him and had told her about the American heiress.

CHAPTER XVIII

Orsino made his preparations for returning to Sicily with a heavy heart. His situation was desperate at present, for he had exhausted his ingenuity in trying to discover some means of seeing Vittoria a last time. To leave San Giacinto to do what he could with Camaldoli and refuse to go back at all, for the present, which seemed to be his only chance of a meeting with Vittoria, was a course against which his manliness revolted. Even if there had been no danger connected with the administration of the new estate, he would not have abandoned his cousin at such a time, after promising to help him, and indeed to undertake all work connected with the place. San Giacinto was a busy man, to whom any sacrifice of time might suddenly mean a corresponding loss of money, for which Orsino would hold himself responsible if he brought about the delay. But as it was, since the position he had promised to fill was a dangerous one, nothing could have induced him to withdraw from the undertaking. It would have seemed like running away from a fight.

It was a consolation to have his brother's company, as far as anything could console him, though he could not make up his mind for some time to confide in Ippolito, who had always laughed at him for not marrying, and who could probably not understand why he had now allowed himself to fall in love with one of the very few young women in the world whom he might be prevented from marrying. He was grave and silent as he put together a few books in his own room, vaguely wondering whether he should ever read them.

Ippolito was collecting a number of loose sheets of music that lay on the piano, on a chair beside it, on the table among Orsino's things, and even on the floor under the instrument. He had taken off his cassock, because it was warm, and he wore a grey silk jacket which contrasted oddly with his black silk stockings and clerical stock. From time to time, without taking his cigar from his lips, he hummed a few notes of a melody in the thin but tuneful voice which seems to belong to so many musicians and composers, interrupting himself presently and blowing a cloud of smoke into the air. Now and then he looked at Orsino as though expecting him to speak.

At last, having got his manuscript music into some sort of order, he sat down at the piano to rest himself by expressing an idea he had in his head.

"How glad you will be not to hear a piano at

Camaldoli," he said, stopping as suddenly as he had begun.

"It is a horrible instrument," Orsino said, "but it never disturbs me, and it seems to amuse you."

Ippolito laughed.

"That is what you always say, but I know you will be glad to be rid of it, and it will do me good to play the organ at Santa Vittoria for a change. As that is three-quarters of a mile away, it will not disturb you."

"Nothing disturbs me," replied Orsino, rather sadly.

Ippolito made up his mind to speak at last.

"Orsino," he began quietly, "I know all about you and Donna Vittoria. As we are going to be so much together, it is better that I should tell you so. I hate secrets, and I would rather not make a secret of knowing yours — if it is one."

Orsino had looked round sharply when the priest had first spoken, but had then gone back to what he was doing.

"I am glad you know," he said, "though I would not have told you. I have spoken to our father and mother about it. The one calls me a fool, and the other thinks me one. They are not very encouraging. As for her family, her mother curses me for having killed her favourite son, and her brothers pretend that she is mad and then intrench themselves behind her to say that it is impossible. I

do not blame them much — Heaven knows, I do not
blame her at all. All the same, Vittoria and I love
each other. It is an impossible situation. I cannot even see her to say goodbye. I wish I could
find a way out of it!" He laughed bitterly.

"I wish I could," echoed his brother. "But I
am only a priest, and you call me a dilettante
churchman, at that. Let us see. Let us argue
the case as though we were in the theological
school. No — I am serious — you need not frown.
How many things can happen? Three, I think.
There are three conceivable terminations. Either
you part for ever and forget each other —"

"You may eliminate that," observed Orsino.

"Very well. Or else you continue to love each
other, in which event you must either succeed in
getting married, or not, and those are the other two
cases."

"One does not need to be a theologian to see
that. Similarly, a man must either live or die, and
a door must be either open or shut, on pain of not
being a door at all."

"I have not finished," objected Ippolito. "In
fact, I have only begun. For the sake of argument,
we will assume first that you continue to love each
other, but cannot get married."

"That is the present position."

"It is not a position which usually lasts long.
At the end of a certain time you will naturally

cease to love each other, and we obtain a second
time the case which you at first eliminated."

"Eliminate it again," said Orsino, gravely.

"Very well. There remains only one possible
issue, after your eliminations. You must be
married. On any other assumption you will forget each other. Now in such cases as yours, how
do people act? You are a layman, and it is your
business to know."

"When both are of age they 'respectfully re-
quire' their respective parents to give their consent.
If it is refused, they marry and the law protects
them."

"So does the church," said the priest. "But it
does not provide them with an income afterwards,
nor in any way guarantee them against the consequences of family quarrels. Those are subdivi-
sions of the case which you can neither modify
nor eliminate."

"Well," said Orsino, wearily, "what do you conclude for all this?"

Ippolito's gentle face grew suddenly grave, and
seemed squarer and more like his brother's.

"From what I know of the world," he answered,
"I conclude that men who mean to do things, do
them, and let the consequences take care of themselves. If you mean to marry Vittoria d'Oriani,
you will marry her, without any help and without
anyone's advice. If you do not mean to marry her,

you will not, because, under the circumstances, she can assuredly not marry you, as women have been known to marry husbands almost against their will."

"You have a singularly direct way of putting things," observed Orsino, thoughtfully.

"That is simply the result of your eliminations," answered the priest. "If you do not love her enough to take her in spite of everything and everybody, you must restore into the list of possibilities the certainty that before long you will not love her at all. For I conceive that half a love is no better as a basis of warfare than half a faith. I do not mean to breed war with our father and mother. That is a serious matter. I am only pursuing the matter to its logical conclusion and end, in words, as you will have to do in your acts, sooner or later."

"Meanwhile I am doing nothing," said Orsino. "And I am horribly conscious that I am doing nothing."

"You are going away," remarked Ippolito. "That is not inaction."

"It is worse than inaction — it is far worse than doing nothing at all."

"I am not so sure of that. It is sometimes a good thing to force an interval between events. In the first place, I often hear it said that a separation strengthens a great passion, but destroys a small one. All passions seem great when the object is present, but distance brings out the truth. By the time you have been a month at Camaldoli you will know whether it is essential to your happiness to marry Vittoria d'Oriani, or not."

" And suppose that it is ? We come back to the same situation again."

" Yes — we come back to the eternal situation of force against force."

" And you mean that I should use force ? That is — that I should marry her and take all the consequences, no matter what they may be ? "

" I do not mean that you should. I distinguish. I mean that you will, that is all. I am not considering the moral ground of the action, but the human source of it. Your marriage may be the cause of great difficulties and complications, but if you are persuaded that it is quite necessary to your life to marry that young lady, you will marry her. It is by no means an impossible thing to accomplish, nor even a very difficult one."

" You do not tell me how far it is a matter of conscience to consider the consequences."

" It is of no use to tell courageous men that sort of thing," said the priest. "They take the consequences, that is all. No man who ever wanted a thing with his whole heart ever stopped to consider how his getting it would affect other people, unless the point of honour was involved."

"And there is no point of honour here, is there?" asked Orsino, as a man asks a question to which he knows the answer.

"You know what you have said to Donna Vittoria," answered Ippolito. "I do not."

"I have asked her to marry me, and she has consented." Orsino laughed a little dryly. "That is the way one puts it, I believe," he added.

"Then I should say that unless she, of her own accord, releases you from your word, the point of honour lies in not withdrawing it," replied the priest. "If you did, it would mean that you were not willing to take the risks involved in keeping it, would it not?"

"Of course it would. I wish you could make our father see that."

"People of the previous generation never see what happens in ours. They only infer what ought to happen if all their own prejudices had been canonical law for fifty years."

"That is sedition," laughed Orsino, whose spirits had risen suddenly.

"No, it is criticism, and criticism is only called sedition under despotic governments. There is no reason why grown men, like you and me, should not criticise their fathers and mothers up to a certain point, within limits of respect. We honour them, but they are not gods, that we should worship them. When we were little boys we supposed

that our father knew everything about everything.
We are aware, now, that we understand many
things which have grown up in our day much better than he does. To go on supposing that he
knew everything, in spite of evidence, would be
a gross form of superstition. Superstition, I suppose, means a survival, to wit, the survival of some
obsolete belief. That is exactly what it would be
in us to artificially maintain the belief of our
childhood in our parents' omniscience. Has your
love for Donna Vittoria anything to do with the
actual amount of her knowledge at any moment?
No. But love appears to be made up of passion
and affection. Therefore affection is independent
of any such knowledge in its object. Therefore
we love our parents quite ·independently of what
they know or do not know about life, or mathe-
matics, and we may, consequently, criticise such
knowledge in them on its own merits, without in
the least detracting from our affection for themselves."

"You are a very satisfactory brother," said Orsino, smiling at his brother's speech. "But I am
not sure that you are a strictly orthodox priest on
the question of family relations."

"I give you a theory of such relations," answered
Ippolito. "In actual practice I believe that our
mother is one of the wisest women living, without being in the smallest degree intellectual. It

is true that my experience of women is limited,
but I hear a great deal of talk about them. She is
fond of Donna Vittoria, I am sure."

" Yes — very. But she sees fifty reasons why I
had better not marry her."

"So do I," said Ippolito, calmly.

"You? Why, you have been urging me to marry
her in spite of everything!"

" Oh, no. I have only proved to you that if you
love her enough, you will marry her in spite of
everything. That is a very different thing."

" Priest!" laughed Orsino. "Sophist!"

"Anything you like," answered Ippolito, swinging round on the piano stool and striking a chord.
" All the same, I hope you may marry her, and
have no bad consequences to deal with, and I will
help you if I can."

"Thank you," said Orsino; but his voice was
drowned by a burst of loud and intricate music,
as Ippolito's white fingers flew over the piano while
he stared at the ceiling, his head thrown back, his
cigar sticking up from between his teeth, he himself apparently unaware of what his hands were
doing, and merely listening to the music.

Orsino was momentarily cheered and encouraged
by all his brother had said, but the situation was
not materially improved thereby. It was, indeed,
almost as bad as it could be, and an older and
wiser man than Orsino would have expected that

something must occur before long, either to improve it, or to cut it short at once and for ever, for the simple reason that it could neither last, as it stood, nor be made more difficult by anything which could happen.

CHAPTER XIX

WHEN Orsino and Ippolito reached Camaldoli
everything seemed to be quiet, and San Giacinto
himself was greatly encouraged by the turn matters had taken. During the first day or two after
Orsino's departure there had still been considerable curiosity among the people of Santa Vittoria,
and more than once San Giacinto had made little
speeches, in his direct manner, to the peasants and
villagers who hung about in the neighbourhood of
the big old house. But after that he had not been disturbed, and everything appeared to be progressing
favourably. The year was one of abundance, the
orange crop, which in Sicily is all gathered before
May, had turned out well, the grapes promised
an abundant vintage, and even the olives had blos-
somed plentifully, though it was still too early to
make accurate predictions about the oil. On the
whole the prospects for the year were unusually
satisfactory, and San Giacinto congratulated himself
on having chanced to buy the place in a good year.
In an agricultural country like that part of Sicily,
the temper of the people is profoundly affected by
the harvest.

The outlaws had not been heard of in the neighbourhood since Ferdinando Pagliuca's death. They were said to be in the region about Noto, at some distance from Camaldoli, towards the south-west. San Giacinto was surprised at not having even received an anonymous letter from one of Ferdinando's friends. He did not suppose that the present pacific state of things could last for-ever, but he had been prepared to meet with a great deal more opposition in what he did.

On the other hand, he was hindered at every step by small difficulties which always seemed to be perfectly natural. If he wished to build a bit of wall, he found it impossible to obtain stone or quicklime, though there were plenty of masons professing themselves ready to work. He pointed to a quantity of slaked lime drying in a deep tank near the gate of Santa Vittoria.

"Eh," said the head mason, shaking his head, "that belongs to the mayor, and he will not sell it."

And, in fact, the mayor flatly refused to part with a single hodful of the lime, saying that he himself was going to repair his house.

The masons said that by and by it could be got from the lime-burners, who had sold their last burning to a man in Randazzo. Stone was to be had for the quarrying, in the black lands above Camaldoli, but there were no quarrymen in Santa

Vittoria, and the gang of them that lived higher up Etna had taken a large contract.

"Patience," said the head mason, gravely. "In time you will have all you want."

As the bit of wall was not a very important matter, San Giacinto did not care to go to the expense of bringing material from a great distance, and decided to wait. Meanwhile he hired certain men from Bronte to come and clear out all the bush and scrub from among the trees. They came without tools. He gave them tools that belonged to the tenants of Camaldoli, the same which the latter had lent him on the first day to make a clearing close to the house. The Bronte men worked for two hours and then came out of the brush and sat down quietly in the sun.

"The tools are not good for anything," they said gravely. "We cannot work with them."

"What is the matter with them?" asked San Giacinto.

"They are dull. They would not cut strings."

"Take them away and have them ground," said San Giacinto.

"Are there knife-grinders in this country?" asked the men. "Where are they? No. They come, they stay a day, perhaps two days, and they go away."

San Giacinto looked at the men thoughtfully a moment, then turned on his heel and left them to their own devices. He began to understand. The men neither wished to refuse to work for him, nor dared to do the work they undertook, when its execution would in any way improve the defensive conditions of Camaldoli. San Giacinto came back when the men were gone, with two or three of the soldiers, took a hatchet himself, and leading the way proceeded to cut away the thorns and brambles, systematically clearing the ground so as to leave no cover under which an armed man could approach the house unnoticed. He regularly devoted a part of each day to the work, until it was finished.

As soon as Ferdinando's body had been removed, there had been no difficulty in getting men to work indoors, and by the time Orsino arrived, considerable improvements had been effected. But the men would not have begun work in a house where an unburied dead person was still lying.

The three Saracinesca strolled up to Santa Vittoria late in the afternoon, San Giacinto and Orsino carrying their rifles, while Ippolito walked along with his hands behind him, just catching up his little silk mantle, staring hard at all the new sights of the road, and mentally wondering what sort of instrument he should find in the little church.

The place was a mere village without any mediæval wall, though there was a sort of archway at the principal entrance which was generally called the gate. Just beyond the shoulder of the mountain, away from Camaldoli, and about fifty yards from this gateway of the village, was a little white church with a tiled roof. It had a modern look, as though it had been lately restored. Then the village straggled down the rough descent towards the shallow valley beyond, having its own church in the little market place. It was distinctly clean, having decently paved streets and solid stone houses with massive mullions, and iron balconies painted red. There were a few small shops of the kind always seen in Italian villages. The apothecary's was in the market place, the general shop was in the main street, opposite a wine-seller's, the telegraph office — a very recent innovation — was over against the chemist's and was worked by the postmaster, and in what had once been a small convent, further on, at the outskirts of the town, the carabineers were lodged. At San Giacinto's request, fifty men of the line infantry had been quartered in the village within the last few days, the order having been telegraphed from Rome on Orsino's representations to the Minister of the Interior. The people treated the men and their two young officers civilly, but secretly resented their presence.

Nowadays, every Italian village has a walled cemetery at some distance from it. The burial ground of Santa Vittoria overlooked Camaldoli;

being situated a quarter of a mile from the little white church and on the other side of the hill, so that it was out of sight of the village. It was a grimly bare place. Four walls, six feet high, of rough tufo and unplastered, enclosed four or five acres of land. A painted iron gate opened upon the road, and against the opposite wall, inside, was built a small mortuary chapel. The cemetery had not been long in use, and there were not more than a score of black crosses sticking in the earth to mark as many graves. There was no pretence at cultivation. The clods were heaped up symmetrically at each grave, and a little rough grass grew on some of them. There was not a tree, nor a flower, nor a creeper to relieve the dusty dreariness of it, and the road itself was not more dry and arid. The little grass that grew had pushed itself up just in the gate-way, where few feet ever passed, and everyone knows what a desolate look a grass-grown entrance gives to any place, even to a churchyard. There were low, round curbstones on each side of the gate.

The three gentlemen strolled slowly up the hill in the warm afternoon sunshine, talking as they came. Ippolito was a little ahead of the others, for he was light on his feet, and walked easily.

"That is the cemetery," observed San Giacinto to Orsino, pointing at the hill. "That is where they buried your friend Ferdinando Corleone on the day

you left. I suppose they will put up a monument
to him."

"His brothers will not," answered Orsino. "They
disown all connexion with him."

"Amiable race!" laughed San Giacinto. "There
is a figure like a monument sitting outside the
gate," he added. "Do you see it?"

"It is a woman in black," said Orsino. "She
is sitting on something by the roadside."

They were still a long way off, but both had
good eyes.

"She is probably resting and sitting on her
bundle," observed San Giacinto.

"She is sitting on a stone,—on one of the
curbstones," said Ippolito. "She has her head
bent down."

"He sees better than either of us," said Orsino,
with a laugh. "I wonder why nobody ever expects
a priest to do anything particularly well except
pray? Ippolito can walk as well as we can, he sees
better, he could probably beat either of us with a
pistol or a rifle if he tried, and I am sure he is far
more clever in fifty ways than I am. Yet everyone in the family takes it for granted that he is no
better than a girl at anything that men do. He
was quite right about the woman. She is bending
over — her face must be almost touching her knees.
It is a strange attitude."

"Probably some woman who has a relation buried in the cemetery — her child, perhaps," suggested Ippolito. "She stops at the gate to say a prayer when she goes by."

"Then she would kneel, I should think," answered Orsino.

Almost unconsciously they all three quickened their pace a little, though the hill grew steeper just there. As they drew near, the outline of the woman in black became distinct against the dark tufo wall behind her, for the sunlight fell full upon her, where she sat. It was a beautiful outline, too, full of expression and simple tragedy. She sat very low, on the round curbstone, one small foot thrust forward and leading the folds of the loose black skirt, both white hands clasped about the higher knee, towards which the covered head bent low, so that the face could not be seen at all. Not a line nor fold stirred as the three men came up to her.

Orsino recognized Concetta, though he could not see her features. Her exceptional grace betrayed itself unmistakably, and he should have known anywhere the white hands that had been lifted up to him when he had stood at the window in the grey dawn. But he said nothing about it to San Giacinto, for he understood her grief, and he could not have spoken of her without being heard by her just then.

But Ippolito went up to her, before his brother

could hinder him. She was a lonely and unhappy creature, and he was one of those really charitable people who cannot pass by any suffering without trying to help it. He stood still beside her.

"What is your trouble?" he asked gently. "Can anyone help you?"

She did not move at first, but a voice of pain came with slow accents from under the black shawl that fell over her face, almost to her knee.

"God alone can help the dead," it answered.

"But you are alive, my child," said Ippolito, bending down a little.

The covered head moved slowly from side to side, denying.

"Who are you, that speak of life?" asked the sorrowful young voice. "Are you the Angel of the Resurrection? Go in peace, with Our Lady, for I am dead."

Ippolito thought that she must be mad, and that it might be better to leave her alone. His brother and cousin had gone on, up the road, and were waiting for him at a little distance.

"May you find peace and comfort," said the young priest, quietly, and he moved away.

But he turned to look back at her, for she seemed the saddest woman he had ever seen, and her voice was the saddest he had ever heard. Something in his own speech had stirred her a little, for when he looked again she had raised her head, and was lift-

ing the black shawl so that she could see him.
She was about to speak, and he stopped where he
was, two paces from her, surprised by her extraordinary beauty and unnatural pallor.

"Who are you?" she asked slowly. "You are
a stranger."

"I am Ippolito Saracinesca, a priest," answered
the young man.

At the name, she started, and her sad eyes
opened wide. Then she saw the other two men
standing in the road a little way off. Slowly, and
with perfect grace, she rose from her low seat.

"And those two—there—who are they?" she
asked.

"They are also Saracinesca," said Ippolito. "The
one is my brother, the other is my cousin. We are
three of the same name."

He answered her question quite naturally, but he
felt sure that she was mad. By this time San Giacinto was growing impatient, and he began to move
a few steps nearer to call Ippolito. But the latter
found it hard to turn away from the deep eyes and
the pale face before him.

"Then there were three of you," said Concetta,
in a tone in which scorn sharpened grief. "It
is no wonder that you killed him between you."

"Whom?" asked Ippolito, very much surprised
at the new turn of her speech.

"Whom?" All at once there was something

wild in her rising inflexion. "You ask of me
who it was whom you killed down there in the
woods? Of me, Concetta? Of me, his betrothed?
Of me, who prayed to your brother, there, that
I might be let in, to wash my love's face with
my tears? But if I had known to whom I was
praying, there would have been two dead men
lying there in the chapel of Camaldoli — there
would have been two black crosses in there, behind the gate — do you see? There it is! The
last on the left. No one has died since, but if
God were just, the next should be one of you,
and the next another, and then another — ah,
God! If I had something in these hands —"

She had pointed at Ferdinando's grave, throwing
her arm backwards, while she kept her eyes on
Ippolito. Now, with a gesture of the people, as
she longed for a weapon, she thrust out her small
white fists, tightly clenched, towards the priest's
heart, then opened them suddenly, in a despairing
way, and let her arms fall to her sides.

"Saracinesca, Saracinesca," she repeated slowly,
her voice sinking; "three Saracinesca have made
one widow! But one widow may yet make many
widows, and many mourning mothers, and the
justice of Heaven is not the justice of man."

San Giacinto and Orsino had gradually approached Ippolito, and now stood beside him,
facing the beautiful, wild girl, in her desolation.

Grave and thoughtful, the three kinsmen stood side by side.

There was nothing theatrical nor unreal in the situation. One of themselves had killed the girl's betrothed husband, whom she had loved with all her soul. That was the plain fact, and Orsino had never ceased to realize it. Unhesitatingly, and in honourable self-defence, he had done a deed by which many were suffering greatly, and he was brought face to face with them in their grief. Somehow, it seemed unjust to him that the girl should accuse his brother and his cousin of Ferdinando's death.

As she paused, facing them, breathless with the wave of returning pain, rather than from speaking, Orsino moved forward, a little in front of Ippolito.

"I killed Ferdinando Corleone," he said, gravely. "Do not accuse us all three, nor curse us all three."

She turned her great eyes to his face, but her expression did not change. Possibly she did not believe him.

"The dead see," she answered slowly. "They know — they know — they see both you and me. And the dead do not forget."

A flying cloud passed over the sun, and the desolate land was suddenly all black and grey and stony, with the solemn vastness of the mountain behind. Concetta drew her shawl up over her head, as though she were cold, and turned from the three men with a simple dignity, and knelt down on the rough, broken stones, where the blades of coarse grass shot up between, close to the gate, and she clasped her hands together round one of the dusty, painted iron rails.

"Let us go," said San Giacinto's deep voice. "It is better to leave her, poor girl."

She did not look back at them as they walked quietly up the road. Her eyes were fixed on one point, and her lips moved quickly, forming whispered words.

"Maria Santissima, let there be three black crosses! Mother of God, three black crosses! Mother of Sorrows, three black crosses!"

And over and over again, she repeated the terrible little prayer.

CHAPTER XX

THE three men entered the village and walked
through the main street. The low afternoon sun
was shining brightly again, and only the people
who lived on the shady side of the street had
opened their windows. Many of them had little
iron balconies in which quantities of magnificent
dark carnations were blooming, planted in long,
earthenware, trough-like pots, and hanging down
by their long stalks that thrust themselves between the railings. Outside the windows of the
poorer houses, too, great bunches of herbs were
hung up to dry in the sun, and strings of scarlet
peppers had already begun to appear, though it
was early for them yet. Later, towards the
autumn, the people hang up the canteloup melons
of the south, in their rough green and grey rinds,
by neatly made slings of twisted grass, but it was
not time for them yet. In some of the houses the
people were packing the last of the oranges to be
sent down to Piedimonte and thence to Messina
for England and America, passing each orange
through a wooden ring to measure it, and rejecting
those that were much too small or much too large,

then wrapping each one separately in tissue paper, while other women packed them neatly in thin deal boxes. The air smelt of them and of the carnations in the balconies, for Santa Vittoria was a clean and sweet village. The cleanliness of the thoroughbred Oriental, a very different being from the filthy Levantine, begins in Sicily, and distinguishes the Sicilians of the hills from the Calabrians and from the Sicilians of such seaport towns as Messina. Moreover, there are no beggars in the hill towns.

San Giacinto had his pocket full of letters for the post office, and wished to see the lieutenant in command of the soldiers; but Orsino had nothing to do, and Ippolito had made up his mind not to return to Camaldoli without having seen the organ in the church. The two brothers went off in search of the sacristan, for the church was closed.

They found him, after some enquiry, helping to pack oranges in a great vaulted room that opened upon the street. He was a fat man, cross-eyed, with a sort of clerical expression.

"You wish to see the organ," he said, coming out into the street. "Truly you will see a fine thing! If you only do not hear it! It makes boom, boom, and wee, wee — and that is all it makes. I wager that not even ten cats could make a noise like our organ. Do you know that it is very aged? Surely, it remembers the ark of Noah,

and Saint Paul must have brought it with him.
But then, you shall see; and if you wish to hear
it, I take no responsibility.”

Ippolito was not greatly encouraged by such a
prospect.

“But when you have a festival, what do you
do?” he enquired.

“We help it, of course. How should one do?
Don Atanasio, the apothecary, plays the clarinet.
He is a professor! Him, indeed, you should hear
when he plays at the elevation. You would think
you heard the little angels whistling in Paradise!
I, to serve you, play the double bass a little, and
Don Ciccio, the carpenter, plays the drum. Being
used to the hammer, he does it not badly. And
all the time the organ makes boom, boom, and
wee, wee. It is a fine concert, but there is much
sentiment of devotion, and the women sing. It
seems that thus it pleases the saints.”

“Do not the men sing too?” asked Orsino,
idly.

“Men? How could men sing in church? A
man can sing a ‘cantilena’ in the fields, but in
church it is the women who sing. They know all
the words. God has made them so. There is that
girl of the notary in Randazzo, for instance — you
should hear her sing!”

“I have heard her in Rome,” said Orsino. “But
she sings in a theatre.”

“A theatre? Who knows how a theatre is made? See how many things men have invented!”

They reached the door of the church.

“Signori, do you really wish to see this organ?” asked the sacristan. “There is a much better one in the little church outside the gate. But the day is hot, and if you only wish to see an organ, this one is nearer.”

“Let me see the good one, by all means,” said Ippolito. “I wish to play on it — not to see it! I have seen hundreds of organs.”

“Hundreds of organs!” exclaimed the man to himself. “Capers! This stranger has travelled much! But if it is indeed not too hot for you,” he said, addressing Ippolito, “we will go to Santa Vittoria.”

“It is not hot at this hour,” laughed Orsino. “We have walked up from Camaldoli.”

“On foot!” The fat sacristan either was, or pretended to be, amazed. “Great signori like you, to come all that distance on foot!”

“What is there surprising in that?” enquired Ippolito. “We have legs.”

“Birds also have legs,” observed the man. “But they fly. It is only the chickens that walk, like poor people. I say that money is wings. If I were a great signore, like you, I, would not even walk upstairs. I would be carried. Why should I walk? In order to be tired? It would be a folly, if I were rich. I, if you ask me, I like to eat well, to drink well, and then to sleep well. A man who could do these three things should be always happy. But the poor are always in thought."

"So are the rich," observed Ippolito.

"Yes, signore, for their souls, for we are all sinners; but not for their bodies, because they have always something to eat. What do I say? They eat meat every day, and so they are strong and have no thought for their bodies. But one of us, what does he eat? A little bread, a little salad, an onion, and with this in our bodies we have to move the earth. The world is thus made. Patience!"

Thus philosophizing, the fat man rolled unwieldily along beside the two gentlemen, swinging his keys in his hand.

"If I had made the world, it should be another thing," he continued, for he was a loquacious man. "In the first place, I would have made wine clear, like water, and I would have made water black, like wine. Thus if the wine-seller put water into his wine, we should all see it. Another thing I would have done. I would have made corn grow on trees, like olives. In that way, we should have planted it once in two hundred years, as we do the olive trees, and there would have been less fatigue. Is not that a good thought?"

"Very original," said Orsino. "It had never struck me."

"I would also have made men so that their hair should stand on end when they are telling lies, as a donkey lifts his tail when he brays. That would also have been good. But the Creator did not think of it in time. Patience! They say it will be different in Paradise. Hope costs little, but you cannot cook it."

"You are a philosopher," observed Ippolito.

"No, signore," answered the sacristan. "You have been misinformed. I am a grocer, or, to say it better, I am the brother of the grocer. When it is the season, after Santa Teresa's day, I kill the pigs and salt the hams and make the sausages. I am also the sacristan, but that yields me little; for although there is much devotion in our town at festivals, there is little of it among private persons. Sometimes an old woman brings a candle to the Madonna, and she gives a soldo to have it lighted. What is that? Can one live with a soldo now and then? But my brother, thanks be to Heaven, is well-to-do, and a widower. He makes me live with him. He had a son once, but, health to you, Christ and the sea took the boy when he was not yet twenty. Therefore I live with him, to divert him a little, and I kill the pigs, speaking with respect of your face."

"And what do you do during the rest of the

year?" enquired Orsino, as they neared the gate.

"Eh, I live so. According to the season, I pack oranges, I trim vines, I make the wine for my brother, and the oil, I take the honey and the wax from the bees, I graft good fruit upon the wild pear trees — what should I do? A little of every- thing, in order of eat."

"But your brother seems to be rich. Have you nothing?"

"Signore, to me money comes like a freshet in spring and runs away, and immediately I am dry. But to my brother it comes like water into a well, and it stays there. Men are thus made. The one gives, the other takes; the one shuts his hand, the other opens his. My mother, blessed soul, used to say to me, ' Take care, my son, for when you are old, you will go in rags!' But thanks be to Heaven, I have my brother, and I am as you see me."

They came to the little church with its freshly whitewashed walls and tiled roof.

"This is the chapel of Santa Vittoria," said the fat sacristan. "The church in the town is dedi- cated to Our Lady of Victories, but this is the chapel of the saint, and there is more devotion here, though it is small, and at the great feast of Santa Vittoria, the procession starts from here and goes to the church, and returns here."

"It looks new," observed Ippolito.

"Eh, if all things were what they seem!" The man chuckled as he turned the key in the lock. "You shall see inside whether it is new. It is older than Saint Peter's in Rome."

And so it was, by two or three centuries. It was a dark little building, of the Norman period, with low arches and solid little pillars terminating in curiously carved capitals. It had a little nave with intercommunicating side chapels, like aisles. Over the door was a small loft containing the organ, the object of Ippolito's visit. In the uneven floor there were slabs with deep cut but much worn figures of knights and prelates in stiff armour or long and equally stiff looking robes, their heads surrounded by almost illegible inscriptions. Over the principal altar there was a bad painting of Saint Vittoria, half covered with ex-voto offerings of silver hearts, while on each side of the picture were hung up scores of hollow wax models of arms, legs, and other parts of the human body, realistically coloured, all remembrances of recoveries from illness, accident, and disease, attributed to the beneficent intervention of the saint. But above, in the little vault of the apse, there were some very ancient and well preserved mosaics, magnificently rich in tone. There was, of course, no dome, and the dim light came in through low windows high up in the nave, above the lower side chapels. The church was clean and well kept, and on each side there were half a dozen benches painted with a vivid sky-blue colour.

The two brothers looked about, with some curiosity, while the fat sacristan slowly jingled his bunch of keys against his leg.

"Here the dead walk at night," he observed, cheerfully, as the two young men came up to him.

"What do you mean?" asked Orsino, who had been much amused by the man's conversation.

"The old Pagliuca walk. I have seen their souls running about the floor in the dark, like little candle flames. A little more, and I should have seen their bodies, too, but I ran away. Soul of my mother! I was frightened. It was on the eve of Santa Vittoria, five years ago. The candles for the festival had not come, though we had waited all day for the carrier from Piedimonte. Then he came at dark, for he had met a friend in Linguaglossa, and he was a drunkard, and the wine was new, so he slept on his cart all the way, and it was by the grace of the Madonna that he did not roll off into the ditch. But I considered that it was late, and that the office began early in the morning, and that many strangers came from Bronte and the hill village to our festa, and that it would be a scandal if they found us still dressing the church in the morning. So I took the box of candles on my back and came here, not thinking to bring a lantern, because there is always

the lamp before the altar where the saint's bones
are. Do you understand?"

"Perfectly. But what about the Pagliuca?"

"My brother said, 'You will see the Pagliuca'
—for everyone says it. But I had a laugh at him,
for I thought that a dead man in his grave must be
as quiet as a handkerchief in a drawer. So I came,
and I unlocked the door, thinking about the festival, and I came in, meaning to take a candle from
the box and light it at the altar lamp, so that I
might see well to stick the others into the candle-
sticks. But there was the flame of a candle burning on the floor. It ran away from me as I
came in, and others ran after it, and round and
round it. Then I knew that I saw the souls of
the old Pagliuca, and I said to myself that presently I should see also their bodies — an evil thing,
for they have been long dead. Then I made a
movement — who knows how I did? I dropped
the box and I heard it break, and all the candles
rolled out upon the floor as though the dead
Pagliuca were rattling their bones. But I counted
neither one nor two, but jumped out into the road
with one jump. Santa Vittoria helped me; and it
was a bright moonlight night, but as I shut the
door, I could see the souls of the Pagliuca jumping
up and down on the pavement. I said within me,
when the dead dance, the living go home. And
my face was white. When I came home, my

brother said, 'You have seen the Pagliuca.' And I said, 'I have seen them.' Then he gave me some rum, and I lay in a cold sweat till morning. From that time I will not come here at night. But in the daytime, it is different."

Orsino and Ippolito knew well enough that in old Italian churches, where many dead are buried under the pavement, it is not an uncommon thing to see a will-o'-the-wisp at night. But in the dim little church, with the dead Pagliuca lying under their feet, there was something gruesome about the man's graphic story, and they did not laugh.

"Let us hope that we may not see any ghosts," said Orsino.

"Amen," answered the sacristan, devoutly. "That is the organ," he said, pointing to the loft.

He led the way. On one side of the entrance a small arched door gave access to a narrow winding staircase in the thickness of the wall, lighted by narrow slits opening to the air. Though the loft had not appeared to be very high above the pavement, the staircase seemed very long. At last the three emerged upon the boarded floor, at the back of the instrument, where four greasy, knotted ropes hung out of worn holes in the cracked wood. The rose window over the door of the church threw a bright light into the little forest of dusty wooden and metal pipes above. The ropes were for working the old-fashioned bellows.

Ippolito went round and took the thin deal cover from the keyboard. He was surprised to find a double bank of keys, and an octave and a half of pedals, which is very uncommon in country organs. He was further unprepared to see the name of a once famous maker in Naples just above the keys, but when he looked up he understood, for on a gilded scroll, supported by two rickety cherubs above his head, he read the name of the donor.

'FERDINANDUS PALIUCA PRINCEPS CORLEONIS COMES SANCTAE VICTORIAE SICULUS DONAVIT A.D. MDCCCXXI.'

The instrument was, therefore, the gift of a Ferdinando Pagliuca, Prince of Corleone, Count of Santa Vittoria, probably of one of those Pagliuca whose souls the fat sacristan believed he had seen 'jumping up and down on the pavement.'

The sacristan tugged at the ropes that moved the bellows. Ippolito dusted the bench over which he had leaned to uncover the keys, slipped in, swinging his feet over the pedals, pulled out two or three stops, and struck a chord.

The tone was not bad, and had in it some of that richness which only old organs are supposed to possess, like old violins. He began to prelude softly, and then, one by one, he tried the other stops. Some were fair, but some were badly out of tune. The cornopean brayed hideously, and the

hautboy made curious buzzing sounds.   Ippolito
promised himself that he would set the whole
instrument in order in the course of a fortnight,
and was delighted with his discovery.   When he
had finished, the fat sacristan came out from
behind, mopping his forehead with a blue cotton
handkerchief.

"Capers!" he exclaimed.   "You are a professor.   If Don Giacomo hears you, he will die
of envy."

"Who is Don Giacomo?"

"Eh, Don Giacomo!   He is the postmaster and
the telegrapher, and he plays the old organ in the
big church on Sundays.   But when there is the
festival here, a professor comes to play this one,
from Catania.   But he cannot play as you do."

Orsino had gone down again into the church
while Ippolito had been playing.   They found him
bending very low over an inscription on a slab near
the altar steps.

"There is a curious inscription here," he said,
without looking up.   "I cannot quite read it, but
it seems to me that I see our name in it.   It would
be strange if one of our family had chanced to die
and be buried here, ages ago."

Ippolito bent down, too, till his head touched
his brother's.

"It is not Latin," he said presently.   "It looks
like Italian."

The fat sacristan jingled his keys rather impatiently, for it was growing late.

"Without troubling yourselves to read it, you may know what it is," he said. "It is the old prophecy about the Pagliuca. When the dead walk here at night they read it. It says, 'Esca Pagliuca pesca Saracen.' But it goes round a circle like a disk, so that you can read it, 'Saracen esca Pagliuca pesca' — either, Let Pagliuca go out, the Saracen is fishing, or, Let the Saracen go out, Pagliuca is fishing."

"'Or Saracinesca Pagliuca pesca' — Saracinesca fishes for Pagliuca," said Ippolito to Orsino, with a laugh at his own ingenuity.

"Who knows what it means!" exclaimed the sacristan. "But they say that when it comes true, the last Corleone shall die and the Pagliuca d'Oriani shall end. But whether they end or not, they will walk here till the Last Judgment. Signori, the twilight descends. If you do not wish to see the Pagliuca, let us go. But if you wish to see them, here are the keys. You are the masters, but I go home. This is an evil place at night."

The man was growing nervous, and moved away towards the door. The two brothers followed him.

"The place is consecrated," said Ippolito, as they reached the entrance. "What should you be afraid of?"

"Santa Vittoria is all alone here," answered the

man, "and the Pagliuca are more than fifty, when they come out and walk. What should a poor Christian do? He is better at home, with a pipe of tobacco."

The sun had set when they all came out upon the road, and the afterglow was purple on the snow of Etna.

END OF VOL. I